THE
DISCREET CHARM
OF THE
BIG BAD WOLF

By Alexander McCall Smith

THE
DISCREET CHARM
OF THE
BIG BAD WOLF

ALEXANDER McCALL SMITH

abacus
books

ABACUS

First published in Great Britain in 2023 by Abacus

1 3 5 7 9 10 8 6 4 2

A CIP catalogue record for this book
is available from the British Library.

Hardback ISBN 978-0-349-14601-0
Trade paperback ISBN 978-0-349-14603-4

Typeset in Galliard by M Rules
Printed and bound in Great Britain by Clays Ltd, Elcograf S.p.A.

Papers used by Abacus are from well-managed forests
and other responsible sources.

FSC
www.fsc.org

MIX
Supporting
responsible forestry
FSC® C104740

Abacus
An imprint of
Little, Brown Book Group
Carmelite House
50 Victoria Embankment
London EC4Y 0DZ

An Hachette UK Company
www.hachette.co.uk

www.littlebrown.co.uk

CHAPTER ONE

More RAM Now!

The invitation came in the form of a letter delivered to Ulf Varg, senior detective in Malmö's Department of Sensitive Crimes, driver of a classic silver Saab, and owner of a hearing-impaired dog known as Martin. It arrived with one other letter, an unsolicited offer from a local building company to renew his windows and, in their words, 'Do away with chilly draughts forever with our one-hundred-year guarantee'. That was absurd, thought Ulf, and smiled at the very thought. How could any firm seriously offer a century's guarantee in a world as uncertain, and as temporary, as ours? Not only would the customer be long gone by the time the guarantee expired, but the firm itself would doubtless have ceased trading. Nothing lasts forever, Ulf reminded himself: everything we see around us, people, buildings, roads, even Sweden itself would in due course disappear, leaving only traces to puzzle future archaeologists, if there were to be any. Sweden ... We thought of our countries as permanent, but they were not. Whatever happened to Tanganyika? Countries and civilisations waxed and waned; populations moved or died out; empires crumbled, their throne rooms deserted, their grumbling legions evaporated. Would people still speak Swedish in two or three hundred years?

No, the guarantee made no sense, other than as a cheap boast of the sort that some manufacturers might make about their over-hyped products. Ulf had recently fallen for one of these when he purchased a toothbrush which it was claimed had the effect of lifting plaque through the action of the rare and special material of which the bristles were made. It was not clear to him how this worked, and he regretted the purchase almost immediately, especially as it cost four times what a normal toothbrush cost. He would feel the same, he imagined, about new windows, even those with a one-hundred-year guarantee.

He tossed the building company's letter into the bin. But then he reminded himself that the builders, a father-and-son team, were no more than doing their job, trying to make a living in a hard world, and he mentally apologised to them. He was sorry, but new windows were not a priority for him right at the moment.

He retrieved the letter from the bin. It had been printed on cheap paper, but care had been taken with the design. At its head, underneath the name of the company, *Northern Windows*, was a photograph of the proprietor and his son. Their names were printed in italics: *Mikael* and *Loke*. Mikael was the father, who looked somewhere in his forties – although Ulf always found it difficult to estimate ages with any accuracy – and Loke was the son, who appeared to be in his early twenties, if that. Mikael, the text then explained, had worked abroad on construction before returning to Sweden to set up his own company. Loke had served an apprenticeship with a firm in Stockholm and, on its completion, had joined his father in the window business. Loke was a keen ice-hockey player, it was revealed, a sport at which his father had once been an amateur coach. Then the text turned to windows and the need to replace them from time to time. *No window lasts forever*, the letter warned. That could be a recurring line in a poem, Ulf thought: *no window lasts forever*.

Ulf smiled. If no window lasted forever, was it wise to offer a one-hundred-year guarantee? He looked at the photograph once again. These two men were honest. He had been a detective long enough to develop that sixth sense that only long experience with erring humanity could engender: that instinct that told one when people were honest and when they were not. Care had to be taken about judging on facial appearance, but it was one of the factors that could be taken into account. Faces revealed internal processes – of course they did. We talked about looks of anguish, or haunted looks, or looks of regret. These all pointed to emotional states within. And so it was with honesty: the anxiety brought about by dissemblance could easily be translated into a small furrow here, a shifting of the gaze there. You just had to be ready to spot the signs.

Ulf thought: I never have to solicit business. I sit at my desk and my work comes to me. These two have to go out, like fishermen casting their nets upon the water, and hope that they attract clients. They can never be sure that anybody will respond, and it is easy to see how that might lead to desperation and the offering of one-hundred-year guarantees. That was entirely understandable.

He folded the letter before slipping it into the drawer in which he kept odds and ends for which he had no other particular place. Some of his windows did need attention, now that he came to think of it, and he remembered that a year or two ago he had even bought sandpaper and a tin of white paint to do something about it himself. But it had gone no further than that, and he had forgotten about it. His own handiwork, of course, would never be guaranteed for a year, let alone a century. Perhaps he would get in touch with *Northern Windows* and ask them to take a look.

He examined the second envelope. His name and address had

been handwritten, which intrigued him. Physical letters were rare enough in an age of electronic communication, and had largely disappeared, just as physical banknotes had done in Sweden. Letters had become special, and one with a personal aspect to it would always be more interesting than the dull missives of officialdom – tax demands, insurance premium reminders, and so on.

He slit open the envelope and extracted the letter within. 'Dear Ulf,' he read, 'It's over twenty years now since that day when we walked out of the Gymnasium on our last day of school. Remember? And since then a lot has happened in our lives. But now a few of us – Per and Margarita, as well as myself – have decided to organise a class reunion. It won't be anything big – just a lunch. We are hoping to invite the current principal to come and speak to us about the plans that the school has for the future. It's much bigger now and I think it's doing well. The invitation is attached and gives the details. Please let me know if you can make it – we hope you can! Best regards, Harald (Olavson).' There was a brief postscript written in a different-coloured ink. 'PS I went on to work in aviation: a landing-gear company. It pays the rent and is reasonably secure, which is all one can ask for, really. I heard that you became some sort of detective. *Selective Crimes*, Per said. Maybe you'll explain when we meet.'

Ulf looked out of the window. Harald Olavson. Of course. He saw him now, on the racing bike that he sometimes rode to school. He was remarkably thin – one of those people who seemed to carry not an ounce of spare flesh – and even the skin on his face seemed to be pulled tight, like parchment. That must have been because there was no subcutaneous fat. People said that if Harald stood side on to you, you might easily just not see him, he was so thin and insubstantial. And then Per, who had an extraordinary memory for facts and figures. They called him *Guinness*, after the *Guinness Book of Records*. And Margarita, whose ambition it had been to go to medical school and become a doctor. She had succeeded at that, Ulf remembered, and become an army doctor. He had seen her photograph in the paper, taken when she was serving with a Swedish peacekeeping force in Mali. He would be interested in asking her about that, and could do so at the reunion, he thought. He would certainly want to attend, even though the date conflicted with an arrangement he had made with Juni, the veterinary receptionist he was now seeing. He had offered to take her to a jazz concert at which a well-known saxophonist would be performing, a player considered to be one of the best alto saxophonists in Europe.

She had been lukewarm about going – she had never liked saxophones, she said – and would probably be relieved when he suggested a change of plan. He had been surprised by her distaste for the saxophone: how could anybody dislike an instrument that Rossini, no less, had said produced the most beautiful of all sounds? Or not be interested in the invention of a man called Adolf Sax, who devised elaborate keywork that would have given rise to envy in the heart of even the most accomplished of plumbers? He would work on that. The saxophone was so versatile an instrument, and Ulf thought that he might introduce Juni to its full range, including its repertoire of early music. It was wrong to think – as he felt she did – that the sax was only about jazz.

He pulled out his phone and began to write an email. Harald had given his address, and Ulf now typed his response. He would love to come to the reunion, he said. And yes, he would bring somebody with him. He then pointed out, tactfully, that it was the Department of Sensitive Crimes, not Selective Crimes. It was not a big thing, of course, but one might as well get it right. He sent the message, and put his phone back in his pocket. It was time to go to work. *Selective Crimes* . . . really! What did people think he did? Chose what to investigate and what to ignore? He paused. That was the way things had gone. Perhaps people thought that because the police ignored so many minor matters these days.

Perhaps Selective Crimes was not an entirely inaccurate name after all. Ulf smiled. The Department of Seductive Crimes (crimes that appealed in some way)? The Department of Speluncean Crimes (crimes committed in caves)? There were numerous possibilities, should the department wish to rebrand itself, as had occasionally been suggested by the Commissioner himself, an incorrigible enthusiast for renaming and restructuring things, other than his own department, of course. The Department of Sensitive Crimes had escaped such attentions because of a precautionary memo that Ulf himself had drafted and circulated. This had argued that any interference with the department would be seen as *insensitive* in the current climate, and should therefore be avoided *sine die*. He had been proud of the inclusion of that Latin iteration of *indefinitely*. He knew that nobody in the wider police force would know what it meant, but that obscurity would add authority and his proposal would go unchallenged. That was exactly what had happened, and nothing had been done. His colleague, Blomquist, though, had looked up the expression, and over the weeks that followed Ulf had heard him using it several times with real confidence, on one occasion glancing at Ulf as he uttered it, as if expecting approbation.

'Quite so, Blomquist,' Ulf had said.

Three months later, at a ceremony marking the graduation of the latest cohort of police recruits, the Commissioner himself had said *sine die* in his speech – in an incorrect context, but Ulf had nonetheless warmed to him, because a solecism was a sign of humanity, and there was something reassuring about the stumbling of a great personage.

He parked his silver Saab in the parking place reserved for him at the police offices. He had only recently been granted the privilege of a reserved space, and felt a strange, almost schoolboyish pride in the fact that his name now appeared on a small painted sign:

Varg, Sens. Crim. Dept. His spot was at the far end of the car park, along with the places allocated to the heads of other small departments. He was next to Environmental Crime, the head of which pointedly parked his bicycle in the middle of his place, suggesting that others should similarly resort to more environmentally responsible means of transport. On the other side was Commercial Crime, fittingly occupied by a sleek Mercedes Benz. At the far end were the places allocated to more senior officers, deputy commissioners and the like. Ulf had noticed that these senior spaces were wider than those in his section, and he pointed this out to Tomas Engelman, the Head of Commercial Crime.

'Typical,' Tomas had snorted. 'Have you seen their coffee cups? Bigger. Desks? Bigger. Telephones? More buttons. Computers? Lots more RAM. I could go on.'

'Oh, well,' said Ulf. 'It doesn't make them any happier, I imagine.'

'Doesn't it?' challenged Tomas. 'I'm not so sure, Ulf. Give me a bigger desk and I'd be very happy. And my computer freezes sometimes or sends a message saying I'm almost out of memory. Give me more RAM right now and I'd be really pleased.'

'Oh, well,' repeated Ulf. He almost said something about what the Buddhists taught us about the impossibility of ever satisfying material appetites, but did not, because if one went on about Buddhism to one's colleagues one would acquire a reputation of being eccentric or other-worldly, and that could be problematic. So Ulf simply said, 'I hope you get more RAM soon, Tomas.'

'So do I,' muttered Tomas. 'If we were in the private sector, we'd have plenty of RAM, you know. My brother-in-law works for a finance firm and he gets a new laptop every year. Every year, Ulf! It doesn't matter if the old one is still working fine and has plenty of memory – that doesn't seem to matter in the private sector. You get a new laptop, no questions asked.'

Tomas shook his head, and the conversation had come to an

end, although Ulf remembered it now as he nosed the Saab into its modest parking place. He looked at his watch and saw that he had twenty minutes in hand, the traffic, for some reason, having been unexpectedly light. Twenty minutes was perfect: he would go to the coffee bar opposite the office and phone Juni about the reunion. Then he would read his brother's column in that day's newspaper. Ulf's brother, Björn, the leader of a minority political party, the Moderate Extremists, had been given a weekly column in one of the local papers. Ulf had not been pleased by this development, as he disagreed with Björn on most matters, but he nonetheless felt he had to read what he had to say, even if only to be prepared for the comments the column would provoke amongst his colleagues. He was tired of telling people that he did not share his brother's opinions, and had become used simply to shrugging when people tackled him on the subject. 'He's him and I'm me,' he would say, and leave it at that.

There were few people in the coffee bar when Ulf went in. It was not uncommon for one or two colleagues to be ensconced within, but not now, and Ulf settled unobserved at his favourite table near the window. He looked at his watch: Juni would already be at work, as Dr Håkansson liked to open his veterinary clinic early. She did not mind his calling her at the office, though, unless she was assisting, as she sometimes did, with some veterinary procedure. He had once called her when she was trying to push a reluctant cat back into its carrier, and their conversation had been punctuated with feline growls and gasps of concern from an anxious owner. They had not talked for long.

She answered immediately.

'I'm sitting here having coffee,' he said. 'Thinking about you.'

He had not planned to say that; it came out, naturally, in a spontaneous burst of affection.

She sounded pleased. 'And I was thinking about you only fifteen minutes ago.' She paused. 'Nice thoughts, of course.'

'That's good to know.'

He told her about the reunion and about the clash with the jazz concert. She said that she did not mind at all.

'I'm going to have to change your view about the sax,' he said. She caught her breath. 'About sex?' she asked.

'No,' said Ulf, and laughed. 'Not sex: sax. About the saxophone.'

The woman behind the bar glanced in his direction. She raised an eyebrow.

'Oh, of course,' said Juni. 'I thought you said sex. That's what it sounded like.'

'Well, it wasn't. Anyway, this reunion . . . it could be a bit dull for you, I suppose.'

She assured him that it would not be. 'I'd like to meet the people you were at school with,' she said.

'They're pretty average. Nothing spectacular.'

She steered the conversation towards an end. Dr Håkansson had buzzed his buzzer and she would need to see what he needed. They agreed to meet for dinner the following day. Ulf asked Juni to come to his apartment, where he would cook crab linguine. He knew she liked that.

'Yes, I do like it,' she said. 'But I don't like it so much that I want to eat it all the time.'

He felt slightly hurt by this. How many times had he made her crab linguine? He had lost count, but that in itself did not mean that he made it too often.

'I could make something else,' he said, trying not to sound offended.

'No. Crab linguine will be fine. I like it – I really do.'

Dr Håkansson buzzed again, and they rang off. Ulf took that morning's newspaper from the rack near the table, his eye caught by a boxed headline on the front page. *How I'd deal with the graffiti problem: Björn Varg, page 4.* Ulf's heart sank. This was his brother playing to the gallery, as his party always did. He doubted whether his brother believed in half the policies he proposed; the criterion for their adoption, as far as Ulf could make out, being only that they would resonate with dyspeptic and dissatisfied people – people who felt things were fundamentally wrong, and were looking for a simple, viscerally appealing solution.

With an inner sigh, Ulf turned to page 4. There was a photograph of his brother, taken at least ten years ago and projecting an image of confidence and virility. And there, beneath the photograph, was the weekly diatribe.

'Every day,' Björn wrote, 'the senses of ordinary people are assailed by a form of visual pollution that scars our cities. Buildings, walls, even monuments are defaced by highly coloured scrawls, meaningless to most of us and intelligible only to the young vandals who perpetrate them. The police do nothing. The civic authorities say they are powerless, and the politicians don't even bother to comment on the issue. Well, I say that we have had enough! And I'll say it again, just in case the authorities are not listening: *we have had enough!*'

That was a favourite catchphrase of the Moderate Extremists. It was trite, Ulf thought, but it was also highly effective. Most people, he suspected, felt that they had had enough, and would be pleased to hear politicians declare that they shared their feeling. It did not matter too much what they had had enough of – it was the satiety that counted.

'Is there anything we can do?' the column continued. 'The answer is a resounding *yes*. We could stop this epidemic of graffiti immediately – tomorrow, even – if we spray-painted any young vandals caught doing it. They should be spray-painted from head to toe with paint that would take a few days, or perhaps even longer, to peel off. That would stop them in their tracks – right then and there.

'Of course, the usual lawyers will raise a howl of protest,' Björn continued. 'They always do. I say: let them. Be my guest. But lawyers should not be allowed to dictate whom we decide to spray-paint. That is a political, not a legal decision. I would simply tell these objectors: *we have had enough!*'

Ulf put the paper down with a sigh. The woman behind the counter looked at him. 'Your brother?' she called out.

Ulf made a gesture of helplessness. 'Yes, I'm afraid so.'

'People approve of him, you know,' said the woman. 'He's a direct speaker. Even when he's talking nonsense.'

Ulf laughed. 'Which is most of the time.'

'Well, we're a free country,' said the woman. 'And there's a place for people who talk nonsense.'

'I know,' said Ulf. And then, as if to affirm what she had just said, he saw Blomquist on the other side of the road, preparing to cross. It was too early in the morning for Blomquist, Ulf thought: he simply could not face it.

'I have to dash,' he said to the woman behind the counter.

The woman smiled. 'Poor Blomquist,' she said.

Ulf felt guilty. He hesitated. No, if he stayed, he would be buttonholed by Blomquist on something or other. Vitamins. Skin complaints. Solar flares. The latest developments in wind turbine technology. The list was a long one – seemingly endless.

Ulf apologised to the woman. 'I really have to get to the office,' he said. 'We're very busy.'

They were not. There had been very little crime over the last two weeks, largely because criminals were on holiday, mostly in Aegean resorts. They would come back at the end of August and begin to offend again, but until then the country seemed to be peaceful, even somnolent. If only it could be like this all the time, thought Ulf, wistfully. If only Sweden could be how it used to be. He stopped himself: that was the sort of nostalgia that the Moderate Extremists played upon, and he was determined that he would not fall into their trap. There had never been a golden age of contentment and good behaviour. There had always been dark forces beneath the peaceful exterior. Always.

He made his way towards the door, meeting Blomquist just as he stepped outside.

'I'm so sorry, Blomquist,' he said. 'I seem to be leaving just as you're arriving.'

'Synchronicity,' said Blomquist. 'Do you know that many of the events we think are coincidental are, in fact, the result of—'

'I'm so sorry, Blomquist,' Ulf repeated. 'We must talk about synchronicity some other time.'

'Oh, I would like that,' said Blomquist. 'When shall we do that, do you think?'

Ulf smiled, but did not answer, and Blomquist, looking down, went past him into the coffee bar. Ulf crossed the street. Outside the main door of the police building, he hesitated, and almost retraced his steps to join Blomquist, but did not. Moments of hesitation may occasionally be more morally significant than moments of action. This was the case right now, but Ulf could not quite face going back into the coffee bar. So he did not, and left his conscience to sort out the matter later on, which it might or might not do. One could never tell.

CHAPTER TWO

Where Is My House, I Ask Myself

Ulf looked at his in-tray and sighed. This was not because it was piled high with pressing matters; it was not – it was empty, apart from a memorandum about micro-aggressions in the workplace that the Human Resources department had recirculated. Ulf had heard that they felt people were not paying sufficient attention to their memoranda, and were proposing in future to send two copies of every memorandum or letter.

Ulf's colleague, Anna, had been incensed over this. 'You'd think they'd have something better to do,' she complained. 'In fact, sending a memorandum about micro-aggression amounts to a micro-aggression, in my view. Certainly sending two copies does. It's like sending an email in capital letters. That's a micro-aggression if ever there was one.'

Ulf had been more moderate. 'I suppose there's something in it,' he said. 'Looks can hurt. Things unspoken can be damaging. People need to bear in mind how others feel.'

Anna pursed her lips. 'Denying a micro-aggression can amount to a micro-aggression, you know.'

Ulf stared at her, and then realised that she was not being serious. 'I don't think you can legislate for courtesy,' he said. 'You just have to hope that people will treat one another well. And, by and large, they do.'

'Yes,' said Anna. 'And the exceptions end up here. In our in-trays.'

Now Ulf gazed at his empty in-tray. He was concerned: the Commissioner was always weighing up the work statistics of the various departments, and nobody wanted to be underemployed. That was the quickest route, they said, to reallocation to the traffic and parking department, an unglamorous corner of police work from which most people never re-emerged.

From across the room, Anna looked up from a report she was reading. She had seen him gazing at his in-tray and had correctly diagnosed the cause of his concern. 'Don't worry,' she said. 'You have an appointment. Somebody called just before you came in. He wanted to speak to you.'

'Personally?' asked Ulf.

'Yes. He was very insistent. I offered to help him but he wanted you. By name. Ulf Varg, he said. Brother of . . .'

Ulf groaned. Occasionally his brother's friends approached him if they were facing difficulties of some sort. He usually succeeded in putting them off, but he had to at least hear every caller out.

'Did he say what he wanted?'

Anna shook her head. 'He said it was sensitive. He said that's why he's coming here.'

'When?' asked Ulf.

'This morning. Ten o'clock. He said he'd be here on the dot.'

'OCD type,' said Ulf.

'Passive-aggressive?'

They sometimes played a game of psychologically typecasting their clients. There was a category for everyone, Anna said.

'And for us?' asked Ulf.

'Depressingly normal,' said Anna. 'Or normally depressing.'

They laughed. Anna made the office fun, thought Ulf. He wondered what it would be like without her – if he just had his male colleagues. He would go mad, he thought. He would become passive-aggressive. And yet, much as he appreciated Anna, he had to preserve clear boundaries. He could not become too fond of her; he had denied himself that possibility in the past, and he should not waver. Anna was married to somebody else. Their relationship was professional, and it should remain that way. It had to.

Then Anna said, 'It's Blomquist's birthday today, you know.'

Ulf lowered his eyes. He felt a warm blush of shame. He had been brutal in his getting away from Blomquist a few minutes ago, pretending to be busy when he was not. And Blomquist, he suspected, would know that he was not busy, because he was in the Department of Sensitive Crimes too, even if only seconded to it from some obscure branch of the uniformed force, and not occupying a permanent desk in the office. And he, Ulf, had more or less snubbed this poor man simply because he could not spare him a few minutes of his time. And he had done this on his birthday – the one day of the year when each of us feels we have the right to a little bit of kindness and consideration.

All that Ulf could think of to say was, 'Are you sure?'

Anna looked puzzled. 'Of course I'm sure. I put people's birthdays into my contacts file and the computer reminds me first thing when I switch it on. Today is Blomquist's birthday, it said. Ping. Automatically.' She paused. 'Don't you enter their date of birth when you add a new contact? It's pretty easy.'

Ulf looked away. 'Perhaps I should.'

'Yes,' said Anna. 'Mind you, men don't remember birthdays – for the most part. It's something that women do.'

They had been alone in the office, but now their colleague Carl came in. He tossed a newspaper down on his desk and removed his jacket. 'Did I hear you mention birthdays?' he said.

'Yes,' said Anna. 'It's Blomquist's birthday today.'

'I know,' said Carl. 'It came up on my computer.'

Anna gave Ulf a reproachful stare. 'And I was just observing,' she continued, 'that it's women who remember birthdays.'

Carl shrugged. 'Women keep everything together. No surprises there.'

'These things are changing,' suggested Ulf.

'That's true,' said Anna. 'My husband says that he sees it in the young doctors coming into his department. He says that the men are far gentler than they used to be. They're not afraid to discuss their feelings.'

'I think that's true,' said Carl. 'Men can cry these days.' He shook his head. 'Poor Blomquist. One doesn't think of him having a birthday, and yet I suppose he must, even if very few people notice it. Very few people are nice to Blomquist, I imagine – even on his birthday.'

Ulf bit his lip. That's me he's talking about, he thought. Me.

'We should get him something,' said Anna. 'A cake, maybe. Blomquist likes sweet things.'

Ulf shook his head. 'He's off them at the moment. You know how he goes on about diets. I think he's avoiding sweet things right now.'

'A bottle of wine?' suggested Anna.

Ulf remembered that Blomquist had said something about the carbohydrates in wine. 'I don't think so,' he said. 'Maybe just a birthday card.'

'Something that simply says "Happy Birthday, Blomquist"?' asked Carl.

'You can't go wrong with that,' said Ulf. 'And, anyway, what else is there to say? "Well done"? There's hardly any credit in simply making it through another year. I don't know why people congratulate others on their birthday.'

Anna disagreed. 'It's quite an achievement to get through a year these days. Look at the strains and the tension. The international situation. Humanity's problems, and so on. Making it through a year is quite a challenge, I'd say.'

Ulf remembered something. 'Albert Camus,' he said.

Carl frowned. 'Is he that suspect we were—'

'No. The French philosopher: Albert Camus. Big existentialist.'

'What about him?' asked Carl.

'He said that the only real philosophical problem was whether to carry on with life. That's all. *Tout simple*, as he might have said.'

Carl looked thoughtful. 'I can see what he means. Sometimes I wonder what the point of it all is. Know what I mean? What's the point in coming in here and sorting out the mess that other people make of their lives—'

'Or the lives of others,' Ulf interjected. 'And surely that provides a point: if we don't do something for the people who are being messed up by others, then who will? God? I don't think he always notices these things, does he?'

Anna corrected him. 'She. God may be a she – if she exists.'

'Human Resources said something about that in one of their memos,' said Carl. 'They said we should watch our pronouns.'

Ulf sighed. 'I would hope we can talk to one another freely – without worrying about getting pronouns correct.'

Anna smiled. 'I know where you two stand,' she said. 'I know that you're both new men.'

Ulf returned her smile. As he did so, he thought: but do you know how I feel about *you*? Because I still love you, you know. I know I shouldn't, and I'm trying hard not to. I'm trying to love somebody else, instead of you, but it's hard – it's really hard. Because often we can't decide whom we're going to love, because love happens to us, just like that, and we can't help ourselves. We love the wrong people. People do it time and time again.

He stopped himself. Anna was staring at him, and for a few moments he wondered if she could, in some unfathomable way, tell what he was thinking. Of course she could not, but there were other reasons why he should not allow himself to think that way. It was wrong – it was as simple as that. She was married to somebody else, to her anaesthetist with his tubes and gases and so on, and she had two young daughters who belonged to a swimming club. It would never be right for him to do anything to imperil the happiness of that little family.

And he had Juni now. He was fond of her. She was attractive and vivacious, and he thought that there was every chance he would love her in the fullness of time. Perhaps it would happen the following evening, when they looked at one another over their plates of crab linguine. Perhaps love would choose that moment to descend upon him, touch him, as might a passing bird that brushes past one with its gentle wing, its feathers.

Ulf's visitor was punctual, arriving downstairs at reception at precisely ten o'clock. The receptionist on duty called Ulf on his extension to tell him that one Fridolf Bengtsson was on his way up to the interview room. Ulf rose from his desk, glanced quickly at Anna, and made his way down the corridor to the sparsely furnished room in which interviews were carried out.

Fridolf was already waiting for him. Ulf introduced himself.

'You're very punctual,' he said.

Fridolf smiled. 'I can't help myself. I always like to arrive for anything at the agreed time. There's nothing worse than making somebody wait.'

Ulf took the opportunity to size up his visitor. He saw a well-groomed man somewhere in his early forties, wearing a blazer of the sort popular with yachtsmen, a pair of khaki chinos and a navy-blue turtleneck sweater. The clothes looked expensive, as did the watch that Ulf could see half obscured by the sleeve of the blazer. It was one of those watches that conveyed far more information than the wearer could possibly need. Who wanted to know the time in Mumbai and New York (contemporaneously)? Who needed to be aware of the barometric pressure of the water about them – other than divers, of course, and would they want to submerge such an elegantly styled timepiece in sea water? And the shoes? Ulf's gaze moved discreetly downwards. Red socks with … He had to look harder. Yes, there was a tiny pig's head motif. That suggested a sense of humour – or a rejection of conformism. Having a pig on one's socks was a statement: the pig was not a fashionable creature, but it was *fun*. And when it came to the shoes themselves, Ulf suspected these were English. Nobody made brogues with quite that look to them other than the English. It was hard to say why: some things had the appearance they did because for centuries people had been doing things in that precise way.

Ulf invited Fridolf to sit down while he himself took the chair on the opposite side of the table.

Fridolf was looking at him with a slightly disconcerting air, as if summing him up. Perhaps, thought Ulf, he's doing what I've just done to him.

'You're Björn's brother,' Fridolf began. 'Am I right? Your colleague confirmed—'

Ulf cut him short. In an interview, he liked to be the person to speak first – all his colleagues were like that too. 'Yes,' he said. 'I take it that you read his column.'

Fridolf grinned. 'I most certainly do. He's a very witty writer.'

Ulf's surprise showed itself. 'Do you think so? I'm afraid that I find my brother—'

Fridolf did not let him finish. 'Oh, he's extraordinarily funny. Sometimes, you know, I start to read his column and have to stop

19

because I'm laughing so much. I wear reading glasses, you see, and they mist up if you're crying with laughter.'

Ulf stared at Fridolf. Was this man serious? Somewhere within him, family loyalty gave him a nudge. Björn was his brother, after all, and it was tactless, to say the least, to poke fun at somebody's brother in his presence.

Fridolf continued. 'Take today's paper: have you seen it? I read it over breakfast and had to put my coffee cup down and take a deep breath. It was a real classic. He has a plan for dealing with graffiti artists. Spraying them with paint, would you believe it? Hilarious stuff. He must have a ball making that up. Can you imagine him sitting there and thinking: how can I parody these people? And then he hits the nail on the head. Bang. Out it comes.'

Ulf sat tight-lipped.

'I've never met him, of course,' Fridolf went on. 'I imagine, though, that he must be hilarious company. He must be: making that stuff up must require a real ear for the absurd. It's a fantastic talent. He'd make a fortune writing scripts for stand-up comics. They'd love him.'

Ulf was unsure how to react. To begin with, he had imagined that his visitor was speaking ironically, but now he was not so sure. It occurred to him now that Fridolf actually believed that Björn's column was a send-up, a pillorying of attitudes that he found absurd. If that were so, then how should he disabuse him of the wholly erroneous impression he had formed?

'I'm not sure my brother has his tongue in his cheek,' Ulf ventured. 'He's always been a fairly literal person . . .'

Fridolf laughed dismissively. 'Oh, come on! He couldn't mean any of it. Spray-painting vandals? Or, as he suggested the other day, making it illegal to play Russian composers on the radio? Nobody in his right mind could possibly . . .'

Fridolf trailed off as he saw Ulf's expression remain impassive. He cleared his throat. 'I really don't think he can be *entirely* serious, surely?' His voice rose as the statement became a question. Ulf noticed him shift in his seat, clearly embarrassed.

'Well,' said Ulf, 'I'm sure that you didn't come here to discuss my brother – interesting though he undoubtedly is.'

Fridolf was relieved to change the subject. 'No, of course not. I was referred to you – to your department – Significant Crimes . . .'

'Sensitive Crimes,' Ulf corrected him. 'The Department of *Sensitive* Crimes.'

'Of course, yes. The Department of Sensitive Crimes. I was referred by my local police station. They said this was a matter I might take up with you.'

Ulf nodded. 'And the matter in question?'

'Theft of a house,' said Fridolf.

'Breaking in?' asked Ulf. 'Theft *from* a house?'

Fridolf shook his head. 'No. Theft *of* a house.'

Ulf folded his arms across his stomach and leaned back. 'You mean squatters? Has somebody moved into your house and is now denying you access?'

Once again Fridolf shook his head. 'No. My house has been stolen. My country house, that is – I still have my house in town, but my house in the country has been taken from me.'

'You've been evicted?' asked Ulf. 'If that's the issue, then I should tell you that it's clearly a civil matter and we may not be able to be involved.'

Fridolf leaned forward. 'I'm sorry if I'm not making myself clear enough. My complaint is this: somebody has taken my house *away*. They have physically lifted it from its foundations and taken it somewhere else – where, I haven't the faintest idea. All I know is that my house was there, and now it's not. It's gone.'

For a few moments Ulf said nothing. He was thinking: a few days previously, he had been driving along a road and had encountered an abnormal load coming in the opposite direction. There had been an escort vehicle in the front, lights flashing, and an illuminated sign that said *Extra Wide Load*. And then there had been the truck with the wooden house strapped onto its chassis. It had been a large enough house – entirely wooden, of course, with two or three bedrooms, Ulf thought – not a mere cabin or shed. And Ulf had thought how convenient it might be, if one had to move, to be able to take one's house along too. There would be no need to pack possessions – they would just need to be secured to withstand the journey.

'This sounds very strange,' said Ulf, adding, 'You did the right thing in coming here. We're used to unusual offences in this department.' He paused. 'We've never had theft of a house before, though.'

'Well, it's gone,' said Fridolf. He began to smile. 'I haven't simply mislaid it, you know. That's always a possibility when something goes missing.'

Ulf shared the moment of levity. 'Car keys are the classic example of that.'

'Yes.'

Ulf opened a drawer in the interview desk. He took out a pad of paper and wrote a brief note at the top. 'Conversation with Fridolf Bengtsson.' To this he added the single word, 'Background'.

'Tell me about yourself,' he said. 'In these unusual cases, we need to know a little bit more about people. It allows us to see offences in context.'

Fridolf said that he could see the reasoning behind that. 'Nothing happens without there being a reason,' he said. 'Mind you, I can't for the life of me see why anybody would wish to steal my house.' He shook his head. 'I've tried, but I just can't.'

'The cause of any particular event,' said Ulf, 'is often not at all obvious. That is, it's not obvious until one identifies it – and then it might become extremely obvious.'

'The hindsight effect,' said Fridolf.

'Exactly,' said Ulf.

'Where would you like me to start?' asked Fridolf.

'At the beginning,' said Ulf.

Fridolf laughed. 'Really?'

Ulf nodded. 'The beginning,' he said, 'is where things start.' And in case Fridolf should think that he was not entirely serious, he said, 'I mean that, you know. Sometimes, in fact, the things that happen today had their roots back in the affairs of a previous generation. Our story doesn't begin when we are born. It begins way before that.'

And as he delivered this truism, he thought of his brother, Björn. Where had his peculiarities come from? He had his theories, of course, but he had never been entirely sure. Perhaps Björn's personality and its attendant quirks were simply the result of aberrant coding in the replication of DNA – the sort of thing that could happen to any of us. In chemistry, perhaps, was our true destiny – a thought that gave him little comfort. There had to be more to life than that bleakly reductionist conclusion. There had to be.

He looked at Fridolf. 'Please tell me about yourself,' he said. 'Where you're from; what you do; how you acquired this house, and so on.' He felt he had to offer further explanation. 'How you acquire things, you see, often has a bearing on how you lose them.'

Fridolf looked interested. 'I suppose that's right,' he said. 'I hadn't thought of it that way.'

'Well, I'm the detective,' said Ulf. 'That's how we're taught to think.' He paused. 'Yes, I'm a detective, and you ... May I ask your profession?'

'We process bacon,' said Fridolf, before adding, with an apologetic smile, 'Mostly for export these days. And we have another division that's doing crispbread. That makes up more and more of our business – in these health-conscious times.'

Ulf's eyes drifted to the socks. A small clue could be as eloquent as a large one – sometimes even more so.

CHAPTER THREE

Don't Do Anything
at the Moment

'My father, you know, died three years ago,' Fridolf began. 'He was a wonderful man. He was eighty-seven and he was still going for long walks. And swimming. He swam twenty lengths of the local swimming pool every morning without fail. Twenty lengths! When you think of that generation, and then you look at us, or the generation below us. Oh, my goodness, what a difference.'

Ulf made a note on his pad *Father died, 87.* That was very much a background detail, but it was precisely the sort of fact that could provide a key to the entire issue. The death of parents could cause more ill feeling amongst offspring than one might imagine. Arguments over succession could be the kindling that fuelled disputes lasting for years. So the death of Fridolf's father was entirely relevant.

'He sounds quite a man,' said Ulf. He did not want to say too much – a narrative was always best when unshaped by the one to whom it was told – but it helped to give encouragement.

Fridolf was pleased with Ulf's remark. 'Oh, he was. He was a countryman, you know – a farmer. He started off running the farm he had inherited from my grandparents. It wasn't much of a place – but he improved the land and slowly acquired more and more hectares. He had a dairy herd to begin with, but he switched to pigs. Eventually he became one of the biggest pig farmers in Sweden. Then he started to process bacon.'

'To give the Danes a run for their money?'

Fridolf smiled. 'He had views on the Danes, and that might have been a factor. I suspect, though, it was all about money. Farmers are more interested in money than bankers are, you know. They know what everything costs. They don't splash it around. They tend to be hoarders, given half the chance.'

'It worked?'

'It certainly did. We now have two big plants here in the south, and we own one in Denmark. I acquired that. Unfortunately, it was too late for my father to see. He would have loved the idea of actually owning a Danish bacon factory. Still, you can't dictate the way life is going to work out.'

'No,' said Ulf, and noted on his pad: *Father successful. Danish bacon factory acquired – presumably after some local (Danish) competition?* He looked up. 'Do you have brothers and sisters?'

Fridolf looked away: the question seemed to touch a nerve. Ulf made a mental note. Sibling rivalry? he thought. And again the issue of succession came to his mind.

'I do,' Fridolf answered. 'I had a brother. My parents were divorced and they did something that I don't think would be much approved of these days. They split us up. My brother went off with my mother and I stayed with my father. My mother had a lover, you see – that's what led to the divorce. He was a bridge teacher in Copenhagen – one of the best players in Denmark, if not in the whole of Europe.'

'Danish?' asked Ulf.

Fridolf nodded. 'Yes. She met him through a cousin of hers who lived in Aarhus. They were on a weekend bridge course and he was the instructor.' He shrugged. 'I was ten at the time and my brother was twelve. These things happen.'

Ulf picked up his pen. *Brother*, he wrote. *Estranged?*

'Did you see much of your brother after the divorce?'

Fridolf shook his head. 'He was brought up in Copenhagen. I saw him about once a year, I suppose. We weren't very close.' He paused. 'We weren't enemies or anything like that. He was a bit distant, I suppose. He went to university in Copenhagen and then lived in Germany for some time. He was an engineer. Siemens. He's back in Copenhagen now. He married the daughter of a merchant banker and he went into the firm. He's very well off.'

They exchanged glances. It was clear to Ulf that Fridolf had understood the drift of his questioning. This brother would have been an obvious candidate for enmity, but if he was independently wealthy, then an argument over succession to the bacon-processing business would be less likely. *Brother well off*, he wrote. *Not close.*

'My brother would hardly be interested in stealing my house,' Fridolf said. 'He has a country house of his own – a house, not a cottage. Stone and mortar. And a house in Italy. Somewhere near Siena. He sends me a Christmas card each year with a picture of one of his houses on it. Last year it was the Italian house. The picture showed Oscar – that's my brother's name – with his wife, his children, and two German shepherd dogs. They were beside the infinity pool he's built at the front of the villa.'

Ulf nodded. He found himself on the point of writing *Infinity pool*, but stopped. This was an interview, not a short story.

'I'm not sure I approve of infinity pools,' Fridolf said. 'They're a bit unnatural. And a bit flashy, too.'

Ulf was interested. 'Do you disapprove of your brother's lifestyle?' he asked.

Fridolf did not answer immediately. Eventually he said, 'No, not really.' But then, in the same breath, he went on, 'Or, perhaps, a bit. I not sure that I like . . .' He stopped.

Ulf waited.

'I'm not sure that I feel comfortable about financial people – bankers and fund managers and so on – paying themselves whatever they want. These people get eye-watering salaries, you know.'

Ulf required no persuasion of that. 'Very few of them are on the breadline,' he said.

'And yet what do they actually make?' Fridolf asked. 'Do they actually make anything useful?'

Ulf laughed. 'I suspect they'd say that they *make* money. That's what they make.'

Fridolf shook his head in disagreement. 'They *handle* it,' he said. 'The actual value is created by the people who do the physical work.' He paused. 'Not that I'm a Marxist – don't get me wrong on that. I believe in free enterprise. I don't think the state should control everything.'

'No, the all-powerful state is not a particularly attractive proposition,' said Ulf. 'It seems to be incompatible with individual freedom.'

'Although the state must have some powers,' said Fridolf.

'Of course. It's a question of balance. We need the state to assume some responsibilities – but not all.' Ulf sighed. There was nothing new in what he was saying; in fact, it was all rather bland: a political philosophy designed to avoid discomfort, but not one that promised much to anybody. And yet, perhaps that was what a political philosophy should do: refrain from any claims to be a complete solution. 'Achieving that balance isn't ever easy.'

They looked at one another, both uncertain where the conversation was headed. Ulf found himself warming to his visitor, and Fridolf, for his part, was pleasantly surprised by the sensitivity of the detective. Of course, he was in the Department of Sensitive Crimes, so perhaps that was not surprising.

Ulf returned to Fridolf's career. 'So, you stayed with your father,' he said. 'Did you take over the farms?'

'I did,' replied Fridolf. 'We had managers, of course, so there was not all that much for me to do – at least on a day-to-day basis. I looked after accounts and so on. Marketing.'

'All of which is important,' said Ulf.

'Yes. But it still gave me time to do other things.'

Ulf knew that he would have to find out what those other things were. Somewhere, in a list of innocent pursuits, might be the key to this otherwise inexplicable crime.

'I got married,' said Fridolf. 'I married my secretary. I'm afraid that we're no longer together.'

Ulf wrote, discreetly, *Wife. Acrimonious divorce/separation?* Once again they were on the borders of territory that could be rich in possible motives. Spurned or abandoned spouses or lovers had long memories, and wrath that could fester for years. And of course, arguments over the ownership of matrimonial assets could spill over into attempts to snatch back property to which one side or the other felt morally entitled.

'It was an entirely amicable divorce,' Fridolf continued. 'We sorted everything out without any real disagreement. There were no children.'

Ulf did not say it, but he was always sceptical of claims that divorces had been amicable. As often as not, people who said that were rewriting history, trying to portray in a positive light a process that had in reality been bitter and acrimonious.

'Did either of you remarry?'

'We both did. She married a chef. They run a small family hotel. She does front-of-house things and he looks after the kitchen. They're in all the guidebooks, and one of the newspapers did a piece on them in which they were described as a local *power*

28

couple. They loved that. Personally, I would hate to be considered part of a power couple, whatever that may be.'

Ulf made a quick note: *Power couple*. 'And you?' he asked. 'Did you find somebody else?'

'I married my secretary,' said Fridolf. 'Again. Different secretary, of course.'

We repeat ourselves, thought Ulf.

'My new wife is called Linnéa. She's half Swedish and half Filipino.'

'Children?'

'One. A boy of three. He's all right.' He smiled. 'I think she might want another. If I have the energy.'

Ulf moved on quickly. 'Does Linnéa work?'

'In the business,' said Fridolf. 'She's very good when it comes to logistics. We send bacon off in large refrigerated trucks. She arranges all that.'

'You mentioned time for other things,' Ulf said. 'What sort of things might those be?'

Fridolf hesitated. 'You mean: how do I spend my time? You'd like to know about what I do in my spare time?'

Ulf felt that he had to explain further. 'It's useful to know that sort of thing. It helps establish the overall picture.'

Fridolf looked out of the window. 'I lead a rather conventional life. Some may even say it's dull.' He sighed. 'You know, I really think we don't need to go over all of this. You're presupposing that the person who has taken my house has been motivated by some sort of antipathy towards me. But what if it's a simple theft? Somebody wanted a house and decided to help themselves. Surely the victim's private life has no bearing on straightforward thefts like that.'

Ulf conceded that this might be so if the motive was property-related, but the theft itself was so unusual that it would be unwise to exclude there being some sort of personal reason behind it. 'I assure you,' he said, 'that the more I know about you and your life, the greater our chances of doing something about this.'

Fridolf made a gesture of acceptance. 'All right. What do I do? Well, I'm a golfer – not a very good one, but I do play. I collect stamps – a rather unfashionable thing to do these days, but I inherited a large collection from an uncle and I've kept it going. I enjoy cycling and I play the flugelhorn in an amateur brass band. That's it, I think.' He gave Ulf a challenging look. 'Can you see anything there – anything at all – that makes you think I've . . . I've *asked* for this to happen?'

Ulf could not. But he asked again about enemies. 'Is there anybody you may have offended – even unwittingly?'

Fridolf answered this with a shake of his head.

'Have you dismissed anybody from your farms or factories?'

Fridolf frowned. 'Every so often the managers get rid of somebody, but it's always for a good reason. Dishonesty or bad time-keeping. But that's very rare: we're considered to be good employers.'

'Could you give me a list of anybody who's been dismissed over, say, the last eighteen months?'

'I'll ask,' he said. 'But I don't think there'll be more than one or two names – at the most. As I said, we have a good reputation as employers.'

'I'd still like to see it,' said Ulf. 'And if you remember anybody who might feel hostile towards you, just let me know.'

Fridolf agreed that he would, and Ulf rose to his feet. The interview was over, apart from the taking of the address of the house. Fridolf had drawn a map, and he handed this over to Ulf. 'This is how you get there, if you want to take a look at the place. And here's a photograph of the house itself – taken about a year ago.'

Ulf studied the photograph of a two-storey cottage of the sort that one might find anywhere in Sweden. It was the sort of house

that urbanites liked to build beside a lake, or deep in a forest somewhere: a retreat from the stresses and strains – and crime – of the
city. It was in an enviable position, close to the shore of a small
lake. At the end of the lawn in front of the house, a jetty projected
into the lake. A small wooden rowing boat was tied to this jetty.

'It's very attractive,' Ulf said.

'Yes,' said Fridolf. 'I've always loved it.' His face clouded. 'And
then, one afternoon, when I went out there, I discovered it had
gone. Can you imagine that? You arrive at your house and there's
nothing there – just a bare patch of earth where the house used
to be. To begin with, I imagined that I must be dreaming. How
can a house disappear? It can, it seems.'

Ulf felt a stab of anger within him. How could people do
something like this? How could anybody take away from another
something as important and as personal as a country cottage?

'I hope that we'll find out who did this,' said Ulf.

'Thank you,' said Fridolf. Then, rather tentatively, he asked
whether there would be any chance of getting the house back.

Ulf considered this. 'If we find it,' he said. 'If we manage to do
that, then presumably we can get it jacked up again and trans-
ported back to where it belongs – unless it has been taken abroad.'

He knew that it might be difficult if the house had been taken
over the border to Denmark, or further afield, into Germany.
Cars disappeared like that – they were whisked over the border
and then taken down to southern Europe and Turkey. Or they
were spirited off to the Balkans and disappeared into Serbia or
Croatia. Swedish cars. Our cars. Ulf felt the back of his neck get
warm. That always happened when he reflected upon a manifest
and major wrong. And it was that reaction that had inspired
him to become a detective. He believed it was important to
apprehend people who caused harm to others, or wronged them
in some way, or made them unhappy in their lives. He believed
in punishment – not severe punishment, but a sufficient measure

of punishment to make it clear to anybody who might be watching that people could not always get away with it, and that now and then justice would be done and malefactors would be called to account.

He walked towards the door to open it for Fridolf, and it was then, just as he was about to usher his visitor out, that it occurred to him that the answer to this case might be staring him in the face. He turned round. 'These bacon-processing factories of yours – are they large places?'

'Yes,' said Fridolf. 'They're massive.'

'How do they work?' asked Ulf. 'Do the pigs go in alive at one end and then—'

Fridolf cut him short. 'No, there are places like that, but mine aren't. We take our pigs to slaughter and then the carcases are delivered back to us. Then we slice them up and smoke them in some cases, and just cure them in others. It's production-line stuff.'

'I take it that there are people who find the whole process distasteful,' said Ulf.

Fridolf looked surprised. 'People who don't like bacon?'

'I meant, people who object to the thought of pigs being treated in this way.'

Fridolf's eyes narrowed. 'Animal rights people?'

'Yes. They wouldn't like it, I imagine. And frankly, I don't think I would either. I know somebody who became a vegetarian after twenty minutes in one of those places. And stuck to it, and never went back to eating bacon – or any other sort of meat, as it happened.'

'And you think that's what may be behind the theft of my house?'

'Possibly,' said Ulf. 'It's just that if you were finding it difficult to imagine anybody being determined to hurt you, perhaps you've missed a rather large cohort of people who would, quite cheerfully, target you for physical violence – let alone for an act of theft.'

Fridolf looked alarmed. 'Do you really think so?'

'I do,' said Ulf. 'It's possible. And if it is those people, then I must remind you that some of them are very determined.'

'What do you think I should do?' asked Fridolf.

'At the moment,' Ulf said, 'you shouldn't do anything – other than be very careful.'

CHAPTER FOUR

Did Dogs Want Much?

On returning from work the following day, Ulf retrieved Martin from his day-care with Mrs Hogförs before he began to prepare the crab linguine and salad for his dinner with Juni. The help he received from Mrs Hogförs in the care of Martin had started informally but had now become a full-time and permanent arrangement. Ulf would take Martin for his morning walk himself and then drop him at Mrs Hogförs' apartment, where he would remain until the early evening. Ulf had been hesitant about imposing on his neighbour in this way, but she had made it quite clear that she enjoyed Martin's company and would miss him if Ulf were to make alternative plans. The affection she felt for the dog seemed entirely reciprocated, as Martin would leap up in his eagerness to lick her face when she answered the door to them in the morning. It was as if they had been separated for weeks or months, rather than for a single evening – a phenomenon that Ulf believed was explained by the nature of canine memory. A dog who sees its owner walk out of the door believes that the owner is going forever – dogs do not remember that when the same thing happened the previous day, the owner duly returned. So, each morning the delight of discovering that Mrs Hogförs was still there was experienced afresh by Martin – and it filled him with joy.

Ulf had thought about Juni on and off throughout that afternoon. They had now been seeing one another for eight months, and he felt that sooner or later a decision would have to be made about their future. There was no question but that they got on well: Juni was easy company and, for the most part, undemanding. She was appreciative of Ulf's attention, and on more than one occasion had remarked that he was infinitely better than her previous boyfriend, a marine engineer, who had been both moody and possessive. She had eventually extricated herself from that relationship, but only with considerable difficulty. The engineer had tried to persuade her to continue, and had taken to telephoning her at odd hours with promises to do better, if only she'd give him the chance. Eventually she had blocked his number and he had finally accepted that things were over, but it had left her cautious about another involvement. Ulf, though, was entirely different, and had restored her faith in men.

Ulf was pleased that he had been able to make her happy in this way, but he was worried that there was, nonetheless, an absence at the heart of their relationship. He had never asked Juni whether she loved him, and she had never volunteered that she did. And yet he felt sure that her feelings for him went beyond the ordinary feelings that one sometimes finds between lovers: an acceptance of the comfort and security that comes with having a regular partner, even if any element of the grand passion is lacking. For his part, he was not exactly sure what he felt. He certainly *liked* Juni; he was fond of her, and was happy to spend time with her. They shared a sense of humour, enjoyed watching similar films, and even if they did not listen to the same music, at least they did not actively dislike the other's choice. But was there much more to it than that? He had been in love several times, even before he fell for Anna, and he knew that fondness and love were two quite different things. Love involved a quickening of the pulse, a feeling of yearning. People talked about being filled with love, but Ulf had always thought that was to misdescribe what was felt by one in love. It was emptiness, rather than fullness: a feeling within that there was an inner space, an incompleteness, that could only be filled by the other. Ulf did not feel that about Juni. He had never counted the minutes until she appeared. He had never been unable to concentrate on his work for thoughts of her. He had never waited anxiously for her telephone call, willing the phone to ring.

He knew the dangers. You could wait for the grand passion to arrive in your life, and wait indefinitely, until eventually it was too late. Nobody was perfect and the perfect woman, the perfect man, might simply never turn up. Life was a matter of compromise in so many respects. You compromised in your choice of job: not every position brought the challenges or variety you might want. Jobs could be dull and repetitive; they could offer few chances for promotion; they could involve boredom, frustration and even humiliation. But they were jobs, and you had to do them, and so you compromised. There were compromises, too, in the renting or purchase of a place to live: not every window looked out in the right direction; not every neighbourhood offered all that you might want of it.

Ulf was aware of his situation. He was by himself, unencumbered by children, and without much close family. If he found nobody with whom to share his life, he would wake up one day and find himself lonely. He was at the middle point of his career, and retirement was many years away. But what would happen to him when he no longer had to go into the office of the Department of Sensitive Crimes? How would he fill his days? Martin had the mortality of all dogs and would by that time have long gone. How would Ulf fill his days if he were by himself?

Ulf had not asked Juni her age but had discovered it when he saw her driving licence left out on the kitchen table. She was, he saw, thirty-four, which was, he thought, a good age to be. Thirty-four was not too old to have children, whatever people said about the ticking of the biological clock. There were women who gave birth to their first child after the age of forty, although that, he understood, was considered very late. If she wanted children, then she would have to make up her mind within the next few years. He wondered whether she was sizing him up as a suitable father; she had made one or two remarks that could be interpreted as suggesting just that. She had asked him whether he liked children, and he saw that she was watching him closely as she waited for his reply. He had said that he did and thought: only a curmudgeon, surely, disliked children. Then she had gone on to ask, 'And babies? What about babies? Do you like them too?' He had been about to answer when she had continued, with a note of embarrassment in her voice, 'Of course, most men are less interested in babies than women are. Its biological, isn't it? It's the maternal instinct. One shouldn't expect men to feel quite the same.'

Ulf realised that it was acceptable for women, but not for men, to say such a thing.

Ulf had said, 'Oh, I don't know. I quite like babies. As long as . . .'

She waited.

'As long as they aren't crying, I suppose.'

It was a weak caveat, and he grinned sheepishly; this was an uncomfortable discussion. Then he added, 'I know they can't help it. Babies cry. I wouldn't think less of a baby because it's crying.'

She looked away. 'I should hope not.'

The discussion had ended there, but it had given Ulf pause for thought. If Juni was keen on having children, then it would be wrong for him to give her cause to hope that she might have children with him – if he had no intention of allowing the relationship to develop in that direction. A mature, honest discussion was what was needed, in which the two of them could express what their expectations were. The problem for Ulf, though, was that he was not sure what he wanted. And now, as he asked himself the question, he answered *Anna*. He wanted her. He closed his eyes. He would not allow himself even to entertain that thought. He could not have Anna. There was no point; no point in wanting what one could never have: *crying for the moon* was the expression that summed up the futility of that. There was no point in crying for the moon, as all children who have ever cried for it are told.

Juni was late. 'I'm sorry,' she said, as Ulf let her into the flat. 'We had an emergency at the last moment. It often happens.'

It was a casualty from a cat fight, she explained. 'A badly torn ear. Dr Håkansson had to put in several stitches. Poor cat. He's a regular: he's always fighting.'

'Arguments over territory?'

She nodded. 'Cats are fiercely territorial. Far more so than dogs.'

'Most conflict is about that, don't you think?' said Ulf. 'Isn't it why human beings fight?'

Juni shrugged. 'Probably. Although there are other reasons, surely. People fight over other things. Don't they say there are going to be plenty of water wars in the future?'

'Probably,' said Ulf. 'But would you like a drink?'

She looked at him. 'Sometimes it seems that you don't want to talk to me.'

He frowned. 'I don't see why you would say that.'

'It's just that when we get on to a topic like the one we've just been discussing, you change the subject.'

He sighed. 'I'm sorry. I didn't mean to ... to stop you talking about whatever it was that we were meant to be discussing.'

'There you go again,' she said. 'It's as if you haven't been paying attention.'

Ulf felt a momentary irritation. It was as if she was looking for an excuse for an argument. He decided to be conciliatory.

'I really am sorry,' he said. 'If I seem unwilling to get involved in a serious discussion right now it's because when I'm at the office, I have to think all the time about issues that people have with one another. Arguments. Disagreements. Problems. All of those things are the daily lot of a detective. And so, when I come home, I prefer not to have to dwell on things that make me . . .' He searched for the right way of expressing what he wanted to say. He was fed up with disagreement, with conflict. Why couldn't people live in *harmony*? He sighed. He feared that the only way of his achieving what he yearned for would be to do something entirely different – to hand in his resignation and leave the Department of Sensitive Crimes altogether. There were plenty of other things he could do with his life. He was young enough to become something quite different. He could acquire a trade – he could train as a plumber or an electrician, as one of the members of the Commercial Crime department had done a few years previously. He had become a heating engineer and had never been happier than when he was busy calculating radiator size and the thermal requirement of his clients' living rooms. But then it had all gone wrong, as he had discovered that many of the other tradesmen he encountered in his work – carpenters, plasterers and so on, were engaged in lucrative schemes of overcharging and, in some cases, downright fraud. Bills were submitted for work not done, or done to a different specification than that which had been agreed upon. He had been outraged, and found himself investigating these wrongs, intent on exposing them. The inner policeman had been only briefly silenced, and, when confronted with criminality, had surfaced once more. The clients, of course, were grateful – even if embarrassed, as victims may often be – but the reaction of some other tradesmen had been resentful. He began to find that work he had done on a building might be discreetly undone, sometimes in a way that was actually dangerous to the inhabitants. He had returned to the police and was still campaigning for the creation of a new department devoted to the investigation and prosecution of construction crime. Thinking about this now, Ulf wondered whether he might tell that colleague about the theft of the house. Was this the sort of thing to which his corrupt plumbers and electricians might have graduated?

Juni interrupted his thoughts. 'I understand, Ulf. I'm sorry. I forget just how demanding – and emotionally draining – your work must be. All those murders . . .' She shuddered.

He shook his head. 'No, we don't have anything to do with murder. We don't have to touch anything like that.'

'But surely . . .'

'No, the matters we investigate are rather . . . how should I put it? Rather offbeat. In fact, they're sometimes downright peculiar.' He thought of examples. The man who'd found rotten fish placed on the front of his car? Intimidation was not all that uncommon, but the form it had taken in that case had ensured that it ended up in the Department of Sensitive Crimes. Or that case involving the nudist asset strippers? How could something like that be investigated by any other department? It was commercial crime, of course, but there was also quite another dimension to it.

'But even the cases that end up with you must have their challenges?'

Ulf nodded. 'Yes. And they all involve the thing that I find most stressful.'

'Which is?'

'Which is, I suppose, a fundamental failure between people. An absence of human sympathy.'

Juni thought about this. 'Wickedness?' she asked.

Ulf smiled. 'Now there's a word we don't hear very much these days. Yes, wickedness – good, old-fashioned wickedness. We try to persuade ourselves that wickedness no longer exists; that it's something that belongs to the past when people believed in things like the Devil and original sin and so on. But we don't realise that talk of the Devil might just be another way – a rather picturesque way – of speaking about something that has always been there in our nature – a capacity for wickedness.'

Juni crossed the room to where Martin was lying on his favourite mat. She bent down to stroke his flank, and the dog gave a brief, contented grunt of appreciation. She stood up and turned to Ulf.

'Poor Martin,' she said.

Ulf waited. He thought she was going to say something more, but she did not.

Ulf shrugged. 'He's all right. Not much happens in his life, but he's happy enough.' He thought for a moment. Did dogs *want* much to happen in their lives? Did it make any difference to them – as long as they were taken for regular walks and given regular meals? What else did they want? Companionship? Martin had plenty of that. During the day there was Mrs Hogförs, who doted on him, and in the evenings and early mornings he was rarely out of the dog's sight. Martin was not unhappy.

Juni looked down at the dog, who, as if he realised he was being observed, half opened an eye and wagged his tail. 'I was thinking of his deafness,' she said. 'It's such a pity.'

Ulf glanced at Martin, who had now closed the eye he had half opened. 'According to what I've read,' he said, 'dogs are unbothered by their deafness.'

Juni looked doubtful. 'I don't see how you can say that. Who can tell what goes on in a dog's mind?'

Ulf replied that for much of the time he could tell, with some accuracy, he suspected, what Martin was thinking. 'I often know

41

what he's going to do before he does it,' he pointed out. 'He communicates pretty well.'

Juni did not seem convinced. 'The problem is that we project our feelings onto animals – then we think that we understand. But we may not. I've discussed that with Dr Håkansson, you know. He has strong views on anthropomorphism. He says that most of his clients act as if their animals understand what they're saying to them.'

Ulf looked embarrassed. He spoke to Martin – of course he did – but he did not, for a moment, imagine that Martin understood him, except when it came to a few clearly enunciated words that Martin could lip-read and certainly understood.

'I know that you speak to Martin,' Juni continued, 'and I'm not saying that you think he understands you. All I'm saying is that we just can't tell what makes an animal happy or unhappy.' She paused. 'Pain's different, of course. We can tell when an animal feels pain.'

'Martin's fine,' muttered Ulf, reaching for the pot in which he was proposing to cook the linguine.

'Have you thought of surgery?' asked Juni.

Ulf shook his head. 'No point,' he said. 'Dr Håkansson told me some time ago: nothing can be done to help Martin. He can't hear, and that's all there is to it. I don't think—'

Juni cut him short. 'That may have been so then – now it's different.'

Ulf waited for her to explain.

'You see, I've been reading one of the veterinary journals Dr Håkansson gets. It's an American journal and the latest issue has a report on cochlear implants for dogs. I asked Dr Håkansson whether he had read the article, and he said that he had. He said, "Very interesting." And then he said, "It'll make a big difference to deaf dogs." That's what he said. He said *big difference*. That means he thinks that dogs do mind being deaf.'

Ulf was non-committal. 'People disagree.'

Juni persisted. 'I think that Dr Håkansson knows what he's talking about.'

'I don't disagree,' said Ulf. 'And he may be right about this. Perhaps dogs do mind being deaf. Perhaps Martin remembers what it was like to hear and wonders why he can't hear any longer. Perhaps he feels a sense of loss. Dogs pine, after all, which suggests that they can experience loss – and the sadness that may come with loss.'

'So, if there was a chance that something could be done?'

Ulf inclined his head. 'I'd listen. Of course I'd listen. Tell me about it.'

'Have you heard of cochlear implants?'

Ulf said that he had. In fact, Blomquist had said something about these, but, as was often the case when Blomquist was explaining something, Ulf had not been paying attention to what was said.

'They put wires in the ear,' he said. 'In the ... what do you call it?'

'The cochlear. It's a bit of bone in the ear. It's full of nerves that pick up signals from special sorts of hairs. When you're deaf, those signals don't get through. They implant titanium electrodes in the bone and transmit the signals that way.'

'I see.' Blomquist had told him you should never put anything into your ears, as you could damage those hairs. He had remembered that – at least some of Blomquist's dire predictions and warnings registered.

He gave Juni a searching look. 'Are you telling me that they can do this for dogs?'

She looked excited. 'Yes. Isn't it marvellous?'

'Well ...'

'People think that animals don't deserve these sophisticated treatments. People say it's a waste of time and money, but I don't agree. What's the difference between human suffering and animal suffering? Can you tell me that?'

Ulf was not sure how to answer that. Most people would argue that there was a moral difference between killing another person and killing an animal – and that, in the absence of hypocrisy, would surely have to be the position of any non-vegetarian. And by the same logic, most systems of morality to date had held that cruelty towards a human was somehow worse than cruelty towards an animal. But the grounds for making that distinction were not always apparent. We valued our interests more highly than those of other species, but against what scale did we make the comparison?

He sighed as he tried to answer her question. 'Oh, I don't know. I suppose it's because we only have the time or energy to worry about ourselves. It would be impractical for us to spend too much time thinking of other creatures. They don't think about us, after all.'

'Except for dogs,' she said. 'Dogs will do anything for us.' She paused. 'And we owe it to them to do what we can for them.'

Ulf turned away. This was a reproach – he was sure of that. And yet he had nothing to be ashamed of in his treatment of Martin. He glanced quickly at Juni, and then looked away. He felt a momentary doubt, which he struggled to repress. But if the doubt had been about her, it quickly became a doubt about himself. There was an inherent danger in entering into any relationship after a long period of being single. It was only too easy to get set in one's ways and become oversensitive to any criticism, however mild.

'I do my best by Martin, you know.' He spoke quietly, trying not to sound peeved.

'Oh, I know you do, Ulf. But you have to be open to . . .'

'To what?'

'To new possibilities. You see, there's a veterinary school in

America that's been experimenting with cochlear implants in dogs. The original research for these implants was done on Dalmatians and monkeys before they tried it on humans. It works.'

Ulf remained silent. Juni was looking at him expectantly.

'I asked Dr Håkansson whether it was something that he could do. He said that he did not feel he had the necessary expertise, but that, as it happened, he had heard of a vet who specialised in animal hearing issues and was prepared to perform the procedure.'

Ulf was surprised by this information. 'Here? In Sweden?'

Juni smiled. 'No, but as good as. He's in Copenhagen.'

Ulf pursed his lips.

'Well, I don't know . . .'

Ulf sensed that she had made up her mind, and that she now expected him to take Martin to this new vet in Copenhagen. But he had not agreed to anything, and he would not be browbeaten.

'I'm not sure I want to put him through it,' he said. 'It's a new procedure – even experimental, when applied to dogs. I really don't want to sign up for something like that.' He paused. 'And I assume that it's pretty expensive. Did Dr Håkansson say anything about that?'

Juni did not reply immediately. Ulf pressed her. 'I imagine it costs a fortune,' he said.

'A bit,' replied Juni, grudgingly.

'How much?'

'Well, it's not cheap. He talked about twenty thousand dollars in the USA – something like that. So it would probably cost that, or a little bit more, in Sweden.'

Ulf corrected her. 'Denmark.'

She laughed. 'Sweden, Denmark: that's not the issue.'

Ulf had not been surprised by the cost. Twenty thousand dollars was two hundred thousand krona. Dr Håkansson was expensive enough; a specialist vet, performing an extremely advanced procedure, could easily involve that much. But it was all academic, as he now pointed out that he did not have twenty thousand dollars. 'Sorry,' he said. 'But there it is. We can't always do the things we want to do.'

That was a mistake, and he realised it immediately. Juni pursed her lips. 'You could get a bank loan.'

Ulf stared at her. 'Are you serious? Do you really think I'd go to the bank and get myself into debt over a veterinary bill – and not even a life-or-death one?'

He tossed several handfuls of linguine into a pot and began to cover it with water. There was crab meat in the fridge – a rough unattractive block of it, once compressed and frozen, but now thawed out and ready for the saucepan. He took this out and then began to chop up two bulbs of garlic.

Juni came to stand beside him, watching him. 'Don't forget the chilli pepper,' she said.

'Of course I won't forget it.' He had not intended to appear touchy, but that was how it seemed. He muttered, 'Sorry. Thanks for reminding me.'

'I'm only trying to be helpful,' said Juni.

Ulf made an effort. 'I'm so glad that we both like crab linguine. Could you imagine going out with somebody who didn't?'

Juni looked at him. 'Would it matter to you? I wouldn't mind.'

She had not detected his irony. 'Of course it wouldn't matter to me,' he said. 'I wasn't exactly serious, you know. I was trying to—' He broke off. It was difficult to explain humour, and often it was best not to try. But the fact that she had not understood the spirit of his remark worried him. There had been one or two instances of that in the past, and he had not paid any attention to them; now he was more concerned.

She sat down on one of Ulf's kitchen stools. 'I've met him, actually.'

'Who?'

'The vet in Copenhagen. I went to see him.'

Ulf had been deseeding the chilli. He stopped. 'You went to Copenhagen?'

'Yes,' she said airily. 'I think I told you I went over there to see my cousin a few weeks ago. Afterwards, I drove past this vet's place. I stopped to have a word with him. He was very nice.'

'I'm sure he was,' said Ulf. 'But that's not the point. I can't afford it – I just can't.'

Juni ignored this objection. 'He showed me a picture of the device. It's amazing. They have an outside sensor, clipped onto the skin on the side of the head, you see, and it transmits to the wires implanted in the cochlear. The dog has to wear a special collar. The batteries are in that.'

'Juni,' said Ulf. 'There's no point. I don't have two hundred thousand krona.'

Her airy dismissal of the expense was unabated. 'We could find a way. What really counts is Martin.' She slipped off the stool and came up to Ulf, reaching out to touch his forearm. 'We can make this happen, Ulf. Think of that. Martin will be able to hear.'

He stared at her: Juni was taking over. *We*. Martin was his dog. He was, in a sense, *in loco parentis* to him – he was his guardian. And any decision about veterinary procedures really should be his, and his alone. And yet what was the point of being in a relationship if you did not share in life's important decisions? And it was hard to think of a more important decision than that of whether or not to spend two hundred thousand krona that you did not have on something that you did not want.

CHAPTER FIVE

Albanian Beer

Ulf had told Fridolf that he planned to see the site of the missing house. He had been given instructions as to how to get there, or at least how to negotiate the final part of the journey, the one not covered by his sat-nav. When he came to do the trip, he was accompanied by Blomquist, who had heard of the case and had specifically asked to be involved. 'I'm shocked,' Blomquist had said. 'It's bad enough to have to put up with the usual sorts of crime – minor thefts and so on – and now these people are actually stealing people's houses.' He shook his head. 'What's happening to the world, Ulf? That's what I'd like to know.'

These people. Blomquist had said *these people.* But who exactly did he mean?

'You said *these people*,' Ulf remarked. 'Does that mean you have an idea who might have done this?'

Blomquist looked out of the window. 'I think you know as well as I do.'

Ulf was at the wheel of his silver Saab, with Blomquist beside him in the passenger seat. There was a satisfying smell of old leather from the car seats. That was part of the charm of an old car: real leather, cracked and weathered, but redolent of a time when . . . a time when people didn't have their country cottages stolen from under their noses.

'No, I'm not sure I do know,' he said. 'You tell me.'

Blomquist was silent for a few moments. 'This is not a local crime,' he said. 'This has organised crime written all over it.'

Ulf smiled. Blomquist had his theories, and his enthusiasms, and one of them was a tendency to look for a global explanation for crime. It was true that there were mafia-type gangs operating in Sweden, as there were in many other countries. It was true that a great deal of the drug trade had fallen into the hands of these gangs. But it was unhelpful – and unfair – to blame one group of people for everything.

'Don't stereotype, Blomquist,' Ulf said. 'There are plenty of innocent foreigners.'

Blomquist continued to look out of the window. 'And the Naserligan? Those people over in Gothenburg – the ones who had the gunfight on the beach? We all know what's going on. There are official reports – from Brussels and so on. They spell it out. There are Balkan gangs.'

'True enough,' said Ulf. 'But there are plenty of Swedes up to their neck in it too. It's not just outsiders.' He paused. 'And frankly, one of the things we should *not* do as detectives is stereotype people.'

'Even if they deserve it?' asked Blomquist.

'But that's the whole point, Blomquist,' said Ulf, his voice rising in exasperation. 'Stereotypes are never deserved.'

Blomquist was sullen. 'Why not? Why not – if they're based on fact?'

'Because they don't look at the facts,' Ulf countered. 'That's what makes a stereotype a stereotype. You don't look at the facts of the case. You don't ask what a particular individual is like – you judge him on the basis of where he's from, what he looks like, how he talks, and so on. Those are things that may have nothing to do with the real question – which is, what he, that actual person, is like.'

Blomquist was silent as Ulf continued, 'And from our point of view, Blomquist – from our point of view as detectives – if we allow ourselves to be influenced by stereotypes, then we can very easily end up looking for criminals in the wrong place.'

There was more silence from Blomquist.

'So,' Ulf went on, 'if we start off assuming that this is the work of a foreign gang, while all the time it may be no such thing, then we could walk right past very obvious clues. We could waste a lot of time looking for outsiders to blame when in reality they may have nothing at all to do with it. It's unfair to innocent foreigners; unfair to the victim of the crime; unfair to everybody.'

Blomquist shrugged. 'I see what you mean.'

'Good.'

'Although it still *might* be foreigners.'

'It might be,' agreed Ulf. 'But let's keep an open mind.'

Blomquist turned to face Ulf. 'Have you ever been there, Ulf?'

'Albania? No, never. I've been to Croatia, but that's . . .'

'A different country,' supplied Blomquist.

'That's right. And you, Blomquist: have you ever been there?'

Blomquist shook his head. 'I've read about it – quite a lot, in fact. I picked up a book about the northern part of the country.'

'Oh, yes? And?'

'It's mountainous up there,' Blomquist went on. 'I know I'm stereotyping the place, but it does have mountains. If you go there, even if you're determined not to stereotype, you'll encounter very high mountains.'

Ulf had the grace to laugh. There were times when Blomquist, even poor old Blomquist, with his rambling theories about vitamins, and his loquaciousness about just about everything, could be amusing.

'Very funny, Blomquist. No, I mean it: very funny.'

'Northern Albania is far from funny,' Blomquist continued. 'It has always been a lawless place. They love their blood feuds up there – they always have.'

'So I've heard,' said Ulf. 'And they've never been too keen on governments.'

'No,' agreed Blomquist. 'And who can blame them? They had the Ottomans for a long time. King Zog and his crew. And then Mussolini turned up.'

'More than enough to put anybody off government,' Ulf mused.

'And then they had a particularly unpleasant dictator for a long time. Hoxha. So, if you're living up in the mountains, with a big moustache and a gun slung over your shoulder, you're obviously not going to be too keen on any government, I wouldn't have thought.' Blomquist paused. 'Hoxha was worse than most of the other Communist dictators. Worse than Ceausescu. Every bit as bad as Stalin – although on a smaller scale.'

'Poor people,' said Ulf. 'They've suffered.'

'No civil society,' said Blomquist, 'means a lot of crime.'

'True.'

'And an inadequate diet too,' Blomquist went on. 'If you don't have enough to eat, then you might have to turn to crime.'

'Understandably.'

Blomquist looked thoughtful. 'Would you steal a loaf of bread if you were starving?'

'Of course I would. Who wouldn't?'

'That's why so much crime is exported from southern Europe,' Blomquist said. 'Desperation coupled with a lack of respect for the law. Put the two together and you get what you get.' He paused. 'Not that I'm excusing anything. Once you start to excuse things, then our job becomes impossible.'

Ulf did not disagree, but he felt he had to remind Blomquist not to blame Albanian gangs for everything. There was too much pointing of the finger, he said. There was plenty of Swedish crime – quite enough to go round, and he pointed this out now.

Blomquist listened to the gentle reprimand and assured Ulf that he had an open mind. 'I'm not one of those prejudiced people,' he said, looking reproachfully at his senior colleague. 'I'm prepared to suspect everybody.'

Ulf struggled not to laugh. 'Suspect *everybody*, Blomquist? Surely that's going a bit far.'

Blomquist frowned. 'You know what I mean.'

'Yes, I do,' Ulf assured him. 'Mind you, it might be a good idea to suspect everybody. How many times have we missed the guilty because we've narrowed the field down too early? That's as bad a mistake as casting the net too wide.'

They were nearing the point at which they were to leave the main road. Fridolf had told them what to look out for – an unpaved road marked *Larsen*. That, he explained, led to his nearest neighbour's farm, a half-cleared stretch of land, badly tended and now the dominion, in some places, of feral chickens and turkeys. Larsen had largely stopped farming, but still kept a few discouraged cows and an ancient tractor. If Ulf followed that road until it forked, he should turn off to the left and he would find himself in woods that continued down to the shore of a small lake. There he would find the clearing in the trees in which the purloined house once stood. 'You'll see the foundations,' Fridolf said. 'You'll see how it's been literally lifted from the ground.'

They passed the fork in the road that led to Larsen's melancholy farmhouse, the roof of which was just visible through a stand of birch trees. The track now became rougher, and Ulf had to negotiate his way round several potholes in which rainwater had gathered. Through the trees they could now just see the lake – small patches of silver reflecting the morning sun.

'I don't know what people see in places like this,' observed Blomquist. 'I imagine that our friend has a comfortable enough house in town – so why does he come to this godforsaken neck of the woods?'

'To reconnect with nature, Blomquist,' said Ulf. 'The discomfort is part of the charm.'

Blomquist peered anxiously through the window, as if looking for hidden dangers. '*Ixodes ricinus*,' he muttered.

Ulf did not say anything. He suspected that Blomquist was about to launch into one of his expositions, but with any luck they would soon arrive and he would be distracted.

Blomquist turned to Ulf. 'That's a tick, you see. And they're everywhere in this part of Sweden. Not that you can see them, of course.'

'There have always been ticks,' Ulf said. 'Martin used to get them until I started treating him.'

'Well, we can't treat ourselves with that stuff you put on dogs,' Blomquist warned. 'Don't try it, Ulf.'

'I wasn't going to.'

'Good. Because I think that stuff causes brain damage in humans. It's best to use a tick repellent powder or specially treated clothing. You do know, don't you, that you can get trousers – and shirts too – that have been treated with a chemical to repel ticks? You know that, I take it?'

Ulf nodded.

'And the interesting thing,' Blomquist continued, 'is that the treatment survives washing. You can wash the clothes normally and they'll still work.' He paused. 'How many times do you think you can wash them, Ulf? Guess. Go on, guess.'

Ulf shrugged. This was Blomquist at his most trying.

'Oh, I don't know. Ten times? Fifteen?'

'Wrong,' said Blomquist, in a tone that suggested he was pleased Ulf had not come up with the right answer.

'Well—' began Ulf, only to be cut off by Blomquist.

'No, go on. Go ahead and guess. See if you can get closer this time.'

'Thirty times,' said Ulf. 'But really, Blomquist . . .'

'Wrong again.'

'All right, two hundred times. You can wash them two hundred times.'

Blomquist snorted. 'Don't be ridiculous.'

Ulf defended himself. 'You asked me to guess.'

'Yes, but I expected you to take it seriously.'

Ulf bit his lip. Any discussion with Blomquist could drag you down into a pointless and meandering exchange out of which it was difficult to escape.

'I take it you're worried about Lyme disease,' said Ulf.

'Yes, I am,' said Blomquist. 'But not only that. There's tick-borne encephalitis too. Not that I'm too worried about that personally – I've been vaccinated. Have you been vaccinated, Ulf? Against tick-borne encephalitis?'

'Possibly,' said Ulf. 'The doctor gave me a couple of shots of something. I tend to forget what I've had.'

'You should keep a record,' said Blomquist. 'I have a book and I enter details of all the injections I have – and all the pills I take. It's all there – going back ten years.'

Ulf kept his eyes on the track. 'I don't see much point in that,' he said. 'Your doctor will have your full medical record – if it's ever needed.'

'And if his clinic goes up in smoke?' Blomquist challenged. 'What then?'

'I assume he keeps it in the cloud,' said Ulf mildly. 'Very few people keep physical records these days. Except you, I suppose, with your notebook . . . There's more risk, surely, of your notebook going up in smoke, Blomquist.'

Blomquist looked smug. 'Actually, Ulf, that's what you might think, but if I were to tell you . . .'

They had arrived: the clearing opened up before them and beyond it, the lake. 'We're here,' said Ulf, not without relief.

He drove the Saab a short distance further before stopping under the shelter of a well-established birch tree. A child's swing had been rigged up on one of the branches of this tree, and one of the ropes was twisted round the seat. It was the only sign of human occupation, apart from the rectangle of light gravel on which the house had been built. From this area there protruded pipes of various dimensions, cut off roughly just above ground level, evidence of severed connection to a drainage system. Here and there, a few pieces of timber, painted green on one side, lay abandoned.

They got out of the car. Ulf drew in his breath. This was a crime scene, but one quite unlike any he had ever seen before. He turned to Blomquist, whose expression of astonishment matched his own.

'It looks as if it really has been stolen,' said Ulf. 'I had my doubts, you know.'

'It's extraordinary,' said Blomquist.

They walked slowly to the vacant site.

'I suppose we should be looking for something,' Ulf said. Serving in the Department of Sensitive Crimes meant that he very rarely had to visit a physical crime scene, and now he had to remind himself of the correct procedures. *Advance slowly over the ground. Keep looking down. Don't disregard any object. Small objects may be big clues.*

They separated. While Blomquist walked in a wide circle round the outer perimeter of the foundations, Ulf started to examine the gravel rectangle itself. The position of the walls was clear enough – depressions where wooden floor-beams must have rested now provided a complete plan of the ground floor. It had all been done so neatly; everything had been lifted, cut out, like tissue removed by a conscientious surgeon – neatly and completely.

Ulf found nothing, apart from sawdust at several points where whoever had removed the house had cut through beams. It was hard to imagine how the whole process had been carried out so neatly, and it occurred to Ulf that the gravel must have been raked afterwards. He looked for footprints, but there were none; nor were there any signs of a vehicle having been driven over the surface. If this had been a legitimate job of demolition, then the contractor would have deserved the highest possible rating for neatness.

He joined Blomquist. 'Anything?'

Blomquist pointed behind him. 'There's something you should see back there.'

Ulf accompanied Blomquist as he retraced his footsteps. 'There,' said Blomquist, pointing to a pattern in the ground. 'That's a tyre track.' He took a few steps forward and indicated a line of indentations in the ground. 'And there: that's another.'

Ulf examined the tracks. He took a tape measure out of his pocket and measured their width. Blomquist wrote down the measurement as it was called out. Then Ulf fished his phone out of his pocket and took several photographs.

'I don't see anything else,' said Ulf. 'The whole thing has been done with surgical skill.'

Blomquist glanced again at the tyre tracks. 'A crane, do you think?'

Ulf thought for a moment. Wooden houses could be moved – he knew that – but he was uncertain how it was done. They'd had to use a crane, he decided, as how would they lift something as bulky as a house otherwise? And if they used a crane, then they must have had another vehicle onto which the structure would be lifted. That would have left tracks too, and yet there was no sign of any other vehicle having been there.

'You'd think we'd find something else,' Ulf said. 'A cigarette end? A scrap of paper?'

Blomquist laughed. 'No self-respecting criminal smokes on the job these days,' he said. 'You leave a bit of your DNA on the cigarette stub, you see.'

Ulf felt embarrassed. He should have known that.

And then he spotted it – at almost exactly the same moment that it caught Blomquist's eye. An empty beer can. Ulf bent down to retrieve it, holding it gingerly before slipping it into a clear plastic bag he had extracted from his pocket.

'Well done, boss,' Blomquist said. 'Now we have something to work on.'

'The thief likes beer,' said Ulf. 'That narrows it down.'

Blomquist looked blank. Of course it narrowed it down. Why should Ulf smile when he said that, he wondered.

'Do you know this brand?' Ulf asked, pointing to the can.

Blomquist nodded. 'I know it,' he said. 'I haven't ever tried it, though. I find that a lot of beers are too gaseous for me. I have to be careful of gas.' He looked at Ulf as if in reproach; as if somehow it was Ulf's fault. 'It's an Albanian beer, you know. Brewed locally, of course, under licence from a brewery in Tirana.' A note of triumph crept into Blomquist's voice. 'Albanian,' he repeated. 'And they'll sell this in that bar they like to hang out in.'

Ulf said nothing. Blomquist was occasionally right; it had happened on a number of occasions before this, and it was possible that this was another instance. For his part, Ulf was always prepared to accept that he himself might be wrong, and so now he said to Blomquist, 'Your suspicions may have been well founded, Blomquist. Foreigners might well be mixed up in this.'

'Or they may not,' said Blomquist. 'We mustn't jump to conclusions.'

'No,' said Ulf. 'But at the same time we might ask ourselves: why else would there be a can of Albanian beer in the middle of a forest?'

'When you put it that way,' said Blomquist, 'foreign involvement does seem to be a possibility.'

They drove back along the track, successfully avoiding all the potholes, bar one into which the near front wheel of the Saab dipped with a sudden shudder. Then they were at the junction with the road to Larsen's farm where, on impulse, Ulf turned the car off to the left.

'He's the only person for miles around,' Ulf said. 'He may have seen something. Farmers usually don't miss much.'

Blomquist agreed. 'Stealing a house must be a noisy business. His dogs may have barked, although ...' He frowned, remembering something.

'Although what, Blomquist?'

'Although dogs don't always bark,' Blomquist continued. 'Have you read that story by Conan Doyle? "Silver Blaze"? Sherlock Holmes was able to identify the culprit for precisely that reason. The dog must have known the person who committed the crime. That's why he didn't bark.'

Ulf laughed. 'We could do with Holmes,' he said.

Blomquist looked hurt. 'Instead of me?'

'Not at all,' Ulf reassured him quickly. 'As well as you. You'd be the perfect team, Blomquist – you and Holmes.'

This pleased Blomquist. 'Do you really think so, Ulf?'

Ulf said that he did. 'The two of you would get to the bottom of this case in days,' he said.

'I've read a lot of Conan Doyle,' Blomquist said. 'I think Sherlock Holmes might have been the reason why I went into the police in the first place. He was my inspiration, so to speak.' He gave Ulf a quizzical look. 'What about you, Ulf? What were your reasons?'

'I studied criminology,' Ulf replied. 'It seemed the natural next step. And I suppose I wanted to help people. Does that sound a bit grandiose?'

'Not at all. At heart, most of us want to help other people.' Blomquist hesitated. 'That brother of yours . . .'

'Björn?'

'Yes, him. The one who's in the Extreme Moderates.'

Ulf corrected him. 'No, he's the other party: the Moderate Extremists.'

'Yes, him. What drives him, do you think? Does he *believe* in what he says?'

They were nearing the farmhouse, and Ulf did not think he had time to do justice to the question. But it was too important to ignore. So he said, 'Does he believe in any of it? I'm not sure. I think he says what he thinks people want to hear. A lot of people do that, of course, but *real* belief is another thing altogether. People who really believe in what they say tend not to worry if others agree.'

'So he'll say anything if it's going to get him votes?'

Ulf took a few moments to answer. Björn was his brother, and he felt a degree of loyalty to him, but Blomquist, once again, was right. There was nothing Björn would refrain from saying if he thought that it might be to his electoral advantage. Did he really believe in spray-painting graffiti artists? Ulf thought not; but Björn would most certainly believe that the broader public would be tickled by the thought of taking direct action of that sort against those who disfigured the public space. Björn, like many a populist, understood the public and its peculiarities. He knew the issues that would raise public hackles; he knew where the public red lines were.

'My brother is not a very principled man,' he said quietly, almost to himself. 'He has many good points, I suppose, but I'm afraid that the thing he wants above all else is power. It's as simple as that. He wants to exercise power; he wants to be the one who makes the decisions. I don't think it matters what the decisions happen to be.'

Blomquist listened to this gravely. 'How can two brothers be so different?' he asked.

Ulf was unsure how to respond. Blomquist had paid him a compliment, but he was not sure that he deserved it: like all truly good men, Ulf was unaware of his goodness. He looked at Blomquist. 'You're very generous, Blomquist,' he said. 'That was a kind thing to say.'

'We must be kind to one another,' said Blomquist. 'It's the only way.'

Ulf nodded, but he felt guilty inside. He was recalling how he had failed to find the time to speak to Blomquist on his birthday. Now he said, 'Blomquist, I believe it was your birthday the other day.'

'It was,' said Blomquist. 'Not a significant one, though – just an ordinary birthday. My wife forgot it, I'm afraid. And I didn't feel I could remind her. That would have made it worse for her, I think.'

'Oh dear,' said Ulf. This made it so much worse. Yet at least Anna had remembered and had ordered a cake. It had been delivered at a time that Ulf had been called out of the office, and he had not been there to share in the celebrations.

'She remembered the next day and felt very bad about it,' Blomquist continued. 'I had to pretend that I had forgotten too, or she would have been very upset. The fact that I had also forgotten made it easier for her.'

They drew up in Larsen's farmyard and Ulf parked the Saab next to an ancient blue tractor. Behind the house, the door of a barn creaked loudly on its hinges. A few chickens pecked at the ground. Ulf gestured for Blomquist to follow him to the house, where a porch door, half open, suggested that somebody was about.

'Mr Larsen?' asked Ulf as a thin man, frail and elderly, came to the door. He was wearing a pair of working dungarees, the material worn smooth at the knees.

'That's me,' said the farmer.

Ulf identified himself and Blomquist. 'We are from the police,' he said. 'The Department of Sensitive Crimes in Malmö. My name is Varg and this is Blomquist.'

Larsen stared at his visitors, his gaze moving from Ulf to Blomquist, and then back again. Ulf saw that the farmer's eyes were light blue and seemed to have a piercing light to them.

'What?' Larsen asked.

'The Department of Sensitive Crimes,' Ulf repeated.

Larsen frowned. 'Why?'

'Why what?' asked Ulf.

'Why there?'

'Where?'

'There. Where you come from. Why sensitive?'

Ulf and Blomquist exchanged glances. 'I wonder if we could come in and have a word with you.'

Larsen was blocking the doorway. He did not move. He seemed to be calculating something. 'No harm,' he said eventually, and turned back into the house.

Ulf and Blomquist followed him into a sparsely furnished living room. Somewhere in the background there was the smell of fish soup.

'You having fish soup?' asked Blomquist. 'For your lunch?'

Larsen shrugged. 'Breakfast, maybe. I didn't have breakfast.'

'Fish soup's good at any time,' said Ulf, with forced cheerfulness.

'If it's fresh,' said Blomquist. 'And as long as you don't put too many potatoes in it. Too many potatoes are bad for you. Carbohydrates, you see.'

'Carbon?' asked Larsen.

'No, carbohydrates. Not carbon.'

'I don't like carbon,' said Larsen. 'Kept away from it. My father died of carbon, you know. Killed him.'

Ulf looked at the floor; Blomquist smiled politely. 'I'm sorry to hear that,' he said.

'Yes,' said Larsen. 'He's dead now. But then everybody dies, don't they?'

They were standing awkwardly, Larsen not having invited them to sit down. Ulf decided to take control. 'I'm going to sit down, if you don't mind. Blomquist, you should sit down too.'

Larsen pointed to a sofa and a chair before lowering himself onto a rickety high stool.

'Your neighbour,' Ulf began. 'Fridolf Bengtsson.'

Larsen brightened. 'Yes, Fridolf. He is my neighbour over there. He's a very big pig farmer. They make a lot of bacon, I think. He had a boat on the lake. It sank.'

'Do you know him well?' asked Ulf.

Larsen shook his head. 'He's got money. He wouldn't want to have much to do with me. He blamed me for his boat, you know. It had nothing to do with me. It was that boy from the village – the one with the large ears – you may know him. That boy. He and his friends took his boat and sank it. They didn't drown. They swam ashore.'

'Why did he blame you, then?' asked Blomquist.

'Because he wants me to go away,' answered Larsen. 'He wants my land. He tried to buy it once, but it wasn't for sale. My father's buried in the woods here and you can't sell your father's bones to some pork butcher from Malmö.'

Ulf hesitated. There was something very wrong here. Was Larsen losing his grip on reality?

'Do you know that somebody has stolen Fridolf's house? They've ripped it from its foundations and taken it away.'

Larsen took some time to absorb this news. Then he said, 'You say it's vanished?'

'Yes,' said Ulf. 'It seems to have disappeared completely.'

Larsen closed his eyes. 'I think it was probably me,' he said.

Ulf waited for a few moments. Then he said, 'You *think* it was *probably* you?'

'I can't be sure,' said Larsen. 'But I think I did it. I don't remember things very well these days.'

'Why would you have done it?' asked Ulf.

'Because I don't like that man,' said Larsen. 'I don't like him and I don't like his house.'

'If you did it,' said Blomquist, 'then where did you take it?'

'I can't answer that,' said Larsen. 'I can't answer that because I can't remember where I put it.'

Ulf cleared his throat. He needed to take control of this encounter. 'How would you have done it, Mr Larsen – if you did it, that is?

Larsen seemed to be trying to remember. 'I think I got a contractor. Yes, a contractor. He took it for me.'

'But you don't know where?'

Larsen shook his head. 'No, I have no idea. I'm sorry.' He paused. 'He should have built it more strongly. It was a very flimsy house. Stupid man. That's what comes of not being from these parts. You don't know how to build proper houses. He built his house of straw. Now it's gone.'

'I think it was wood,' said Ulf.

'A bit of wood,' said Larsen. 'Lots of straw too.' He paused. 'Olof Palme will stop that sort of thing. He's planning to, you know. When he gets the time. He's very busy. If you're prime minister you have a lot to do.'

Ulf gave a start. 'Olof Palme?'

'Prime minister,' said Larsen.

'He was,' said Ulf.

Larsen seemed not to have heard him. 'He's busy.'

Blomquist was staring at Larsen, his mouth wide with disbelief. Ulf gave his assistant a glance before he addressed his question to Larsen. 'It's possible that you didn't steal Fridolf's house,' he said. 'It's possible that your memory is a bit faulty. But let's just imagine that you didn't and that somebody else did. If that were so, then would you have heard anything? Or seen anything?'

'If somebody else took the house?' Larsen asked.

'Yes.'

'But I did see something. I saw some men down there. They were doing something.'

'What were they doing?' Ulf asked.

'They were having a picnic. They were drinking. Maybe fishing. Who knows?'

'Beer?'

'I didn't see.'

Ulf waited. 'What sort of men?' he asked.

The answer came quickly. 'Albanians, I think,' said Larsen.

Ulf raised an eyebrow. 'Are you sure?'

'Yes, they were shouting out in their language. It wasn't Swedish and it wasn't Polish or German. Maybe French. Or even English.'

Ulf asked if the house had still been there when he saw the group of men. Larsen shook his head. 'No, the house had already gone, now that you mention it. There was nothing there. It was very odd.' He paused. 'But I think it was there. Yes, houses don't move, do they? I've got some fish soup on the stove. Do you want some? I want to have my lunch, you see, and I don't want the soup to spoil.'

Ulf shook his head. 'You've been very helpful, thank you. We must get back to Malmö.'

'You said you were from Gothenburg.'

'No, we didn't. Malmö.'

Larsen nodded. 'And what is it you say you do?'

CHAPTER SIX

Enfants Sauvages, etc

The following day being the first Tuesday of the month, Ulf went for his regular appointment with his psychotherapist, Dr Svensson. He usually saw the therapist during his lunch hour, taking a sandwich and a flask of coffee with him to the appointment. The therapist did not mind this, and had even encouraged him to do it. 'We talk more readily over food,' he said to Ulf. 'It is because, in the past, that is where we met one another.'

'Around our campfires?' said Ulf.

'Exactly. Our hunting ancestors huddled around the fire for warmth and told one another stories of the day. That is how they transmitted the culture, such as it was.' Dr Svensson shivered involuntarily. 'The fires would have been a small circle of light in enveloping darkness, you see. And just outside the light, waited the wolves.'

Ulf thought of wolves. This was not the first time that Dr Svensson had mentioned them; every so often the topic of wolves came into their conversation. Was that, Ulf wondered, because of his name – composed, as it was, of the word for *wolf* in both Danish and Swedish. Dr Svensson was interested in the works of Lacan, the French psychoanalyst who stressed the importance of language, and might be expected himself to be influenced by linguistic associations.

'Wolves?' asked Ulf.

'Yes. In the night. Can't you see them? I can. They're sitting there, outside this circle of forelight, shrouded in darkness. But every so often their eyes can be seen, reflecting the light. Can you see that? Pinpoints of yellow light in the velvet black. Wolves.'

'I suppose so,' said Ulf. 'They probably picked up the scent of the meat we cooked on our fires.'

'Oh, they certainly did that,' said Dr Svensson. 'They would have sniffed that out. And we gave them scraps, of course. We tossed a bone in their direction. That was how they became habit-uated. Then, as they became bolder and approached the fire more closely, we singled out the friendlier ones and they became dogs. That's where dogs come from – as I expect you know.'

Ulf said that he did know that. 'And, of course, modern canine DNA is virtually indistinguishable from lupine DNA. Or so I've read.'

Dr Svensson nodded, and gazed pensively out of the window, as he often did when talking to Ulf. Ulf noticed his jacket, which was made of blue linen, and his not-quite-matching trousers, also of linen, but in a lighter shade. Dr Svensson was a natty dresser, and his clothes, although relatively low-key, were clearly well made and expensive. He could afford them, thought Ulf, who had once done a rough calculation of Dr Svensson's income, based on what he paid him for his sessions. If he saw only three patients a day, he would still be making a more than comfortable salary.

'Wolves,' said Dr Svensson, 'are laden with symbolism. They carry on their backs so much of our fear and dread that I'm sur-prised they can so much as walk, let alone run for hours through the forests. They represent the dark, the primeval, the elemental. They are the creatures with whom we shall never have any dealings because they *lurk*. Other animals don't *lurk*; they strut or scurry or do whatever it is they do, but they do not *lurk*. Wolves are outlaws.'

'Well—'

Dr Svensson cut Ulf short. 'Of course, that is all from our perspective. Wolves have been more positive in other cultures. The Japanese used to worship them, I believe. And the Romans rather liked them – hence the story of Romulus and Remus being suckled by wolves.'

'Highly unlikely . . .'

'But of course. And yet . . .' Dr Svensson made a cautious gesture. 'One must be careful not to be too dismissive. Many legends are based on historical fact, and there are numerous accounts of the discovery of feral children. Have you read *Les Enfants Sauvages*? No? Perhaps you've heard of Kaspar Hauser and Victor de l'Aveyron. And then there are the children discovered in India, who were thought to have been raised by wolves. One was actually discovered in a cave at the age of about six, living with wolves. He was taken to an orphanage and given a name – Dina Sanichar, I seem to recollect. It was quite a famous case. He walked about on all fours and ate raw meat.'

'And howled?'

Dr Svensson smiled. 'Yes, I believe he did. He never learned to speak, although he did learn how to smoke once he joined human society. That wouldn't have done him much good.'

Ulf unwrapped his sandwich, examining the filling as he did so. 'Ham and avocado,' he said. 'And tomatoes. The same as last week – although last week there was no tomato.'

He noticed that Dr Svensson, who was now seated in the chair opposite Ulf's – the therapist eschewed the use of a couch; 'Such a cliché,' he said. 'A gift to cartoonists, of course, but in reality a way of emphasising the dependency of the analysand' – now made a note on his pad. Was he noting down the contents of the sandwich, Ulf wondered? And, if so, why? He resisted the temptation to enquire.

Instead, he said, 'I sometimes feel guilty about eating while you're sitting there without anything. I feel a bit greedy.'

Dr Svensson looked interested. 'Guilt?' he asked.

'Yes. I feel that I'm looking after myself when I should be . . . well, I suppose I should be offering to share my sandwich with you.'

Dr Svensson looked thoughtful. 'That's entirely natural and healthy,' he said. 'The desire to share with others is a feature of our inherent need for community. We eat together, we share our food, and that sharing ensures our survival. All that is completely understandable in evolutionary terms.'

Ulf nodded. 'I can see that. But I still feel guilty.'

'Guilt,' said Dr Svensson. 'Who doesn't feel guilty – other than the psychopath? Tell me, Ulf, what other feelings of guilt do you experience?'

Ulf gave the matter some thought. 'Oh, I feel guilty quite often, I suppose.'

Dr Svensson urged him to give some examples. 'Talking about feelings of guilt is very important. You defuse them by exposing them to the gaze of others. Our cognitive therapy friends are big on that – and they're right, in my view, in so far as they go. But they tend not to go too far below the surface, even if they have a few useful tricks up their sleeves.'

Ulf remembered Blomquist's birthday and his lack of patience with his colleague. 'I work with somebody,' he said. 'There's a man called Blomquist, and he's attached to my unit. He's a nice enough fellow, but he can be extremely trying when he gets going. And he can get going on any number of subjects – often health-related. You know: vitamins, carbohydrates – that sort of thing. On and on.'

Dr Svensson smiled. 'Oh, tell me about it,' he said. 'I have a cousin like that. He's a cosmetic dentist – you know, one of those people who straighten your teeth and give you a better smile, that sort of thing. He's keen on railways and he talks about them non-stop. For hours, if he gets the chance. He does these long railway journeys, you know – all over the world. The Trans-Siberian Express. The journey from Montreal to Vancouver. Last year he went on that train that goes from Darwin to Adelaide – the Ghan, I think it's called. Well, he went on that. And do you know what he did? He counted the number of kangaroos he saw on the trip. He kept a tally. Can you believe it?'

'There must be something wrong with him,' said Ulf. 'He must be a bit . . .' He stopped himself.

'On the spectrum?' supplied Dr Svensson. 'Yes, you'd suspect that, but I don't think he is. I think he just likes to keep himself entertained, and counting kangaroos was a way of doing that. He also counted the camels he spotted from the train. You know there are a lot of feral camels in Australia – thousands of them. They were brought into the country for transport purposes – for crossing the outback – and some of them escaped and bred in the wild. They're a big problem for graziers because they drink a lot of water.' Dr Svensson paused. 'But let's get back to guilt. Do you feel guilty about your relationship with this Blomquist person?'

Ulf inclined his head. 'Very,' he replied.

Dr Svensson made another note on his pad. Then he looked up at Ulf. 'You feel guilty because he's making demands on your attention. I can see that straight away. He's using up your time talking about vitamins and so on and you blame yourself for not paying much attention to what he has to say.'

'That's about it,' said Ulf.

'But of course you don't need to feel that. He has no right to claim more of you. You don't have to *love* Blomquist, you know.'

'I don't love him,' said Ulf. 'I never said I did. I couldn't love Blomquist – ever. I just couldn't.'

'And you feel guilty about that, I imagine. Do you? Do you feel guilty for not giving Blomquist the love that he so clearly craves?'

'I don't know if Blomquist wants me to love him,' said Ulf. 'I don't think he does.'

Dr Svensson did not agree. 'Blomquist needs your love. You are his superior. You are senior to him in rank. You are wiser—'

'Blomquist is pretty intelligent,' Ulf interjected. 'I wouldn't underestimate him.'

'It's not a question of intelligence, Ulf. It has nothing to do with that. The desire for love is a demand of the ego, not of the rational mind. Blomquist feels empty. He is trying to fill his world with irrelevant facts – these things you say he goes on about all the time. He wants to fill the void with that and with the love of others. He wants you to *affirm* that he – that is, his ego – is important. Your love would do that, you see, but you cannot give it because—'

'Because I don't feel it,' said Ulf. 'You can't force yourself to love another person – or a thing. Love is not something that can be turned on like a tap.'

'Possibly not,' agreed Dr Svensson. 'But tell me, Ulf, whom do you love? What are the things or the people that you love? Not Blomquist, obviously; nor, I would venture to suggest, that brother of yours.'

Ulf interrupted the therapist. 'I do love my brother. Of course I love my brother.'

'Why?' asked Dr Svensson. 'You've always told me how embarrassed you are by him and his views.'

'I am,' said Ulf. 'Did you see what he wrote in his last column?'

Dr Svensson smiled. 'That piece about spray-painting graffiti artists? Yes, I read it. I thought it very significant.'

'It wasn't significant,' retorted Ulf. 'It was nonsense.'

'Oh, as a policy it's ridiculous,' said Dr Svensson. 'But it tells us a lot about what your brother really wants.'

Ulf waited.

'He wants to *possess* the graffiti artists,' said Dr Svensson. 'He wants to make them *his*. And his way of doing that would be to paint them, to assert his ownership over them. It's exactly the same motivation that inspires the graffiti artists to scrawl their names and designs over public objects. They're saying: *this is mine because it bears my cypher.* By this act of spraying, I claim this thing, this space. I may be nothing to you, but I am *here*. And your brother is evincing a similar desire. By spraying these vandals with paint he is *claiming* them. It is a form of *jouissance*, as Lacan would have it.' He paused. 'But let us not wander.'

'No,' said Ulf, trying to glance at his watch without being seen by Dr Svensson. 'You asked me about guilt. And I told you about poor Blomquist – with whom I declined to have coffee the other day – on his birthday. That made me feel guilty. And then I felt guilty about entertaining erotic thoughts about my colleague, Anna. And then about feeling irritated with my girlfriend, Juni. I was cross with her because she was trying to make me feel guilty about declining to get my dog's hearing restored.' He shook his head. 'There's so much guilt. Wherever I turn, there's guilt.'

Dr Svensson was interested in hearing about Martin. 'I suspect that you blame yourself for your dog's hearing problems. Do you?'

'Blame myself?'

'Yes. We often blame ourselves for the suffering of others – even if we've done nothing to cause or exacerbate that suffering. There's nothing at all unusual in that.'

Ulf explained that Martin's deafness really had nothing to do with him.

'Of course it hasn't,' said Dr Svensson. 'But guilt can be entirely undeserved. That's one of its main characteristics.'

71

'The operation in question would be very expensive,' said Ulf. 'Over two hundred thousand krona.'

The therapist raised an eyebrow. 'But it would restore his hearing?'

Ulf shrugged. 'There'd be a chance of success.'

'Juni wants you to do it?'

Ulf nodded. 'She's trying to push me into it. She can be persuasive.'

'And you'd like to resist?'

'Yes, I think I would. But I don't want her to think that I'm unfeeling – that I care nothing for Martin.'

'Will she think that?'

'I think she might.'

Dr Svensson took a few minutes to make notes on his pad. Ulf tried to see what he was writing, but he could not make anything out – other than the word *guilt*, which the therapist then underlined. Twice. The notes made, the therapist fixed Ulf with an enquiring gaze. 'I get the impression,' he said, 'that you find yourself trapped at present. You feel hemmed in when it comes to those around you. There's Blomquist at work, and Juni at home. I wonder whether you're getting enough oxygen – in the metaphorical sense.'

Ulf was silent as he thought about this. It was true, he thought. He needed oxygen. But he was uncertain about how he might obtain it.

'You need to take a deep breath,' said Dr Svensson.

Ulf drew in his breath.

'I meant in a metaphorical sense,' Dr Svensson added quickly.

Ulf exhaled.

When he returned to the office, the eyes of his colleagues followed him to his desk. Ulf sat down. There was something in the manner of the other three that suggested something had happened. He looked at Anna first, who caught his eye for a moment before looking away. That told him a great deal. He glanced at Carl, who gave him a bland, uninformative smile. That, too, was eloquent – as was Erik's attempt at a neutral expression.

Ulf looked down at his desk. On it lay an envelope that bore his name. It was an internal delivery – a communication from another department.

He raised his eyes. All three had been watching him, but immediately busied themselves with paperwork when they saw him look in their direction.

'That came for you while you were out,' said Anna. 'I think it may be important. It was brought over from the Commissioner's office.'

Ulf affected nonchalance as he slit open the envelope. 'You'd think he could use the telephone,' he said. 'But there we are.'

Erik could not contain himself. 'It must be important,' he said.

'Cuts,' said Carl. 'They're taking an axe to the budget everywhere. Our turn now.'

Ulf did not respond. He had started to read the note from the Commissioner.

'Please make an appointment to see me as soon as possible,' said the note. 'Preferably today, but by tomorrow afternoon at the latest.'

Ulf looked at his watch. It was barely two o'clock and there would probably be time to see the Commissioner that afternoon. He reached for the phone and dialled. He was aware of the silence in the room. Erik had been about to make a call, but on seeing Ulf lift the receiver, he put his down. They were all listening.

Ulf did not bother to lower his voice as he spoke to the Commissioner's secretary. 'I gather that the Commissioner wants to see me urgently,' he said.

The appointment for an hour later made, Ulf now addressed the office at large.

'Something important, I think,' he said. 'And probably not good news.'

Erik groaned. 'They're going to abolish us. I can tell. Would they think of getting rid of public relations or social compliance or any of the other major wastes of money? No, they would not. So they go for Sensitive Crimes – of course they do.'

Carl told Erik that it could mean early retirement. 'Isn't that what you've been angling for, Erik?' he said. 'If you'll excuse the pun.' Erik was an obsessive fisherman.

Erik shook his head. 'I'd like to do a few more years,' he said. 'My wife is keen for me to maximise my pension.'

'We all have financial obligations,' said Anna. 'Children are ruinously expensive.'

'What about Blomquist?' Carl asked. 'Last in, first out. He's the most recently arrived member of the department.'

'Technically, he's just attached to us,' said Ulf. 'I think he's an item on somebody else's budget.' He paused. 'And I don't think we should be discussing Blomquist's situation when he isn't here.'

Blomquist did not have a desk in the office, but was accommodated in what had previously been a large stationery cupboard on another floor. The notice on the door used to say *Stationery and Supplies*, but had been painted over to read *Blomquist*. Occasionally, older members of other departments still opened it in their search for envelopes or paper clips and were surprised to find Blomquist within. Blomquist would sigh and ask them to knock. 'But we thought you were stationery,' they would say. And he would reply, 'I'm not,' and sigh once more. It was not easy to accept that one might be mistaken for stationery; it was not easy at all.

Ulf decided to end the discussion. 'I think we should refrain from discussing this until I know what the Commissioner wants,' he said. 'There's no point in surmise.'

'I thought that surmise was what we did,' said Anna. 'Professionally, I mean.'

Her tone bordered on the sarcastic, and Ulf gave her a reproachful look. He would never speak like that to her, and he was hurt that she should address him in that way. She did not love him – obviously. But he already knew that, and he told himself that he should just accept it and get on with his life. And that life now included Juni ... except he was not so sure that he wanted it to continue to include her. He felt confused and unhappy. And now the Commissioner was going to make his whole position even more uncomfortable, because no summons to the Commissioner – for whatever reason – boded well.

He busied himself with minor administrative correspondence until it was time for him to make his way to the Commissioner's office in its nearby building. He arrived on time, but was asked to wait in an ante-room while the Commissioner finished a conference call to Stockholm. Ulf sat back in an easy chair and studied the artwork on the walls. It was all reproduction, framed in identical frames, and all of it by well-known Swedish artists of the nineteenth century. One of Ulf's interests was art history, and he had particular knowledge of Nordic landscape art of that period. He recognised one of the paintings immediately: Simeon Marcus Larson's *Waterfall in Småland*, which he had seen in the Nationalmuseum in Stockholm. He gazed at the angry sky that was so typical of the artist's work, and the turbulent torrent below. It was a painting full of turmoil and energy – not one to calm any visitor to the Commissioner who was feeling anxious or perturbed. In contrast, beside it was a painting of a placid lake and an empty, almost white sky. That was more like it; that was more in the spirit of Nordic landscapes: a painting full of thin, northern light. Ulf did not recognise it, and was about to get up to make a closer inspection when a door opened and he was beckoned inside.

'So,' said the Commissioner, 'I seem to recall that you have an interest in art, don't you? We've discussed it before, I think.'

'In a very amateurish way,' said Ulf, and then, immediately correcting himself, he added, 'I mean my interest is amateurish – not our discussion.'

'Oh, very funny,' said the Commissioner. 'You were concerned I might think that you meant I knew nothing of the subject.'

'Which would be the very opposite of what I thought,' said Ulf. 'I'm the one who knows nothing – or very little. I'm sure you know a great deal more than me.' He paused, and then went on, 'About many things.'

The Commissioner smiled. 'You don't need to flatter me, Varg.'

'I wasn't,' said Ulf. 'I was just trying . . .' He waved a hand. 'I was just trying to make conversation.'

The Commissioner pointed to a chair. 'That's fine. Don't worry. I also remember, I think, that you have a dog. We talked about dogs once, I think.'

'I do have a dog,' said Ulf.

'I'm very keen on dogs myself,' said the Commissioner. 'I might have told you that before. In fact, I was visiting our dog unit the other day. We have a couple of new trainers, you know. They're very gifted. Dogs know when somebody is in charge – they're pack animals, aren't they? You have to be assertive. Dogs pick it up if you aren't.'

'I think that's right.'

'You can't reason with dogs,' said the Commissioner. 'Dogs have a sense of hierarchy – they need a firm hand. You tell the dog what's what, and you insist on compliance. That's the way to deal with a dog.'

'I think I'd agree with you,' said Ulf.

'It's the same with people,' said the Commissioner. 'Human beings aren't all that different from dogs, you know.'

Ulf waited politely. 'Oh yes?'

'Yes. We need leadership. We need commands.'

Ulf imagined for a moment the Commissioner addressing a

group of police officers and telling them, sharply, to sit. And they all sat – as dogs will do on being so instructed.

'The problem with society these days,' the Commissioner went on, 'is that we have lost sight of the need for authority. We are adrift. We have no sense of purpose or meaning in our lives.' He paused. 'Ask the average person what the meaning of his life is, and he'll look at you blankly. He'll shrug.'

Ulf did not disagree. But he thought: how would *I* answer that question? What was the meaning of his life? He thought of the others in the office. Erik existed to catch fish. That was what he thought about all the time: fish gave his life its meaning. And Carl? Carl was a member of a chess club and liked jazz. Would those interests give meaning to his existence? Anna, of course, had her daughters and their swimming lessons. As far as he could make out, the two girls and their swimming galas gave an immediate purpose to Anna's life. And she had her husband, of course, and he in his turn had his anaesthetic gases to think about and his patients and their various complaints and operations: that was surely enough to give a purpose to anybody's world.

The Commissioner cleared his throat. 'But I didn't get you in here, Varg, to discuss these large philosophical questions. There is a more pressing matter that I need to raise with you: staff reduction.'

Now here it comes, Ulf said to himself. I'm going to lose my job.

He looked at the Commissioner. It could not be easy for him: people thought it must be wonderful to be a police commissioner, but they did not reckon with the unpleasant aspects of the job – such as firing people.

'In times of financial stringency,' the Commissioner began, 'we all have to tighten our belts. That means reorganising things so that we make the most effective use of the resources we have. That's elementary – as I'm sure you're well aware.'

Ulf inclined his head. 'Economics,' he said simply.

'Yes,' said the Commissioner. 'You obviously understand. I get a budget and I have to operate within it. That's economics. Life is dependent on economics. It's simple. Money: that's what everything comes down to in the end.'

He looked at Ulf, as if waiting for him to challenge this truism.

The Commissioner lowered his voice. 'To turn to specifics,' he said, 'I have to find economies to the tune of ten per cent of our current budget. That may not seem a lot, but it's one item in ten. Think of it that way, and ten per cent becomes difficult enough to find in a budget that's already under pressure.'

'It must be very difficult,' said Ulf.

'Yes,' said the Commissioner. 'And that brings me to the point. Our establishment is too big. You need to lose point seven-five of a person.'

Ulf stared at the Commissioner. 'Point seven-five? Three quarters of a person?'

The Commissioner nodded. 'That's correct. But obviously you can't divide people – hah! – and so you'll have to lose a whole member of staff.'

Ulf hesitated. 'And that person – or that point seven-five of a person – what will happen to him or her?'

The Commissioner raised a finger. 'Now here, as they say, is the good news. That person – that point seven-five of a person – will not be got rid of entirely. He or she will simply be transferred to another department.'

'Which one?' asked Ulf.

'Litter and Waste,' said the Commissioner. 'As it happens, two members of that department – which has an establishment of three at present – have reached retirement age. Those two will be replaced by one person, or by that point seven-five of a person. So, a saving will be achieved without redundancy.'

Ulf digested this information. He was pleased to hear that there would be no outright redundancy, but Litter and Waste . . . That department, which concerned itself with illegal waste disposal, was regarded as the ultimate dead end. Nobody who had been sent to that department had ever come out of it again: it was what everyone called a 'punishment posting'.

The Commissioner brightened. 'I would like the whole thing to be amicable and entirely voluntary,' he said. 'So what I'm going to ask you to do is to find somebody in Sensitive Crimes who would fancy a sideways move into Litter and Waste. There must be somebody who would jump at the opportunity. It's not very stressful. They never actually arrest anybody, as far as I can see.'

Ulf shook his head. 'With the greatest respect, Commissioner, I don't think so. I can't think of any of my colleagues who would favour such a transfer.'

The Commissioner looked surprised. 'Are you sure? There would be no cut in salary, of course.'

'Pretty sure,' said Ulf. 'Litter and Waste is generally considered to be a bit . . . how shall I put it? Dull?'

The Commissioner began to show his irritation. 'I can't see why. The environment is a top priority these days.'

'I understand that,' said Ulf. 'It's just that I feel confident that none of my colleagues will relish the idea of that particular move.'

'Well, they're just going to have to accept it,' said the Commissioner peevishly. 'And if you don't get a volunteer, Varg, then I expect you to choose somebody to make the move. It is either going to happen voluntarily or compulsorily, but it has to happen.' He fixed Varg with an intense gaze. 'This is not a request, Varg – it's an instruction. You know I like to do things discreetly and without coercion, but there comes a point when what must be done must be done.'

Ulf inclined his head. The Commissioner was not a pompous man and it was true that he tried to be tactful in staff matters. If savings had to be made, they had to be made, and the least that Ulf could do was to acknowledge the Commissioner's efforts to avoid redundancy. As he rose to his feet, Ulf said, 'You've been very decent about this, Commissioner. Thank you for that.'

The Commissioner gazed at Ulf with gratitude. 'That's very kind of you, Varg. I do try my best, you know. It's not easy being a police commissioner. You have to do things that you'd prefer not to have to do, you know.'

'I can imagine that,' said Ulf. 'And may I say: you do those things with a very gentle touch. We all see that – and we all appreciate it.'

The Commissioner looked away. 'Are you saying that people in the force actually ... actually *love* me?'

Ulf nodded. 'They do, Commissioner. You are very much loved.'

For a few moments, the Commissioner was silent. Ulf watched him, and briefly imagined that he was even on the point of tears. He felt a surge of sympathy for the other man, this holder of a demanding office who so yearned for the affection of those over whom he exercised authority.

Then the Commissioner said, 'That's such a heart-warming thing to hear – it really is.'

'Well, I mean it,' said Ulf.

'I can see that,' said the Commissioner.

Ulf returned to the office, where he felt the eyes of his colleagues upon him.

'So,' said Anna. 'What was it, Ulf?'

Ulf looked up at the ceiling. He had to tell them. He would prefer not to, but he could not conceal the truth: it was his responsibility to reveal what the Commissioner had said.

'Bad news,' he muttered.

'What?' asked Erik sharply.

'Bad news, I'm afraid,' he replied. 'We have to lose one post.'

There was complete silence as glances were exchanged.

'Not a redundancy, though,' Ulf continued. 'One of us has to be transferred.'

They waited.

'To Litter and Waste,' Ulf said.

Until then, the silence had been ordinary; now it became a stunned silence.

CHAPTER SEVEN

Cochlear Implants

I t was Juni who arranged the meeting with Dr Niklas Wikström that took place the day after Ulf's disturbing meeting with the Commissioner. Ulf was not pleased to have yet another difficult matter to contend with – he was yet to call his colleagues to the meeting that he knew he could not put off – but Juni had been insistent.

'Niklas was going to be calling in on Dr Håkansson anyway,' she said. 'There is something else they need to discuss, so I thought we could kill two birds with one stone.'

Ulf bit his lip. 'I hadn't decided,' he said. 'I need to think about this.'

In fact, he had decided that he would not take the matter of the cochlear implant any further – but Juni had been persistent.

'This would just be a discussion,' she said. 'Nothing's been signed yet. All it would be is a general chat about the procedure – nothing more than that.'

'I don't see the point,' said Ulf. 'As I told you, I don't think I can afford it.'

Juni brushed his objection aside. 'But that won't be an issue, Ulf. I'm sure that Niklas would be happy to allow payment in instalments. Say, one hundred thousand now and the balance in three months' time – something like that.'

Ulf shook his head. 'I haven't got it. I told you. I just don't have the cash.'

'He's a very kind vet,' said Juni. 'And he says that he's looking forward to meeting you – and Martin too, of course. He has a wonderful way with dogs. They sense that he's on their side.'

She threw him a glance as she said this, and for a moment Ulf wondered whether he was being reproached. He glanced at Martin, who seemed to be following this encounter with some interest, his head cocked to one side, as dogs will do when they are anxious to make sense of the human world and its doings. It crossed Ulf's mind that Martin was lip-reading, but he reminded himself that even if he were, the dog's vocabulary was very small – a handful of functional words and phrases: *walk, Martin, biscuits, all gone, good dog, bad dog, squirrels, stop, sit.* That was about it, Ulf thought: and how small a world that lexicon described. Ulf took an interest in language, having taken a linguistics option in his criminology degree. He had enjoyed every moment of that course and its arcane reading lists, and had later reflected, with a touch of remorse, on how different his life might have been had he opted for a degree in art history or linguistics. He might have become a scholar, a minor professor somewhere, exchanging correspondence on obscure issues with colleagues abroad, conducting seminars with students, writing journal papers that it really did not matter too much if nobody read. The infrequency with which certain furrows of scholarship were tilled had no bearing on the effort and enthusiasm devoted to them.

Now it came back to him, just as Juni leaned forward to stroke Martin on the head. She loved him – that was clear enough – but Martin loved her back only out of politeness, Ulf thought, because even as her hand caressed the dog's head, his eyes were still upon his god, who was Ulf, of course. It was an unswerving devotion of which some ancient desert father, some monk, would have been proud.

Suddenly it came to him. It had been in a remote, dusty corner of memory, undisturbed and unlit: the Sapir–Whorf hypothesis. He had not thought about it for years – not since he had sat in that lecture theatre and the professor of linguistics, who looked so like one of the actors in Bergman's *Wild Strawberries*, had mentioned it. Ulf had written the name down, *Sapir–Whorf*, at the head of his notepad because it had intrigued him, just as the hypothesis itself had. And he had never completely forgotten it, because now it had cropped up, uncorrupted by the years: *Sapir–Whorf*. It had seemed to him at that point to be so obvious: of course our inner world was formed by the nature of the words we had; of course how you experienced things was moulded by the words you had for the experience; of course, if you had, in the popular example, twenty words for snow rather than one, then you *saw* snow in a richer, more nuanced way. Ulf had believed it, and then, when the professor went on to discredit it, he had felt disappointment, not unlike the disappointment any believer feels when a cherished belief is shown to be without foundation. *There's no such person as Santa Claus*, his brother Björn had whispered to him in the shared bedroom of their boyhood. *Don't let them fool you, Ulf.* He remembered that moment too, oddly and unexpectedly, and then became aware that Juni had said something to him and was waiting for an answer.

'What?'

Sapir–Whorf would not go away: if dogs had only a few words, Ulf thought, then the canine world was very small indeed, circumscribed by the narrow bandwidth of the language available to dogs.

'Ulf?'

'Sorry, I was thinking about something.'

'I said, Niklas wants Martin to be there when he comes to Dr Håkansson's clinic. He says he wants to examine him.'

Ulf sighed. 'I'm not sure. I'm sorry but—'

Juni interrupted him. 'Martin loves you, Ulf. And you have the power to change his world. Think of that.'

'I know, but . . .'

'Animals rely on us, Ulf. They rely on us and on our kindness. We shouldn't let them down.'

He pointed out that he was not letting Martin down. 'It's just the money,' he said. 'I'd do anything for Martin – you know that.'

She looked at him with an air of near-triumph. 'So you accept that this should happen – if it *can* happen?'

He nodded wearily.

'Then I've had an idea,' she said. 'That car of yours – that old Saab – do you know what it's worth?'

Ulf shrugged. 'Not very much,' he said. 'It's pretty ancient. People want comfort – and electronics – these days.'

Juni smiled. 'You're wrong about it being worthless, you know. I looked up its value. You can find that sort of thing out online. It's worth more than many new cars. Yes, it really is. It's scarcity, you see. There aren't all that many of that particular vintage available. Do you want to know what you'd get for it?'

Ulf waited.

'Almost three hundred thousand krona,' she said. 'Yes, three! So if you were to sell the Saab, you'd get enough to pay for Martin's operation and have enough left over to get another second-hand car to replace it.'

She looked at Ulf with the air of one who has worked out a solution to an uncomfortable problem. Then she added, 'Simple!'

Ulf swallowed. He asked himself how he had got into this situation. Like all impossible situations, he concluded, it had been through small failures, here and there along the line – failure to say no, to take control, to assert himself. That was how it happened. That was how one found oneself trapped in a position that one should have averted through the simple expedient of being firm and unambivalent in the rejection of that which one had a perfect right to reject. Yet he had not done that. He had been too passive. He – Ulf Varg – in spite of his name and its lupine associations, had been, if anything, too ovine. He sighed, and even as the sigh escaped him, he realised that a sigh gave the wrong signal altogether. Sighs were redolent of acceptance, not of resistance. Another sigh came – involuntary and, this time, deeper.

Ulf took the hand extended by Dr Niklas Wikström and shook it politely, but without enthusiasm.

Wikström was a man in his early thirties, well groomed and with a confident air to him. He struck Ulf as being somebody who was probably well aware of just how handsome he was.

'I've been looking forward to meeting you,' Wikström said. 'I realised, when Juni told me what you do, that I had never actually met a detective – not in real life. It's interesting: we watch so many detective dramas – think of them all – and yet we may never actually meet one. Strange.'

Ulf did not like Wikström. He was not one to rush to judgement, but there were occasions on which his instinct warned him against somebody – and this was such an occasion. And yet he knew that he should not allow such snap judgements to influence him. Such views, reached on the basis of little knowledge, were more often wrong than right. And they were unfair, too, in that they denied others the chance of a fair hearing. So he told himself that he should not allow himself to feel this about Wikström, and that he would wait and see what he was like. Juni obviously liked him; as, apparently, did Dr Håkansson, who was beaming indulgently as his receptionist introduced the visitor to Ulf.

'I'm not sure if television films give a true impression of how we actually work,' said Ulf. 'Some may, I suppose, but many, I fear, are misleading.'

Wikström smiled. 'I imagine you're right. I suppose most detectives are really rather dull.'

It took Ulf a moment or two to take offence, but he did. Dr Håkansson, responding to the lack of tact evinced by his colleague's remark, tried to make amends. 'But everybody's daily life can be dull,' he said quickly. 'I imagine that most of us vets could be so described. And certainly, the detectives I've met have not been in the slightest bit dull.'

'Oh, I didn't mean that,' said Wikström, who had realised that he'd expressed himself awkwardly. 'I didn't mean to say that detectives themselves were dull. Heavens, no. I meant that some of the things they have to do – just some of them – must be very routine. The same is true of my life, of course. I do a lot of routine work.'

'No matter,' said Ulf quietly. 'I would never say that my daily round is in any way spectacular. Get up, go to work, do the paperwork, go home. Nothing exciting.'

He glanced at Juni as he spoke, and saw that she was looking at Wikström: she was not listening to him. And perhaps that was just as well, as he had not included her in his description of his day-to-day existence. He turned away and then allowed his gaze to return to her. She was still looking at Wikström, and Ulf felt a sudden pang of jealousy. She was looking at Wikström in a way that did not conceal the interest – the appreciation – that a woman might feel when confronted with a man who looked as he did. It was hard to conceal, and Ulf felt that Juni was not even trying.

Ulf suddenly felt panicky. He had had enough of being single, and he did not want to lose Juni. He did not want to go back to the situation he had been in before she had come into his life. It was true that he had recently had his reservations about their relationship, but now that she was showing an interest in somebody else, he felt that he wanted her once again.

Rashly, and without thinking it through, he said, 'I'm so pleased you're prepared to consider Martin for this procedure,' he said to Wikström.

Juni spun round. 'But . . . that's wonderful, Ulf.'

'Yes,' said Ulf, conscious that he was throwing caution to the wind, and not quite sure why he was doing it. 'I'm very pleased.' And to Juni he whispered, 'I'm going to sell the Saab.'

She blew him a kiss. 'Wonderful. Generous Ulf. Kind Ulf,' she whispered.

He found her tone strange. It was as if she were addressing him as a dog. *Good Boy. Generous Ulf. Kind Ulf.*

Wikström now joined Dr Håkansson in examining Martin.

'I know this dog very well,' said Dr Håkansson. 'He's been my patient for some years now. He's a fine dog. Intelligent. And a lip-reader, you know. I think he's the only lip-reading dog in Sweden.'

Wikström seemed to be impressed. 'That's quite something,' he said. 'Mind you, I gather there's a dog in Gothenburg that has been trained to read basic road signs.'

'Very useful,' said Dr Håkansson.

Wikström inserted an auroscope into Martin's left ear, peered into it, and then repeated the procedure with the right ear. Then he stood back and, holding his hand in front of his mouth, shouted out Martin's name. Martin gazed at him, unflinching. He seemed completely indifferent to what was happening. Things like this happened in Dr Håkansson's clinic – there was nothing unusual in all of this.

Wikström now carried out a full physical examination of Martin. The dog was poked and prodded, and the inside of his mouth was looked into.

'Heart?' asked Wikström.

'Good coronary function,' said Dr Håkansson. 'No record of cardiac issues.'

'So, no anaesthetic issues?' asked Wikström.

Dr Håkansson shook his head. 'Very straightforward,' he said.

The two vets now conferred further while Ulf reassured Martin. Juni reached for his hand, and he looked at her in surprise.

'You're doing the right thing, Ulf,' she said. 'And I always knew you would.'

Ulf gave a non-committal response. 'Oh, well,' he said.

'I can't wait to see his face when he hears,' said Juni. 'Imagine it, Ulf.'

Ulf was not sure whether it would make all that much difference to Martin, but he did not say as much. Now he waited for the vets to finish their clinical conversation. Then he broached the subject of payment.

'Could we discuss the cost?' he asked Wikström.

The younger vet waved a hand carelessly. 'It's manageable,' he said.

'But I need to know,' said Ulf.

Wikström looked annoyed. He exchanged a glance with Juni that Ulf almost missed, but which nonetheless dismayed him. He now knew that there was something between the two of them. But it was too late to withdraw, he felt, and he was not sure that he had the energy to stand in the way of Juni and her veterinary allies. Life had a habit of happening to us, he thought; some of it we controlled, some of it we chose, but often it just happened to us. In such circumstances one could rail against a turn of events or one could accept it and let it roll over one like a stream in a water course.

'I'll send you a detailed note of the costs,' Wikström said, almost grudgingly. 'We'll keep them to a minimum, but the implant itself has to be imported. Each piece is engineered to fit a particular recipient, and so that inevitably makes them expensive.' He paused. 'But worth it, I think. Your dog will thank you, Ulf.'

'Yes, that's right,' agreed Juni. 'Martin will say, "Thank you! Thank you for the gift of hearing!" That's what he would say, Ulf – if he could speak.'

Ulf winced, but did not say anything. He looked down at Martin, who gazed back up at him with adoration. They had been through so much together, including that unfortunate incident in which Martin's nose had been almost totally severed by a rogue squirrel. Martin, Ulf imagined, would accept whatever it was that was happening to him now with the good grace and stoicism with which he accepted everything: bad weather that led to cancelled walks; the taunts of squirrels and cats; all the disappointments and setbacks to which all dogs were subjected and which they bore with such fortitude. Unlike us, he went on to think: we complain and lament, we bemoan our fate, we make a disastrous mess of so much and then transfer the blame to others. We are deeply flawed in ways beyond the understanding of dogs, who see us as simply perfect, entirely fitting objects of their loyal and soul-deep devotion, their unconditional love.

CHAPTER EIGHT

Cannibalism in Fish

U lf met Blomquist early the next morning, by arrangement, in the coffee bar opposite the office. Blomquist had been pleased with the invitation to join Ulf, as he was often to be seen sitting in the coffee bar by himself, waiting for somebody to talk to him but, as often as not, having to settle for only his own company.

'It's good of you to come in early, Blomquist,' Ulf said as Blomquist lowered himself into his seat at the table. 'I find this part of the day a particularly good time to review puzzling cases. The mind is fresh, I find.'

'Oh, absolutely,' agreed Blomquist. 'I do some of my best thinking then.'

Ulf nodded. There would have been a time when any mention by Blomquist of his *best thinking* might have occasioned a smile, but not now. Ulf had discovered that those who thought little of Blomquist – and he had once heard Erik describe him as a long-playing record with a crack in the first groove – were far off the mark. Blomquist was anything but that; yes, he went on about various subjects of interest, principally to himself; yes, he made mountains out of molehills; yes, he had an uncanny ability to go off at a tangent; but he also had the knack of seeing dimensions to an issue that had escaped everybody else. Blomquist's questions might come out of left field, but they were often ones that needed to be asked and that moved an otherwise slow inquiry on by several steps. Blomquist was useful, however much his manner might irritate or bore. Blomquist was no fool.

Ulf took a sip of his coffee. 'This case, this house theft,' he began. 'We need to do something, but, frankly, I'm at a bit of a loss. As you know, one normally starts with the question: who's likely to have committed the crime? That works with safe-breaking, for instance. We know the safe-breakers. We know who's active in the field and who's taking a rest. We know their modus operandi, and we have their fingerprints and DNA on file. But this? Who are the house thieves? I have no idea – none at all.'

Blomquist nodded his assent. 'It's a very unusual crime,' he said. 'I've never encountered anything like it. The closest thing I've ever heard of is aeroplane theft. That was another theft of a big object. Somebody stole a passenger airliner once from an airport in Las Vegas. It turned up in Mexico a year later, painted in the livery of another airline. Corporate crime. But a house? I've done a search online and drawn a blank. It's a totally new crime.'

Ulf was about to agree, when Blomquist remembered something.

'Hold on,' he said. 'I remember reading about a beach being stolen once.'

'A beach?'

'Yes. It was in Jamaica. Somebody stole all the sand from a hotel's beach. They took it off in trucks.'

Ulf's eyes widened. 'I suppose that a rival resort—'

'Exactly,' said Blomquist. 'A rival resort would be the obvious suspect, and, as it turned out, they did it. Then there was

Albert Einstein's brain. Somebody stole that. Whom would you suspect, Ulf, if the Department of Sensitive Crimes had to investigate that?'

Ulf looked thoughtful. 'No, don't tell me. Let me think.'

Blomquist waited.

'The pathologist who conducted the autopsy?'

Blomquist looked disappointed. 'Yes, you're right. He wanted to carry out research on Einstein's brain to see if there was anything about it that set it apart from ordinary brains like yours or mine.'

'And did he find anything?'

'He said he did,' replied Blomquist. 'But his results were discounted. I don't think there are any physical signs of genius. It's in the inner workings, I think.'

'I see.'

'And yet,' Blomquist went on, 'there must be a difference between the brain of somebody of average intelligence and the brain of a person who's really accomplished. Mozart's brain must have been differently wired from other people's. Or these people who remember everything; you know the ones – they can read the telephone directory and then remember every number. That man in America – the Rain Man. People like him.'

'Savants,' said Ulf. 'Yes, don't they have different connections between the hemispheres of their brain? Something like that.'

'That man in records,' Blomquist said. 'You know the one? He also wears that purple sweater – even in summer. Have you looked at his head? It's tiny. He must have a very small brain. And yet he seems to remember everything. You need a file and he gets it straight away – he says, "Oh yes, I remember that case," and off he goes. He always gets it – in spite of his tiny head.'

Ulf took another sip of his coffee. It had been unwise to encourage Blomquist to digress; it could take hours to get back to the subject. So now he said, 'That's very interesting, Blomquist, but to the matter in hand: who would steal a house?'

Blomquist sat back in his chair. 'Somebody who resents your having a particular house? House envy. Such a thing exists, I think. People envy the houses of their neighbours.'

'Possibly,' said Ulf. 'But the thing about this house is that it was very ordinary. And it was tucked away from sight. People would have been unaware of it unless they actually looked for it. It was not what you might call a conspicuous possession, like a Lamborghini or a diamond necklace.'

'True,' said Blomquist. 'So perhaps envy would not be a motive. What about simple desire for the item? People steal things they *want*. Who wants a house like that?'

'Somebody who hasn't got a country cottage? Somebody who would like to have a country cottage?'

Blomquist agreed. But there was a problem, he said. 'You have to have somewhere to put it. You can't just steal a house and leave it at that. And that means you have to have a plot of land. You have to put the house down somewhere.'

Ulf thought this made sense.

'And another thing,' Blomquist continued. 'You probably won't be able to take a house very far. Trucks carrying houses will move very slowly. They'll be very obvious. Technically, they need a police permit and sometimes a wide-load escort.'

'All of that is true,' said Ulf.

'And I've already spoken to the traffic department,' Blomquist said. 'I asked them whether any of their units had seen a house on the road round about the time when we think the theft was committed. The answer was no. There were no reports of any unusual loads slowing down traffic.'

Ulf looked at Blomquist with admiration. This was why the other officer was so useful. Blomquist could act on his own initiative. And the way his mind worked meant he explored avenues that might not occur to others. Ulf had not thought of speaking to colleagues in traffic; Blomquist had.

Blomquist had more to say. 'The important thing about this particular crime,' he remarked, 'is that once we find the house, we find the perpetrator – inside, I should imagine. That makes it different from other thefts. You may find the stolen object, but the object may not lead you to the thief. It may have been abandoned or sold on. The trail to the thief may run cold.'

That was perfectly true, thought Ulf. Thieves usually disposed of stolen goods as soon as they could, to the fences, the dedicated purchasers of such things – but one could hardly sell a house in that way. So if they found the house, then as likely as not they would find the thief. Ulf now pointed out that all they needed to do now was to find the house: had Blomquist any ideas as to how to go about that?

'Yes,' said Blomquist. 'Let's imagine that they have found somewhere not too far away to . . . to put the house down, so to speak.'

'Yes,' said Ulf, encouragingly.

'Now, the area is heavily wooded, isn't it?'

Ulf nodded. 'It would be a good place to hide a house – somewhere in a small clearing. Nobody would see it.'

Blomquist raised a finger. 'Except from the air. You'd see it from the air, wouldn't you?'

Ulf thought about this. 'I suppose so.'

'So,' said Blomquist, 'if we found an old aerial photograph of the area and then compared it with a more recent photograph from the same vantage point, then we might notice any new buildings – even if they are tucked away in clearings.'

'I suppose—'

Blomquist did not let Ulf finish. 'That's how they discover stars, you know. They compare photographs of the sky and they see new spots of light appearing here and there. Those are new stars.'

Ulf looked thoughtful. 'Easier said than done,' he said.

'But I have an idea,' said Blomquist.

Ulf listened. And when Blomquist had finished explaining, Ulf nodded slowly. 'Possibly,' he said.

He looked at his watch. It was time to go into the office and meet his colleagues. Ulf had asked everybody to assemble at nine sharp. He had an announcement to make, and he wanted everybody to be there. He finished his coffee and said to Blomquist, 'We'll talk about this house matter later on. But thank you for your ideas. As usual, they are very interesting ones.'

Blomquist basked in the praise. 'Do you really mean that?' he asked. 'You're not just saying it?'

'I mean it, Blomquist,' said Ulf.

And he did.

Unknown to Ulf, two other members of the Department of Sensitive Crimes – Carl and Erik – had already had a meeting of their own to discuss the issue of the Commissioner's diktat. They had not said anything about this to Ulf, as they wanted to have an agreed position to counteract any move that he might make as the senior member; nor had they involved Anna, whose views, they thought, were likely to be too close to Ulf's. And of course they had not involved Blomquist, because it was clear to them that Blomquist was the solution to the problem.

Carl was the lead conspirator. 'I can tell you this right from the beginning,' he said. 'I'm not going. And if Ulf – or anybody else – tries to transfer me to Litter and Waste, then I'm going to refuse to go. I don't care what the consequences may be. I just won't go.'

His determination impressed Erik. This was fighting talk, and he took the cue from him. 'I agree,' he said. 'I've worked hard to get where I've got, and I'm not going to throw it all away to satisfy some budgetary instruction. Who runs the force? Accountants?'

Carl felt he did not have to answer, as the power of accountants had grown ever greater, and everybody knew it.

Erik now continued, 'I'm happy in my job. I've thought of

96

retiring, as I think you know. But I don't want to go yet. I still have casts to make – fish to catch.'

Carl stared at him. Erik's passion was fishing, and he often used angling metaphors to make a point. But he was not sure whether he was now talking about real fish or something else. It did not particularly matter, though, as his reluctance to move was clear enough.

'The way I look at this,' Carl said, 'is like this. We don't like these penny-pinching accountants, but the reality of the situation is that they have the Commissioner's ear. So, somebody has to go – agreed? Whom can we exclude, so to speak – who's definitely not going anywhere? Ulf. He's the one who has to give the Commissioner a name and I can tell you this as a matter of certainty: he won't self-nominate.'

'He's a very kind man,' observed Erik. 'Perhaps . . .'

Carl shook his head. 'What do they say? Turkeys don't vote for Christmas. They never have. Ulf won't be an exception to that simple socio-biological rule.'

'What's socio-biological about it?' asked Erik.

'Survival,' answered Carl. 'Everybody wants to survive. Our decisions are all directed towards that goal – all of them. We dress them up in the language of principle and altruism and so on. But at heart it's all about individual survival.'

Erik thought about this. 'Interesting,' he said at last. 'It's like that with fish.'

Carl waited for an explanation.

'Fish are driven by a species survival instinct,' Erik said. 'That's why cannibalism in fish is far less common than people used to think.'

Carl raised an eyebrow. 'Oh yes?'

'Yes,' said Erik. 'There's an ichthyologist in South America who studied cannibalism in freshwater fish and discovered that it was far rarer than imagined. Cannibalism has only been observed in one per cent of the thirty thousand fish species that people have studied. One per cent! That's not very much. Of course, there are some fish who definitely eat their own families. There's one species, interestingly enough, where the male persuades the female to release her eggs and then he promptly gobbles them up.'

Carl looked up at the ceiling. 'I've never trusted fish,' he said.

'We need to decide,' Erik said. 'We need to work out what our stance is going to be.'

Carl broke the ensuing silence. 'In my mind there's only one name,' he said. 'I don't like to be uncharitable . . .'

'Of course not,' said Erik. 'Who does?'

'Precisely,' Carl continued. 'I don't like to be uncharitable, but it's perfectly obvious who should go. Blomquist. He's not a proper member of the department. He was tacked on. And you know what he's like. Nobody will miss him.'

'He doesn't do very much,' said Erik. 'He goes on and on about every subject under the sun, but he doesn't do much more than that. He bores the pants off everyone, but that's not the same thing as solving crimes.'

Carl did not disagree with this decidedly uncharitable assessment. 'A department of sensitive crimes needs *sensitive* people. Is Blomquist sensitive?' He broke into a smile. 'I think not.'

Erik looked momentarily uncomfortable. 'Poor Blomquist,' he said. 'There's no doubt that he tries. And yet, and yet . . .'

'Oh, he does his best,' agreed Carl. 'It's just that his best is pretty hopeless.' He paused. 'But I'm not sure that Ulf will see it the same way. He spends a lot of time with Blomquist.'

'True,' said Erik. 'But I've seen him become glassy-eyed when Blomquist gets going about vitamins or microbial disease and so on. Yet Ulf's kind. He puts up with him.'

Erik looked serious, and he spoke with a certain gravity. 'I think we should remind ourselves that we're doing this purely for the good of the department. There must be nothing personal in it.'

'For the good of the department,' Carl echoed. 'And for the protection of the public.'

'The two go hand in hand,' said Erik. 'There's no distinction.'

'What we need to do,' Carl went on to say, 'is to prepare a list of Blomquist's shortcomings. If we present a reasoned case as to why he's not up to the job and then submit it to the Commissioner, he'll put two and two together. He might then propose to Ulf that Blomquist gets the transfer, and Ulf will be pleased that he doesn't have to make the decision himself. It'll be easier for him if he doesn't have to push Blomquist.'

'Good thinking,' said Erik. 'Let's get something down on paper.'

They applied their minds to the drafting of a two-page memo in which the case for transferring Blomquist was set out. Blomquist was ill-suited to sensitive work, they said: he meant well, but he lacked the background to be able to deal with the often rather demanding tasks of the department. Subtlety was not Blomquist's strong suit, they said. Furthermore, Blomquist was not a university graduate. That in itself was no disqualification, but it did mean there were times when he was out of his depth. He tries hard, they said, but effort alone is sometimes not quite enough. He would be good in Litter and Waste, where a determined, unimaginative approach would pay dividends. Blomquist was certainly determined and unimaginative, they said.

Once the letter was completed, the two of them signed it.

'What about Anna?' asked Erik. 'Should we see if she'll sign too?'

Carl shook his head. 'She won't. She's too soft on these things. Let's just head it: *A Memo from Members of the Department of Sensitive Crimes*. Let's leave it at that. It will still sound authoritative.'

Erik had an idea. 'And perhaps we could write, underneath our signatures, the words *thank you*. But we could write them in such an illegible way that it would look like a signature.'

Carl was impressed, but then he shook his head. 'We must remember who we are, Erik. We are the Department of Sensitive Crimes – and we have standards.'

Admonished, Erik said that Carl was right. His suggestion was a bad one, he admitted: tempting, but bad.

The memo signed by the two of them was sent to the Commissioner's office. 'We know that you believe in a consultative approach,' they wrote, 'and it is in this spirit that we submit these observations to you.'

'He likes that sort of thing,' said Carl. 'And you can never go wrong with a bit of flattery.'

Ulf had invited Blomquist to the meeting, and when the two of them entered the meeting room at the same time, he noticed the quick exchange of glances between Carl and Erik, who were already there.

'We shall wait for Anna,' said Ulf, as he sat down at the table around which five chairs were arranged. 'Is she in yet? Has anybody seen her?'

'She said she had to take the girls to a swimming lesson,' said Carl. 'She knows about the meeting, though. She won't forget.'

'I always enter meetings in my phone diary,' said Blomquist. 'It has a little beeper that lets me know when I'm due to be at something. It's very useful.'

Carl and Erik avoided Blomquist's eyes. Ulf noticed this, and wondered why.

'Very useful, Blomquist,' Ulf said.

'It's a sort of alarm clock, effectively,' Blomquist went on. 'And my watch can do it as well. I have one of those watches that does everything.'

Anna arrived. 'I'm sorry I'm late,' she said. 'The traffic.' She shook her head.

Ulf nodded to her and then opened the file he had placed

on the table before him. Carl craned his neck to see what was written on the topmost piece of paper. Erik looked at Anna, and then up at the ceiling. Blomquist scratched the side of his head. Carl noticed that Blomquist's jacket had a large stain on it that looked like it had been made by milky coffee. Poor Blomquist, he thought; but these are socio-biological times. He suddenly thought of fish, and Erik, and of all the life forms that were busy struggling to survive – in the water, and above it. Every species, he imagined, had its accountants – or their equivalent – who circumscribed its world, described the limits of the possible.

Ulf saw their eyes fixed upon him.

'You know the reason why I've called this meeting,' he began.

They all nodded. Ulf then folded his hands before him as he began to say what he had planned to say – the words he had rehearsed that morning in the kitchen, with Martin looking up at him, struggling, and failing, to understand, but aware that there was something worrying his man who took him for walks, fed him, provided him with his reason for existing; the still and unchanging centre of his universe.

'When I saw the Commissioner the other day,' Ulf began, 'he made it clear to me that financial stringency requires the loss of point seven-five of a post – effectively one person. As I explained, this person will go to Litter and Waste . . .'

This provoked looks of distaste, but Ulf persisted. 'That is an important department, in spite of its unglamorous-sounding name. We can't ignore the issue of waste.'

'That's true,' said Blomquist. 'And that means recycling becomes all the more important. The waste side of things in that department keeps an eye on disposal regulations and so on. That's vital if we're to preserve what's left of the earth's resources.'

Carl saw his opportunity. 'It sounds as if you know quite a bit about waste issues, Blomquist,' he said.

Blomquist saw this as a compliment. 'As a matter of fact, I do try to keep myself up to date with these matters. I read a newsletter called *Finite*. It deals with all these questions of depletion.'

Carl and Erik exchanged glances. This was Blomquist more or less *volunteering* to go to Litter and Waste.

Ulf continued, 'The point I'd like to make is this: Litter and Waste is not a dead end. It's a department with a future. And its work is every bit as important as ours is. We're all part of the same effort, after all. We all want the same thing for Sweden.

'At the same time, I fully understand how people get settled into a particular routine, doing work they like, with colleagues whose company they value and enjoy. Change is rarely easy. Change can hurt. I understand all of that. But the world doesn't stand still, and none of us can expect things to oblige us by remaining unaffected by the winds that blow across our familiar landscapes. We must adapt. We must position ourselves so that we can give of our best for the community as a whole. This, then, is not about us; this is about the role that we're called to carry out in this life – our work, our calling, our fight to protect the weak and the vulnerable, the put-upon, the victims of the thoughtlessness, selfishness and cruelty of others. That is what we are called to do.

'So we must accept change. And those of us who are in charge in one way or another must be readier than those whom we lead to show willing to embrace that change. It is for this reason that I tell you now that I am going to put my name forward for transfer to Litter and Waste.'

There were several sharp intakes of breath. Blomquist opened his mouth to say something, but then shut it again. Carl's eyes widened.

'Yes,' Ulf went on, 'that is what I propose doing. I shall suggest to the Commissioner that I remain here for a month or so to finish off various inquiries, but that after that my place be taken by whichever of you he should appoint as senior staff member. I am sure that whoever it is will rise to the challenges of the position and maintain the tradition of service and comity that has always been at the heart of our efforts in the Department of Sensitive Crimes.' He paused, and then repeated the words, 'Service and comity.'

At first, nobody spoke. Ulf cleared his throat. Then Blomquist said, his voice heavy with sadness, 'You, Ulf? You're going? You yourself?'

Ulf confirmed the news with a wordless nod of the head.

'Well,' said Anna. 'This is . . . this is very surprising.'

'Are you sure?' asked Carl. 'I mean . . . Litter and Waste . . . After this . . .' He gestured around the room.

'I have made up my mind,' said Ulf. 'I have never been able to ask anybody to do something that I am not myself prepared to do. So there could only be one answer. I must take that post.'

Once he had finished, Ulf sat back in his chair and surveyed his colleagues. Anna looked confused; Carl was examining his fingernails; Erik had sunk his head in his hands; Blomquist looked shocked.

'Unless anybody has anything to add,' Ulf said, as he rose to his feet, 'I suggest we get back to our desks.' Ulf went back to the office by himself. He glanced over his shoulder as he made his way down the corridor, and saw that Carl and Erik were walking back together. They were deep in whispered conversation.

Blomquist caught up with Ulf.

'I wish you hadn't done that,' Blomquist said. 'It was a noble thing to do, but to tell you the truth, I'm going to miss you so much, Ulf. We work so well as a team.'

'We do, Blomquist,' said Ulf. 'We seem to complement one another, you and me. We've managed to get results, haven't we?'

'Yes,' said Blomquist. 'We had something good going on, Ulf. And now I'll have to see whether any of the others will work with me. They . . .' He paused. He looked embarrassed before he went on, 'They don't think much of me. Oh, they're civil enough, but

I can tell. They laugh at me.' He paused. 'I'm not talking about Anna here – it's the others.'

Ulf's heart went out to him. 'Oh, Blomquist,' he said. 'I don't think that's true.'

'It is,' said Blomquist. 'They don't really like me. In fact, I wouldn't be surprised if they had been plotting to get me transferred. I've seen them, Ulf. I've seen them talking.' He paused. 'I would like you to review your decision. Send me instead. I'll do it. You're what makes Sensitive Crimes the place it is. You mustn't leave it at this critical juncture.'

'Which junctures *aren't* critical?' asked Ulf.

'There must be some,' said Blomquist.

'Possibly,' said Ulf. 'But at the moment it seems to me that the junctures we face are far from simple – or inviting.' He looked at Blomquist. 'You're a good man, Blomquist. And I appreciate your offer, but I must do this. Omelettes cannot be unscrambled.'

Blomquist looked thoughtful. 'Are omelettes ever scrambled in the first place?' he asked. 'You don't stir the eggs in the same way as you do with scrambled eggs, do you? Omelettes are *folded*.'

Ulf was unsure how to respond to this, and decided that it was perhaps best not to try. But he looked at Blomquist with fondness and thought of how, in what he imagined would be a rather dull professional future in the Department of Litter and Waste, he would look back nostalgically on Blomquist's *aperçus*, and even miss them altogether. Possibly.

CHAPTER NINE

The Car as Mother

U lf would hardly have recognised Harald Olavson when his former schoolmate approached him that Saturday at the reunion lunch. Harald was still unusually thin – an ectomorph at the convincing end of the spectrum – but his appearance had been radically changed by the cultivation of an elaborate handlebar moustache and the wearing of rectangular blue-tinted glasses. The effect of these two changes was to give him a slightly mysterious air, making him look more foreign than Swedish. Ulf might have thought him Russian, if he'd met him in the street, or Armenian, perhaps. Certainly he would not have guessed that this was the same Harald Olavson with whom, as a boy of twelve, he used to ride his bicycle on Saturday mornings, or with whom he'd discussed, with passionate intensity, the relative merits of the heroes of hockey.

'Ulf,' enthused Harald, as he stepped forward to shake Ulf's hand. 'After all these years – the same old Ulf.'

Ulf tried not to look at the prominent moustache, and at the way it waved as Harald spoke. But Harald noticed, and said, 'I have a moustache now.'

It hardly needed saying. Ulf blushed. 'It suits you, Harald. Very smart.'

Harald leaned forward and lowered his voice. 'Actually, Ulf, if the truth be known, I'd prefer to be clean-shaven. It's my wife's idea. She wanted me to grow it, and she's the one who does the maintenance. She trims it and . . . and encourages it. She says it gives my face *breadth*.'

Ulf laughed. 'Wives,' he said.

It was, he realised, a rather old-fashioned thing to say. Men used to make a joke of being under the thumb of their spouse, but that sort of attitude was no longer encouraged – at least not in the stereotyping awareness courses that he, and the other members of the Department of Sensitive Crimes, were required to attend from time to time.

Harald fingered the moustache carefully. 'I go along with it,' he said, and added, 'It's the least I can do.' He paused and looked around the room, now filling up with their former classmates. 'You see, here they all are. Per, over there – see him. That's his partner with him. And Margareta – see her, she's standing over there with Lars. I never got on with him, as you may remember, but he's changed a lot. I suppose we've all grown up.'

'So we have,' said Ulf. 'It happens to everyone.'

After half an hour of mingling, they sat down to lunch. Ulf found himself opposite Harald and next to a woman who had been in their class for not much more than a year, and whom he remembered only vaguely. There were speeches, including a long drawn-out one from the current school principal, who dwelt mostly on a change in the mathematics curriculum. Then, over coffee, he talked to Harald while the woman beside him spoke to her neighbour on the other side.

Ulf asked Harald about his work as an aviation engineer. 'It has always seemed miraculous,' he said, 'at least to me, that is, that planes get into the air at all. All that machinery – that massive weight – manages to fly, of all things. It seems so improbable.'

Harald smiled. 'Bernoulli's principle,' he said, and then, looking enquiringly at Ulf, he went on, 'You know about Bernoulli, I take it?'

Ulf shook his head. 'Not really.'

'It's what takes a plane up,' said Harald. 'If you put your hand out of the window of your car when you're driving along, it tends to lift up in the rush of air, doesn't it?'

'Yes.'

'Bernoulli's principle, you see. The compressing of air below the hand leads to a reduction in pressure above it; so the hand rises into the area of reduced pressure. That's what a wing does. Push the wing along fast enough so that the pressure underneath is higher than that above, and you get lift. It's simple, really.'

Ulf said that now he knew.

'And all that I do,' Harald went on, 'is make it possible for the descending plane to land. I work on landing-gear systems – pneumatic arrangements and so on. It's nothing special, really. But you don't want it to go wrong, do you?'

'Certainly not.'

There was a silence. Then Harald said, 'I think you know my neighbour.'

Ulf waited for him to expand.

'Fridolf Bengtsson.'

It took Ulf a moment to make the connection out of context. Then he made it, and was wary. He had to be careful about discussing cases outside the office.

'He said he went to see you,' said Harald.

Ulf nodded. 'He's your neighbour, you say?'

'Yes. He's lived next door for five or six years. We were there before he came to the area. He had a son who was in my son's football team.' Harald paused. 'He mentioned that he had been to see you to report that business of his house. Not the house next to us – his townhouse – but his country cottage. It was a very strange affair.'

Ulf relaxed. Fridolf was not a suspect, and he had clearly made Harald party to the matter. Ulf felt now that he could talk more freely, and he wanted to do that, too, as Harald might be able to throw some light on the case. It was always useful to know more about the parties to an investigation, even if the facts one acquired were of little immediate use. You never knew: a seemingly irrelevant detail might just enable one to understand another, more important dimension of the matter under investigation.

'Yes,' Ulf agreed. 'It's a very strange affair. It's the first case of house theft that we've ever encountered, actually.' He paused. 'Do you know Fridolf well? I suppose you must, living next door to him.'

Harald replied that he would not describe Fridolf as a close friend. 'We see a certain amount of one another, but he keeps to himself much of the time. He got divorced, which was awkward for us, as we knew his previous wife. My wife was on good terms with her, and in fact took the whole thing rather badly. She felt that Fridolf did not behave particularly well. But you never know what happens in a marriage. You have to be careful about blaming one side or the other. Mind you . . .'

Harald left his sentence unfinished. Ulf looked at him expectantly.

'Mind you?' prompted Ulf.

Harald hesitated, as if weighing up whether to impart a confidence. At last, he said, 'He remarried. It must have been about three years ago. She's a dentist. A nice woman. She doesn't deserve it.'

'Deserve what?' asked Ulf.

Harald looked away, as if he found it painful to talk about the matter. 'She doesn't deserve to be treated the way he treats her. He's having an affair, you see. We happen to know that, but his wife, poor woman, is blissfully ignorant of it.'

'And his girlfriend?' asked Ulf. 'Who's she?'

Harald shrugged. 'I don't know her name, but I've seen her with him and I know somebody who's met her. She's Albanian. She works in a coffee bar somewhere.'

Ulf drew in his breath. An Albanian lover. It was of no real significance, but it was strange that an Albanian should be mentioned so soon after Albanians had cropped up in his discussion with Blomquist. And there had been the Albanian beer can and the report from Larsen that the people he had seen at the site of the crime had possibly been Albanian.

'This lover,' said Ulf. 'Do you know anything about her?'

Harald shook his head. 'Fridolf is wild about her – and more fool he. You don't make life any easier for yourself by falling for women half your age.'

'Is she?' asked Ulf. 'Half?'

Harald nodded. 'She's awfully young.' He tapped his brow. 'Not much in the intellectual department, I'm afraid. But young people these days – what do they know?' He held a thumb and forefinger slightly apart, to signify a tiny amount. 'I doubt if she knows what the capital of Italy is, or what the French Revolution was all about. There's nothing in that head, I imagine – or next to nothing.'

'Can you tell me anything else about her?' asked Ulf.

'She's very attractive,' said Harald, giving Ulf a conspiratorial look. 'I suspect that Fridolf's head was turned.'

'Sex is very powerful,' said Ulf. And he thought: yes, it is. When all was said and done, how many of our troubles were caused, at heart, by the dark, anarchic power of sex? If men, in particular, did not feel they had to compete with other men to make the point of their masculinity then there would be so much less confrontation and competition. Jealousy and envy, too, were powerful drivers of antisocial behaviour, and once again could be reduced to the tides and tugs of testosterone.

Harald sighed. 'Very,' he said. 'Unless you master it and show it who's the boss.'

'Who does?' asked Ulf.

'Not me,' said Harald. 'I try, Ulf, but … well, you know how it is.' He looked at Ulf as if for sympathy, and Ulf momentarily turned away: he did not want to become Harald's confidant in some maudlin confession of infidelity – Harald's wife was there, seated further down the table and, even now, was looking in their direction.

'People make their lives unnecessarily complicated,' Ulf said, taking a sip of the cheap Portuguese wine that the reunion organisers had laid on for the occasion.

Harald said, 'Lovely wine, isn't it? I chose it myself, although Per put me on to it. He goes to Portugal, you know. He has a house there. He's invited Bettine and me and we think we might go next year. We've been used to going to Greece, but we want a change. New horizons, you know.'

Ulf returned to the subject of Fridolf. 'You said that you saw him with this young woman: are you sure they're having an affair?'

'Absolutely sure,' answered Harald. 'You can tell, Ulf. You can tell whether two people are sleeping together. It shows. I don't know how exactly – body language, maybe – but you always know.' He lifted his wine glass and gazed fondly at the contents. 'This comes from the place Per has his house, you know. He says that it's going to be a big thing in Sweden when they get a proper distributor. A lot of it goes to China at the moment.' He put down the glass. 'And anyway, the woman who runs our local delicatessen filled me in on the details. She said that they go away together. He tells his wife that he has to go off on business – he's a big bacon producer, you know – and he's actually meeting this woman. She said that she knows the woman who does her hair – the young woman's hair, that is – and she says she opened up to her about it once. You know how people like to talk to their hairdressers. It's like being with a priest – if you're a Catholic, of course – or with a therapist. You want to talk – and you do.'

This was gossip, thought Ulf, but he never dismissed gossip. There were times when gossip was an entirely reliable source of information, as it might be in this case. So, what did this tell him? That Fridolf was having an affair even though he had married, for the second time, only comparatively recently? That he and his lover went away together? That was all, really, and that was hardly very much. But then there was the Albanian connection, and that either meant something, or it meant nothing. It was worth thinking about, though.

He turned to Harald. 'Which coffee bar does she work in?' he asked.

'Who?'

'This young woman whom Fridolf sees.'

Harald hesitated. 'I'm not sure,' he ventured. 'But I think it *might* be something called the Bar Tirana. I saw him going in there once, and, well, consider the name.' He smiled coyly. 'You're the detective, Ulf. Doesn't the name suggest something to you?'

Ulf shrugged. 'It might,' he said. 'And then again, it might not.'

'You're being very obscure,' Harald complained.

'Am I?' Ulf asked. 'Well, perhaps I am.' Then he added, 'Possibly.'

Later, when discussing his actions in this period with his therapist, Ulf raised the possibility that he was, for some inexplicable reason, doing the precise opposite of what he really wanted to do. For Dr Svensson, this was no surprise.

'But that is exactly what we do,' Dr Svensson said. 'We do the opposite of what is in our best interests – time and time again.' He fixed Ulf with one of his melancholic stares. 'I can't tell you the number of people I've had sitting where you are sitting now and telling me about how they've done things they didn't want to do. That's what we do. We do these things and then ask ourselves how we could possibly have done them. *Not me*, they say. *It really wasn't me.* And they're right, as often as not – so much human action comes from a self that is *other* to what we think of as our normal self.'

'But why do we do it?' asked Ulf. 'Why did I sell my Saab – my beautiful silver Saab that I got from my uncle? Why would I have done that? I didn't really believe that Martin needed the operation, after all, and yet I caved.'

'Because we all cave,' said Dr Svensson. 'We cave because we find it hard to cope with the emotional demands made upon us. It's nothing unusual. And in your case, the emotional demand came from Juni ...' He hesitated, as if uncertain whether to vouchsafe some psychological truth that might be just too much for his patient to bear. 'Because Juni, you see, is your mother.'

'No, she isn't,' said Ulf, almost automatically. 'She was my girl-friend. Mothers and girlfriends are not the same thing.'

'But they are,' insisted Dr Svensson. 'At least in one sense. There's a large body of research that shows ...'

Ulf closed his eyes briefly. He had his reservations about any observation that began with *There's a large body of research that shows*, even if it was made by one whom he admired as much as Dr Svensson.

'... that men,' continued the therapist, 'marry people who look like their mothers and women marry men who look like their fathers.'

Ulf opened his eyes again. 'Really?'

'Yes. You can read about it if you wish in the popular psychology magazines. People love that sort of thing because it's information that tends to accord with what they themselves have noticed in their own lives. We all know people who have married along those lines. I had a friend who married a woman who was the image of his mother. That ended in divorce, and do you know what he did? He went out and found somebody who once again looked exactly like his late mother, and married her.'

Ulf thought about this, and realised that he too could think of a friend who'd done exactly that.

'Freud, of course,' Dr Svensson continued, 'would explain that in terms of the Oedipus complex. And you may have heard of the female equivalent – the Electra complex. But even if you don't think of it in Freudian terms, it's still there as an observable phenomenon. Some people, though, have argued that we in fact marry somebody who looks like ourselves – because we are, for obvious genetic reasons, likely to look like our parents. So we effectively marry ourselves.'

'I see,' said Ulf, momentarily unable to say anything else.

'One might take it even further,' Dr Svensson continued. 'One might say that we choose houses that look like the houses we lived in as children. Or we buy a dog that looked like the dog we had when we were young. Or even that our car reminds us of our mother.'

Ulf stopped him. 'Our car?'

'Yes,' said Dr Svensson. 'Even our car.'

Ulf's incredulity showed. 'Are you seriously suggesting, Dr Svensson, that my car – my Saab 65 – resembles my mother?'

Dr Svensson sat back in his chair. He fiddled with his pencil. 'I didn't know your mother. So perhaps that is a question best addressed by you.'

Ulf stared at his therapist. Sometimes Dr Svensson took things too far and became fanciful in his analogies and metaphors. To suggest that Ulf saw his mother in a Saab 65 was an example of the sort of thing that made people mock Freudian theory. Ulf's mother bore no resemblance to ... He stopped. He closed his eyes and saw his mother, seated on a picnic rug on the small island where they had their summer cottage, which was not much more than a bathing hut, really, but which they had loved so much as a family. And he realised then, with shock, that there was more than a passing resemblance between his mother and his Saab – that the soft, feminine curves of the car were redolent of the female lines of her hips and her bust, and that the characteristic Saab grille could be her mouth, the bars of chrome her teeth, the headlights her wide, gentle eyes. He stopped himself: one should not think of one's mother in such terms.

'In selling your car,' Dr Svensson continued, oblivious to the images he had provoked, 'you are performing an act of distancing from your mother. You, the son, feel the need to focus your affection elsewhere, and to do this you must detach yourself from your mother. Perhaps you did not do that sufficiently, and so for that reason you felt you had to cut yourself off from the thing that *stood* for your mother – your Saab.'

Ulf said nothing. It was possible, just possible, that Dr Svensson was right; the psychotherapist had been right before – more often than not, in fact. And now Ulf thought again of that difficult moment when he had driven to his local garage and spoken to Edvard, the mechanic who had looked after the Saab ever since his uncle had given it to him. Edvard loved Saabs with all the passion of one who had spent his youth with his head tucked into the engine compartment of those sleek cars, tinkering with their pipes and tubes and wires. The world had largely passed him by while he cosseted engines: great events had occurred unnoticed by him because of his single-minded devotion to machinery, and, although Ulf noticed this with some degree of bemusement, he also realised that this was not perhaps such a bad thing. To immerse oneself in one's work could protect one from the anxiety inherent in following the news, which was invariably about conflict and disaster. Edvard had none of that: his concerns were immediate and mechanical, and in relieving others of worries over their cars, he made the world a slightly better place. No, there was nothing wrong in being Edvard.

'Sell your Saab?' the mechanic had said, looking at Ulf with a shocked expression. 'Are you quite sure?'

Ulf felt as if he had proposed the imminent sale of his grandmother into slavery.

'I need to raise some money. And I'd do just as well with a more modern car. It would be easier, I think.'

Edvard wiped his hands on a square of blue paper towel. It was the sort of towel that mechanics seemed to prefer – and detectives too, as Ulf now remembered a case in which a suspect had left his greasy fingerprint on just such a piece of paper and had been apprehended as a result.

'It's a pity,' Edvard said. 'These modern cars are so characterless. They're computers on wheels, most of them – especially the electric ones. They don't really need us.'

'But they still have wheels and brakes and suspension,' said Ulf. 'Presumably you people will have to attend to those.'

Edvard sighed. 'Yes, but I'm not sure I want to be that sort of mechanic.' He gave Ulf a melancholy look – the look that the last speaker of a dying language might give to a visiting linguist. 'There's no . . . no poetry in modern cars. There's poetry in these old Saabs, Ulf – a lot of poetry.'

They stood in silence. Then Ulf said, 'I'm sorry, Edvard. I'm grateful for what you've done for this car, but these things, well . . .' He searched for words, but none seemed suitable. *On saying goodbye to a Saab* . . . that could be the title of a poem, since Edvard had mentioned poetry.

But the mechanic had become business-like. 'No, don't worry. I understand. And I have a suggestion to make, if you're all right with that.'

Ulf was relieved. 'Of course.'

'I have a client,' the mechanic said, 'who's looking for a Saab 65.

He's fussy, and wants this exact year. He used to have one exactly like this. There aren't many of them around these days, you know.'

Ulf told him that he had heard that, and that he understood the prices being paid were high. Edvard agreed. 'They aren't cheap, and he knows that. He's well off, anyway, and so there'll be no trouble there. He has four or five Saabs already, including a beautiful 92, a lovely piece of machinery: transverse-mounted two-stroke engine, drag co-efficient of 0.35 – can you believe that? 0.35!'

'Well, they made aeroplanes,' said Ulf.

'That's the secret,' said Edvard. 'Anyway, he – Jurien, he's called – he'll snap this up. All I have to do is call him.'

Ulf hesitated. He had made the decision, but now, at the point of having to act upon it, he questioned it again. But it was too late. If he changed his mind now, he would have to bear Juni's reproach. He would feel guilty – unfairly, of course – but guilt often had nothing to do with fairness.

'All right. Call him.'

Edvard made the call, and half an hour later Jurien arrived to inspect the Saab. He was older than Ulf had imagined, and there was something distracted in his manner – as if he was there, but might have wished to be somewhere else.

Jurien sat in the Saab and started the engine. He got out, peered into the engine compartment, and then cocked his head to listen to the beat of the motor. Then he dropped down to his hands and knees and looked underneath the car. He tapped the bodywork, as a doctor might percuss a patient's chest.

'Jurien knows what he's doing,' said Edvard.

Ulf agreed. This was a man who understood Saabs – that was clear enough.

Jurien turned to Ulf and named a figure. It was twenty per cent higher than the valuation that Juni had mentioned.

'That's generous,' muttered Edvard.

Ulf inclined his head. 'I accept,' he said. 'I'm sorry to see it go.'

Jurien reached out and placed a bony hand on Ulf's shoulder. 'I know, I know. But I promise you this: I shall look after this car. You don't need to worry about that.'

'He's right,' said Edvard. 'Your Saab will be in good hands, Ulf.'

The bargain was concluded.

'I think I know who you are,' said Jurien. 'You work in that special police department, don't you? The Department of Serial Crimes.'

'Sensitive Crimes,' corrected Ulf.

'Yes. That one. I know who you are because you were very helpful to my cousin when her hairdresser was stalking her. Remember? She said that you were very kind to her.'

Ulf remembered the case and its unusual details. It had been complicated by the fact that the hairdresser was the nephew of a government minister and was also blackmailing the minister.

'It was a difficult case, that one,' said Ulf.

'Well, my cousin said that you made it much easier for her,' said Jurien. 'The whole family was very grateful to you. We never thanked you, but we were.'

'I was just doing my job,' said Ulf. 'Nothing more than that.'

'Maybe,' Jurien said. 'But there are some people who just do the job, and then there are those who go out of their way. You did the latter, I think.'

Ulf looked away in embarrassment. It was good to be appreciated, but he had never been one to court praise. 'I hope that everything's going well for your cousin now,' he said.

'Oh yes. She's fine. She has a new hairdresser.'

'That's wise.'

Edvard looked thoughtful. 'My hairdresser had a nervous breakdown. He's Turkish, and he gave these hot shaves – you know, the ones with the open razor. Very comfortable.' He paused. 'But not so comfortable if the barber is ranting. I stopped going after a while – he seemed so agitated and his hands shook.'

117

'Poor man,' said Ulf.

'Yes. He was a nice man, if a bit unbalanced. He went back to Istanbul, and got a job on one of those boats they like out there – a gulet. Apparently he was much happier. I think our winters got to him.'

Jurien was looking intently at Ulf. 'Thank you for what you did,' he said.

Ulf inclined his head. 'That's all right. But when would you like the car?'

'Tomorrow?' suggested Jurien.

Ulf swallowed. That at least gave him time to go for a final drive. He turned to Edvard, 'Can you fix me up with something in the meantime? Something small and practical?'

'I have a nice little Volkswagen Golf,' said Edvard. 'Very clean.'

Ulf said that would do. And it would: it would do. It would never be the same as driving a Saab, but it would do. That was the case with so much in our lives – it might not be ideal, but it *did*.

CHAPTER TEN

Garlicky Lunch

Blomquist asked Ulf whether he could meet him for lunch. It was an unusual request, as Blomquist knew that Ulf preferred a light lunch at his desk – a sandwich or a roll usually sufficed – but Ulf accepted nonetheless.

'I know a bar where they serve soup all day,' Blomquist said. 'I used to have an informer who worked there. He slipped notes under the plates. He was very useful.'

Ulf imagined that this must have been during the two years that Blomquist had spent on the drug squad. He tended not to talk about it, but Ulf knew that Blomquist had been conspicuously brave, as he had served as an undercover agent – always a dangerous assignment. People forgot about that, Ulf reflected; people like Carl could be dismissive about Blomquist, but none of them had ever taken the risk that Blomquist must have assumed during that assignment. That was the trouble with police work: you often got no recognition – or even cursory thanks – for the things you did.

Now he found himself sitting at a table in the Blue Parrot, a small bar in a side street in Varvsstaden, watching people walk past the window that looked out onto the street. It was a bar of little character, patronised, as far as Ulf could see, by office workers and drivers from a nearby taxi garage. It was not the sort of place where drugs would have been traded, and Ulf wondered why Blomquist's informer would have been working there.

When Blomquist arrived, he asked him, 'Your informer, Blomquist – is he still here?'

Blomquist shook his head. 'That was five or six years ago. I was undercover for a while, you know.'

'I was aware of that,' said Ulf. 'And I must say I admire you for it, Blomquist. That can't have been easy.'

Blomquist seemed pleased with the compliment. 'No, I suppose not. I didn't think too much about it, though. If you start to worry, then you end up never getting anywhere. I had one colleague who was undercover as well, and he never left the house. He was just too nervous. He shook all the time, and I think anybody would have noticed it.'

'That's not much good,' said Ulf.

'I called myself Bobby,' said Blomquist. 'I was meant to be a sailor who had been at sea for a long time. That's why nobody would know me in the area. They know people round here. They know who comes from where. Being a sailor meant I could get away with not having much of a local past.'

'And it worked?' asked Ulf.

Blomquist grinned. 'I'm still here, aren't I?'

Ulf nodded. 'I suppose so. We forget just how dangerous it can be.'

'I had a narrow escape once,' said Blomquist. 'We had penetrated a gang that was bringing in cocaine from Colombia. The drugs were hidden on board a ship – pretty skilfully as it turned out. One of the sailors from the vessel in question was in on it, and the gang met him in a flat not far from here. I was there. I

120

was meant to be arranging for the drugs to be passed on up the line to Stockholm. We talked about the ship and I made a bad mistake in using the wrong words. Proper sailors refer to the bow and the stern. I'm afraid I said front and back. The sailor gave me a very suspicious look. He said, "I thought you were meant to be a sailor." There was a horrible silence.'

'That sounds dicey,' said Ulf.

'Yes. They all looked at me, and I must admit I thought: this is it, Blomquist. *Finito*, as they say. But then I just laughed, and said, "Where's your sense of humour?" They carried on looking at me, and then I said, "Those words are very *yesterday*, you know." Then somebody's phone rang, and the moment seemed to pass. It was a close thing, though.'

'You must lead a charmed life, Blomquist,' said Ulf.

A waiter came to take their order.

'And your informer here?' asked Ulf.

'He was a Mormon,' said Blomquist. 'He had been involved in drugs and then he had some sort of experience crossing the bridge to Copenhagen and he became a Mormon. He never told me what it was, but it changed him, he said, and he started to help us. He was very useful.'

'I hope we looked after him,' said Ulf.

'I think we did,' said Blomquist. 'He didn't want payment, though. All that he asked of us was that we read the literature he gave us. Religious literature. All about somebody who found some plates of gold with Egyptian writing on them. He read them through some special spectacles he had. Have you heard of all this?'

Ulf nodded. 'A bit,' he said.

'He married a dairy farmer's daughter,' said Blomquist. 'I saw him once or twice afterwards. He seemed perfectly happy.'

'The routes to happiness are varied,' said Ulf. He looked at Blomquist expectantly. 'You wanted to discuss something?'

121

Blomquist fiddled with the cuff of his jacket. 'Yes, there are two things.'

Ulf waited. 'I'm listening, Blomquist.'

Blomquist fixed him with an earnest stare. 'This business of your transfer to Litter and Waste. I really want you to reconsider.'

Ulf smiled. 'I'm flattered, Blomquist – I really am. It's nice to know that people will miss me. But I'm sorry—'

Blomquist did not let him finish. 'If you go, then I'm going to have to go. I can't stay – not with one of them as new head of department. I can't face that.'

Ulf drew in his breath. He felt for Blomquist.

'You see,' Blomquist went on, 'they're never going to allow me to do anything interesting. They'll expect me to do all the routine stuff – worse than routine, in fact. They have a very low opinion of my abilities.'

Ulf tried to reassure him that this was not so. 'I don't think you're right about that.'

'But I am. They have a nickname for me, you know. The Purgative. Somebody in Traffic said that he had heard them laughing about it.'

'I'm sure they didn't mean to be hurtful,' said Ulf. He would deal with this, he thought. He would speak to them and tell them that if it continued, it would go on their records. There would be no bullying, and he would take action – even in the last days of his tenure of office. He would stamp out this hurtful, juvenile behaviour. And Anna would help him to do this, as he doubted whether she was a party to any of this.

Blomquist was silent. 'You won't reconsider?'

'I don't see how I can,' said Ulf. 'I've made the announcement. I've written to the Commissioner.'

Blomquist bit his lip. For a few moments, Ulf thought that the other man was about to cry, and perhaps there were the beginnings of tears, but they were quickly wiped away.

'I'm so sorry, Blomquist,' Ulf said.

Blomquist shook his head. 'I just thought I'd ask.'

'And you mustn't feel you have to go,' said Ulf. 'Give it a try. See how it works out. I'll speak to the others.'

Blomquist looked alarmed. 'I don't want that,' he said. 'Please don't do that.'

'If you don't want me to ...'

'I don't.'

'Very well.'

Ulf waited. Then he said, 'There was another thing?'

'Yes,' said Blomquist. 'You know that house? The one that's been stolen?'

Ulf nodded. 'Fridolf's place.'

'Yes. Well, I think I've found it.'

Their soup arrived. It was very garlicky, and the pungent sharp odour rose up like an enveloping miasma.

The garlic seemed to cheer Blomquist up. 'I love garlic,' he said. 'And it's very good for the heart, you know. There are lots of studies now that confirm it – beyond any doubt at all. Its alicin, you see. That's the active ingredient and there's plenty of evidence to show that alicin combats viruses and bacteria. I eat several cloves in the morning. I put them on my muesli – chopped up, of course. Alicin, and three Brazil nuts, because they have selenium in them, as I may have told you. But alicin's the stuff you need. Then I have some in the evening. My wife sprinkles it on my kale, because I eat a lot of kale. Kale lowers blood sugar levels – did you know that, Ulf?'

'That house,' said Ulf. 'Have you really located it, Blomquist?'

He wanted to say: 'Forget garlic, forget Brazil nuts; even forget kale.' But he did not. Instead, he gently encouraged Blomquist to tell him how he had found the missing house and why he was sure that it was the right one.

*

Pausing from time to time to take a spoonful of garlic-laced soup, Blomquist now launched into what, in retrospect, Ulf came to realise was the most remarkable and inventive piece of detection ever undertaken by a member of the Department of Sensitive Crimes. Had he been inclined to gloat – which of course he was not – Ulf would have taken pleasure in telling his colleagues exactly what Blomquist had done, but, as it was, Blomquist's achievement remained generally unsung, other than in a confidential report to the Commissioner. There, it had an even greater effect than Ulf could possibly have hoped for, with results that forever endeared the Commissioner to Ulf. Even if the Commissioner had in the past been obliged to act as an unsympathetic cost-cutter, a harbinger of contraction seemingly unswayed by Ulf's pleas for a better dispensation for his department, this was overshadowed by his eventual reaction to Ulf's report on Blomquist's work. This confirmed what Ulf had long suspected: that the Commissioner, at heart, was a just man.

That was still to come. Now he sat with Blomquist over their rapidly cooling soup while the account of the *modus acquirendi* of this significant information was revealed.

'I have a friend,' began Blomquist. There then followed a pause, which made Ulf wonder whether this was a statement complete in itself. Blomquist had never mentioned any friends. There was his wife, of course, who was mentioned from time to time; and, Ulf seemed to recollect, there may have a been a cat too. But there had never been any mention of friends, and Ulf had somehow assumed that Blomquist had none.

But the syntax was only interrupted, and Blomquist continued, 'I have a friend who has an aeroplane – or, shall I say, access to an aeroplane.'

Now there came a further pause, as Blomquist's spoon was dipped once again into the soup.

'There's more evidence come out recently,' Blomquist said,

'about what eating garlic does if you're troubled by colds. Did you know that?'

Ulf focused on his soup. There was no point trying: Blomquist was incorrigible when it came to this sort of thing. The only response was to tolerate it: sooner or later the health facts, the diversions, tailed off and he would return to the subject in hand. One might discourage him by not taking him up on any of the incidental remarks, but one could not stop it altogether. And we all have our faults, Ulf reminded himself. Some of which, he reflected wryly, might be ameliorated by the consumption of garlic.

'We're all troubled by colds,' said Ulf wearily. 'Who isn't?'

It was the wrong thing to say. Ulf had uttered a rhetorical question, but that was not how Blomquist saw it.

'Who isn't? Well, I can tell you, Ulf. Me! And my wife too. I can tell you exactly when we last had a cold. It was nine months ago.' He paused, and fixed Ulf with a look of pride. 'Yes, nine months, almost ten. Neither of us has had so much as a sniffle since then, and in my mind, that proves it. Garlic protects you against colds. We both eat it regularly – as I've told you. I have it on my food, as I've explained, but Cornelia takes it in capsule form. You know those clear capsules they call pearls? That's how she takes it.'

Ulf took a sip of his soup. He would watch for sniffles, he thought.

'Oh yes?'

'Yes. And I happen to know the figures – the actual figures – because I subscribe to a garlic newsletter. I'll give you the web address, if you like. It's free, but you have to sign up – reasonably enough. They publish links to all the important research. And one of these research programmes found that regular use of garlic cut the incidence of colds by sixty-three per cent, Ulf. Sixty-three per cent! Can you believe it?'

'That's a lot,' said Ulf, wearily, and added, 'That's more than half. Comfortably more than half.'

'Precisely,' said Blomquist. 'But there's something else. Those who came down with colds – in spite of the garlic – found that the symptoms lasted for a far shorter time. One and a half days rather than five days. The group taking the placebo had to endure five days of their cold, but the other group . . . well, one and a half days is not all that long, is it?'

Ulf, uncharitably, thought it would be an eternity in *some* company. But he immediately withdrew the thought, which was unkind and should not have been entertained, should not have been allowed to surface. That was the trouble with the subconscious mind, he told himself: it was the source of unwelcome thoughts. The subconscious mind is only too ready to be uncharitable unless it is harnessed by moral control, or, as Dr Svensson would put it, by the super-ego – if Dr Svensson still talked about the super-ego, which Ulf thought he did.

'Who's this friend of yours, Blomquist – the one with access to a plane?'

'He's called Hansson,' said Blomquist. 'Ansgar Hansson. He's married to a distant cousin of Cornelia's. He's not a cousin, of course – just a friend.'

'Of course not.'

'He's a photographer. He used to have an insurance brokerage – quite a big one. They specialised in agricultural insurance. They had a lot of trouble with quad bike theft, you know. Farmers were losing quad bikes all the time, and that could be really difficult for them, as they used them to cart animal feed around – that sort of thing. And who pays in the end? I don't have to tell you: the insurance companies. Or, rather, the people who pay the premiums, although that takes a year or two to filter through.'

Blomquist had now almost finished his soup, and the story of the cousin who had been an insurance broker and then a photographer had to wait while he tilted his bowl to get the last of the benefit of alicin.

Blomquist looked up from his empty bowl. 'You know something? I'm almost tempted to have another helping.'

'You can if you like, Blomquist. Nobody's stopping you.'

Blomquist shook his head. 'No. I've had enough. I don't want to be greedy.'

'Who does?' muttered Ulf.

Blomquist answered. 'Carl,' he said firmly. 'He's greedy.'

Ulf said that he had never noticed this, but Blomquist was adamant: he had seen greedy behaviour on Carl's part on numerous occasions.

'He wants everything,' he said. 'Have you looked at his desk? It's the best in the office – if not in the entire building. I shouldn't be surprised if it's better even than the Commissioner's desk. And his chair too. And when we have a cake in the office, on somebody's birthday, Carl always – and I mean *always* – takes the biggest piece.' He paused, as might a prosecutor before he presents a crucial piece of evidence. 'I know; I've measured it.'

Ulf looked at Blomquist with frank astonishment.

'Measured the slices of cake?'

Blomquist nodded. 'Yes, before handing them round. I measured. Discreetly, of course.'

'Of course.'

Ulf stared down at his empty soup bowl. At times he thought that he understood humanity – that nothing would surprise him. And then, at other times, he realised that there were in others wells of opacity, or pettiness, or sheer absurdity that he would never imagine until they manifested themselves in some unexpected remark or some incomprehensible act. But this was not the time to explore that, to attempt to determine why Blomquist should have bothered to observe which pieces of cake people took.

'Look,' said Ulf, 'time is marching on. You were going to tell me about whatshisname? Ansgar?'

'Yes. The photographer. Well, he's a member of a flying club.

127

They have one of those small single-engine planes . . . I wouldn't care to go in a single-engined plane, you know. A fuel stoppage – something like that – and where are you? Going down, I'd say.'

'Yes,' said Ulf, as briskly as he could. 'So Ansgar goes to a flying club.'

Blomquist did not appear to mind being prompted to continue. 'He does. And it occurred to him a few years ago that he could combine hobby flying with a bit of commercial photography.'

Ulf waited.

'He takes photographs of people's houses and farms. He does this from the air. People love an aerial view of their place.'

'I suppose they do,' said Ulf.

'He's done a lot. He's photographed much of the countryside round here.'

Ulf had been staring at his bowl; now he looked up and saw that Blomquist was smiling. There was a certain triumph in his expression.

'I asked him whether he kept copies of the older photographs,' Blomquist continued. 'And he said he did. Then I asked him if he had recent photographs too. And once again he said that he did. He would be quite happy for me to take a look at them, he said. And I did. I compared them to see if there were any changes in the countryside – you know, new buildings, new roads and so on.'

Ulf realised what Blomquist had done, and he shook his head in admiration.

'You're a real Sherlock Holmes, Blomquist,' he said.

Blomquist beamed. 'I had a book once about aerial reconnaissance during the Second World War. They used to compare photographs, you know, to get a picture of what was going on. One week there would be few signs of activity – and then the next week there would be vehicles on the roads, trains moving, and so on. You could draw conclusions.'

'You did just that,' said Ulf. 'And?'

'And I found several places where there had been forest, and now there was something – a clearing or a house. One place in particular, about half an hour from where the house went missing.'

Blomquist went on to describe what he had seen. There was what looked like a new clearing in the trees, and a building. The roof of the building appeared to match the shape and colour of that of the missing house. 'I'm fairly certain,' Blomquist concluded. 'I haven't checked yet, but I've noted the location.' He paused. 'Should we go there, Ulf?'

They travelled in the Volkswagen that Edvard had found as a replacement for Ulf's Saab. It was a four-year-old model, and it had not been particularly well looked after.

'You may have noticed something, Blomquist,' Ulf said as he picked up his assistant at the start of their journey. 'You may have noticed that my Saab is no more.'

'A new car?' said Blomquist, looking about him with ill-concealed disappointment. 'I liked that Saab, Ulf.'

'So did I,' said Ulf. 'They don't make cars like that any more.'

'Why did you get rid of it?' asked Blomquist. 'Mechanical issues?'

It was odd, thought Ulf, that he felt loyalty to what was only a collection of metal parts. Saabs, though, were capable of being loved, he thought, because of their shape, and because of what they stood for: a Sweden that had perhaps never been what people imagined it to be, but had somehow been simpler and less demanding than the complex Sweden of today. A car, like any artefact, could be redolent of an era, a mood, an outlook; could embody memories of journeys short and long, and what those journeys meant. His Saab reminded him of so much – starting with his uncle, from whom he had acquired it, and of whom he had been so fond, and ending, more recently, with outings with Juni and Martin, and working trips with Blomquist expounding on vitamins and garlic and the sort of thing that seemed to fill Blomquist's small slice of the universe.

'I needed some cash,' said Ulf, without telling Blomquist why he'd needed it. Blomquist would have views on cochlear implants and Ulf did not feel he could face such a conversation.

'Nice car,' said Blomquist.

Ulf realised that this was just politeness. 'Not really,' he said. 'This is just a car. It's functional, which I suppose is all that one really needs.'

Blomquist gave Ulf a sympathetic look. 'Of course,' he said.

They travelled in silence, which was unusual for any journey with Blomquist, and it was not until they were close to the point at which they would need to turn off the public road that anything was said. Then Blomquist remarked, 'Do you think we'll be making an arrest?'

Ulf slowed down to scan the road ahead. He thought the turn-off should be coming up soon. 'It's possible,' he said.

'I suppose,' mused Blomquist, 'that we shall have to say, "Are you the owner of this house?" That's what we'll have to say to anybody we find in the house. That's what you say to people when you stop them in what you think is a stolen car.'

'Or, "Where did you get this house?"' suggested Ulf, smiling.

'They might reply, "We found it." That's what thieves often say, isn't it?'

They arrived at the turning. Blomquist had input into his sat-nav the position of the house he had spotted on the aerial photograph, and now a disembodied voice from his mobile phone instructed them to turn off and drive two miles down a narrow, unpaved track.

After a while, a smaller track branched off to the left. It looked as if it was of recent creation, as the packed earth of its surface was yet to be substantially eroded by rainfall. The forest, too, cut to make room for the track, had yet to green over the incision.

Seeing this, Ulf began to feel confident that they were indeed on to something – that somebody had recently made this track, deep into this profusion of trees, to hide something that needed to be concealed. And had it not been for Blomquist and, indirectly, his photographer friend, that attempt at concealment might have succeeded. But not now, because Ulf had a very strong feeling that they were about to strike yet another blow for the proposition that the perpetrators of egregious crimes would, sooner or later, be made to answer for their misdeeds.

They followed the smaller track for a few minutes and then they were in a clearing. And there it was – the very house that had been in the picture shown to Ulf when he first met Fridolf Bengtsson.

Ulf slowed down. 'There,' he said.

Blomquist pointed. 'Yes. See? See.'

'You were right, Blomquist,' said Ulf. And then he added something that he knew would give Blomquist pleasure, for that was what he felt he wanted to do now. 'Right again, Blomquist.'

Blomquist made a modest gesture. 'I'm not always right. I'm often wrong.'

But he did not sound convinced of this self-deprecating remark. So Ulf went on, 'No, Blomquist – you must be prepared to take credit where it's due. And you deserve it. You've solved this case – you. Not me. You.'

'I didn't do very much,' muttered Blomquist.

'I intend to give you full credit in my report,' said Ulf. 'I'm going to spell it out. *Entirely owing to Blomquist's intelligent and creative inquiries, we managed to locate the stolen house.* Or words to that effect.'

'But we haven't found the guilty party yet,' Blomquist pointed out. 'We've located the stolen goods, but that's not the same thing as wrapping up the case.'

'No, that's true,' said Ulf. 'But let's go and knock on the door and see what we find. I have a good feeling about this whole case now, Blomquist.'

They got out of the car and walked across a small patch of grass towards the front door of the house. Ulf looked up towards the roof, and then turned to look over his shoulder. 'Blomquist,' he said. 'How do you think they got this into this clearing?'

Blomquist shrugged. 'On the back of a big trailer,' he said. 'Or a truck. Something like that.'

Ulf nodded. 'Yes, but . . .' He pointed towards the track down which they had just driven. 'Look at that track.'

Blomquist turned to look. 'Yes?'

'It's not very broad,' said Ulf.

For a few moments, Blomquist was silent. Then he said, 'I see what you mean. The house is wider than the track, I think.'

'I think so too,' said Ulf.

'So that suggests,' Blomquist continued, 'that this house was constructed in this clearing, rather than being brought in ready-made.'

Ulf sighed. 'That seems to follow.' He paused. 'However, let's not jump to any conclusions. We should still take a look.'

They approached the front door, which was open, and Ulf knocked loudly. When there was no response after a minute or so, he knocked again.

'Not in,' said Blomquist. 'And the absence of any vehicles points that way too.'

There was a small window close to the front door, and Ulf now peered through it. 'Nothing much in here,' he said to Blomquist. 'A sort of entrance hall. A table. A couple of chairs. A coat hanging up on a hook.'

Blomquist moved past Ulf to a window just round the corner. Ulf followed him, and the two of them looked through that. Through the slightly dirty glass, they saw what seemed to be a study. There was a wall of bookshelves, a desk, a captain's-style office chair, and a box in which magazines had been stacked.

Ulf strained to make out the title of a large book at the end of one of the bookshelves. It took him a moment to make out the lettering, but what he saw made him take hold of Blomquist's arm in excitement.

'You see that large book on the second shelf, Blomquist? See it?'

'The one with the blue cover?'

'Yes. Can you read the title? Does it say what I think it says?'

Blomquist wiped the window with his handkerchief and then screwed up his eyes. 'I'm going to need glasses soon,' he said. 'This sort of situation brings that home to me.' He pushed his nose up against the glass. 'Modern Pib Breeding,' he said. 'Yes. Modern Pib Breeding.' He turned to Ulf. 'What are *pibs*, Ulf? A breed of dog? You know how they're mixing breeds these days – labradoodles, cockapoos, and so on.'

'Pigs,' said Ulf, laughing. 'Pigs, Blomquist.'

'Ah.'

And then it dawned on Blomquist. 'Fridolf is . . .'

'Yes, he's a pig breeder – a very major one.'

'So this must be his house?'

'I would say so,' said Ulf. 'Who else would have a book of that title in his study? I would venture to suggest that only a pig breeder would own a book like that.'

Blomquist said that he thought Ulf was probably right. 'I think that confirms it,' he said.

Ulf looked at his watch. Ideally he would have liked to have had time to go back to town, pick up Fridolf, then bring him out to identify the house as his own. But now he felt they would not have the time for that, and that it would have to wait until the following day. He was very much looking forward to reuniting Fridolf with his property – it always gave him pleasure to restore to people what was rightfully theirs. If one felt that with a stolen car or something of that sort, how much greater would the pleasure be if the item were something as emotionally significant as a house.

They decided to walk round the house before returning to the car and starting their journey home. They tried a back door, but it was locked, and investigated an empty wooden box lying on the ground at the back. But that afforded no information and they left it where it was. Then Blomquist said, 'Oh.' And after that, he said, 'Oh,' again.

Ulf stopped. 'Have you seen something, Blomquist?' he asked.

Blomquist pointed to the ground. 'What do you think made those?'

Ulf looked down and saw a line of large paw-prints. 'Those are rather large,' he said. 'They're very interesting.'

Blomquist crouched to examine the prints more closely. 'Yes,' he said. 'It would have to be a pretty big dog to make these prints.' He paused. 'Or a wolf?'

'This far south?'

'There are wolves in this country,' said Blomquist. 'And look at the claw marks. Dogs don't have claws like that.'

He straightened up. He looked into the surrounding trees and shivered. 'I know that wolves are meant to be up in the north. And in the west. But wild animals move around, don't they?'

Ulf shook his head. 'Wolves mainly rely on moose for food,' he said. 'They go where they'll find moose – and that's not here.'

Blomquist seemed unconvinced. 'What about those big cats that people see? Panthers and so on? They even see them in England, you know. They're escapees but they can survive in the wild.'

'It's all a question of food sources,' said Ulf. 'Predators need their particular food.'

'They could take pigs,' said Blomquist. 'There are plenty of pigs in southern Sweden.'

Ulf smiled. 'Do you remember the story, Blomquist? The three little pigs and the wolf? Remember the song? "Who's Afraid of the Big Bad Wolf?"'

Blomquist said that he remembered it very well. 'I used to be scared by that story,' he said. 'When I was a little boy. I remember hiding under my mother's skirts when she read the story to me and she got to the point where the wolf huffed and puffed and blew the pig's house down.'

Ulf looked thoughtful. 'The straw one, yes. And the wooden one too. But not the one made of brick.'

He looked at the house. 'Do you think there's some strange connection here, Blomquist? Pigs, wolves, houses?'

Blomquist shrugged. 'Heaven knows,' he said. 'But could we get back to town now? I'm going to take my wife out to dinner tonight. It's her birthday. We're going to a restaurant that specialises in pork, as it happens.'

'I love pork chops,' said Ulf.

'So do I,' said Blomquist. 'People go on about steak, but I find it too strong. Pork is somehow lighter, isn't it? Pork chops and creamy mustard sauce. And then the crackling that comes with them – I can't get enough of that. That lovely crisp texture and the taste . . . oh my.'

They reached the car. 'I suppose one shouldn't eat too much pork,' said Ulf. 'I don't want to spoil your dinner, but it's pretty fatty, isn't it? It's not what you'd call a lean meat.'

'But it *is* healthy,' Blomquist insisted. 'It has more unsaturated fats than beef or lamb. That's a positive thing, because unsaturated fats are better for you, Ulf. I may have told you that before – I don't know – but it's something you should know. And then pork has a lot of iron, zinc, niacin, vitamin B12 . . . all of those, and more. We can definitely eat pork, Ulf. Definitely.'

'I'll take your word for it,' said Ulf. To himself, he muttered, *I'll huff and I'll puff and I'll blow your house down* . . . The things of childhood stayed with us, a layer or two beneath the adult façade – which is what it is, thought Ulf: a façade. Because deeper down, in the basements of our being, we are all still children, with all the fears and insecurities of the child still firmly rooted in our psyches. Dr Svensson would agree with that, of course, but would offer reassurance nonetheless. Wolves should not frighten us, he would say, because in the cold light of day we should be able to see that they bear us no ill will. What should frighten us, the therapist once said, is other people. They're the real danger.

CHAPTER ELEVEN

White Mask Crime

Fridolf did not react in the way that Ulf had expected when he gave him the news that his house had been found.

At first there had been silence. Then, with unconcealed nervousness in his voice, Fridolf stuttered, 'My house? You've found my house?'

'Yes,' said Ulf. 'I'm happy to tell you we have. Unharmed . . .'

It was as if he were giving news of the recovery of a missing person. *The victim was untouched . . .*

'There was no damage to it, as far as we could see,' Ulf continued. 'It was in a clearing about forty-five minutes from . . . from where it used to be.'

Fridolf said nothing.

'I take it that you're pleased,' Ulf said. It occurred to him that Fridolf might have claimed the insurance on the house, and might not wish to refund it; that sometimes happened with stolen property, and then the owner was embarrassed by any restoration.

The silence returned for a few seconds longer, and then Fridolf said, 'I am so pleased – I really am. I thought—'

He did not finish, as Ulf interrupted him. 'We'll need you to identify it.'

'Of course. I'll go round and do so.'

Now it was Ulf's turn to be silent. There were slips – missteps as they were sometimes called – and then there were catastrophic, headlong falls.

'You'll go yourself?' Ulf asked.

'Yes. No need to take up your time. No doubt you have important things to do.'

Ulf held his breath. 'Good,' he said.

He waited. Perhaps Fridolf just needed time to gather his thoughts; perhaps he would now ask where he might find the house. But no such question was asked.

'You might need me to tell you where to go,' said Ulf, his voice calm and even.

Ulf heard an involuntary intake of breath. That was enough. Fridolf might have tried to conceal it, but he had not done so. It was the most fundamental of mistakes – to show knowledge that only the perpetrator could possibly know. That sort of error was one that an inexperienced teenage miscreant might make – not a misjudgement expected of a successful businessman, a man of the world, as Fridolf clearly was.

'Of course,' Fridolf blustered. 'Foolish me.'

Foolish you indeed, thought Ulf. He was tempted to say that aloud, but he did not. As a general rule, he thought it was best to say as little as possible. That meant there was less to regret; less to explain; less to retract.

'I tell you what,' said Ulf. 'Let one of my people accompany you. He can spare the time. He'll show you.'

Fridolf agreed, and Ulf arranged a time when Blomquist might come and pick him up.

'Blomquist knows all the facts of the case,' Ulf said. 'You will find him pleasant company on the journey.'

That comment was not made ironically; nor was it insincere. It was one of those remarks that is made without really meaning anything at all. And Ulf made it because he was, in fact, thinking very hard about how Fridolf's involvement in the disappearance of his own house made any sense. The obvious explanation involved insurance. In fact, thought Ulf, there could be no other explanation. And if that were the case, then the next thing for him to do was to discover whether Fridolf was in financial difficulty. Ulf had a way of finding that out by way of a quick telephone call to his accommodating friend, Irena, in the Department of Commercial Crime. She had ways of finding out which businesses were in difficulty, and which were not. And she rarely took more than a couple of days to do so. If you wanted the information within hours, that could be arranged too, although she would expect a large take-out coffee and a chocolate éclair for that – delivered discreetly, of course – as this was a matter of informal reciprocity, a system that ensured that life within the various departments proceeded smoothly and on a cooperative basis.

After making this arrangement, Ulf spent the remainder of the day dealing with a build-up of paperwork. It was the aspect of his job that he liked least, and it was for this reason that he let it accumulate. Then, when guilt tugged at his sleeve too insistently, he would tackle the backlog in a single cathartic session – which is what he did now. Five o'clock came quickly, and with his work all but finished, Ulf put the one or two remaining files into a desk drawer, slammed it shut, and then left the office.

Juni had a key to Ulf's flat, and she was inside, waiting for him when he arrived home. He could tell immediately that she was excited, as she flung her arms around his neck and gave him a long, lingering kiss.

'What have I done to deserve that?' Ulf asked.

She gave him a reproachful look. 'You don't need to do any-thing special for that,' she said.

'It's just that you seem . . .' He trailed off.

'Pleased?'

Ulf nodded. 'Yes. You seem pleased about something.'

'I am,' Juni said. 'I've got good news for you. Niklas phoned.'

Ulf slipped off his jacket. He did not want to hear from Niklas, but he did not want Juni to see that the mention of the vet's name made him feel uncomfortable.

'Well,' Juni persisted. 'Aren't you going to ask?'

'What did he say?'

'That's better. Niklas has managed to get hold of the compo-nents that he needs for Martin's operation. He ended up getting them from a colleague in the Netherlands. So he'll be able to perform Martin's operation tomorrow afternoon.'

Ulf felt his heart skip a beat. 'That's rather soon, isn't it?'

'No,' said Juni. 'There's plenty of time to starve him.'

It took Ulf a moment or two to realise what she was talking about. 'Do you mean so that he can have an anaesthetic?'

'Exactly,' said Juni. 'There's always a danger of choking if the patient regurgitates.'

Ulf looked away. He resented the fact that she had made this arrangement without consulting him. For all she knew, he might wish to be with Martin during the procedure, and the following afternoon might not have suited him.

It was as if she had read his mind. 'I'll take him to Niklas's clinic,' she said. 'I know that you're likely to be busy, and I have the day off anyway. Niklas says that I can stay with Martin while he's carrying out the operation.'

Ulf bit his lip. It was too much. It was a liberty.

'I would have liked to go with him,' he said.

She seemed to be weighing up alternative responses. Eventually, she struck a conciliatory note. 'I know how you feel, Ulf. You want the best for Martin, and I can see why – he'd feel safe with you there with him. But we mustn't risk losing the opportunity, you know. If Niklas doesn't do the operation tomorrow, it might be weeks before he can fit Martin in. It really could be. Niklas is very busy, you know. He has clients from all over – even Estonia. They book months in advance.'

Ulf closed his eyes briefly. This was not what he wanted, but he felt a curious powerlessness. 'Will you stay with him?' he said.

She hesitated briefly before answering. 'We'll see how he is. He may need to be kept in overnight.'

'Overnight,' muttered Ulf.

She was watching him. Did she really think he was unaware of what was going on? She needed to remind herself of what his profession was.

'It may not be necessary,' she said quickly. 'But if it is, I'll stay down there with him and bring him back the following morning.'

Ulf took a deep breath. 'You'll stay in Copenhagen?'

'Yes. It would be simpler, I think. And Martin will feel less . . . less confused, I suppose, if I'm there.'

Ulf wanted to say that Niklas, too, might like it, but he did not. There was so much that he did not say, even when he knew that he would have been entitled to speak. So now he simply said, 'All right.'

Juni seemed relieved. 'I thought I might make crab linguine tonight,' she said. 'Would you like that?'

Ulf thought: I shall not be bought off with crab linguine. He glanced at her and replied, 'I'm not feeling brilliant. I've had a tough day.'

She looked at him with concern. 'I won't stay then. I'll come back tomorrow morning for Martin.'

'That would be best,' said Ulf.

From his window he watched her walk out to the car that she had parked just beyond his Volkswagen. She looked up as she unlocked the door, and she saw him staring down at her. She waved, and blew him a kiss.

Ulf drew back from the window. He had not returned the kiss, and now he thought, I must do it. I must bring this to an end. It's what she wants, I think, and what I have to do. He had been unwilling to hurt her, but now he was sure that she was ready to leave him for Niklas, he felt less compunction about ending the relationship. I don't need to play second fiddle to anyone, he told himself. I will not be cheated on.

He would wait until Martin was back from his operation, and then he would tell her. 'There's no longer any point,' he would say; and she would be relieved. It would show in her eyes. He would thank her, though, for the time they had spent together, and she would go off to Niklas with his blessing. There was no point in increasing the amount of unhappiness in the world by making others feel bad about themselves and about what they had done – even if, from one point of view at least, it was their fault.

He stopped himself. He was not sure that fault came into it. There were admittedly cases where people treated their lovers selfishly, where they deceived them or took advantage of them, but this was not one of them. Juni had not done that at all; even if she had fallen for somebody else – and Niklas was younger and more attractive than he himself was, thought Ulf – even if that had happened, the fact that she had continued to see him, to come to his flat for evenings of crab linguine and episodes of historical television drama, was evidence, surely, that she was trying not to hurt him. Perhaps she was thinking of letting him down slowly, as people did when their fondness for another prevented them from opting for an abrupt break. And when one looked at it in that way, nobody should be blamed. Feelings for others were not cast in stone; we changed in our affections in much the same way as our other habits and tastes could change. Ulf had once liked marzipan; now he did not. His brother, Björn, had once admired the work of David Hockney and had then decided that he did not. That was strange – and Ulf had sided with Hockney in the one conversation they had had on the subject. But Björn was odd, anyway – most of the senior ranks of the Moderate Extremists were – and was perhaps not the best example to bring into anything, Ulf decided.

A sudden thought occurred to him. He had submitted to the pressure Juni had brought to bear on him over Martin's operation. He should have stood his ground, but he had not. He regretted that, if not entirely – as he wanted the best for Martin, of course he did – but he still should not have allowed himself to be manipulated. But now a fresh doubt began to nag at him. What if the whole thing was an elaborate scam? What if he, Ulf Varg, of the Department of Sensitive Crimes, had fallen for a grubby confidence trick? Juni might be innocent – she might believe Niklas – but what if the Copenhagen vet was cynically taking advantage of people's desire to help their dogs? He might be a properly trained vet, but he might nonetheless be peddling an expensive operation that he knew to be at best of questionable benefit, and at worst, a complete waste of money? Shortly after he had joined the department, Ulf had been assigned to an investigation of a dentist who had been giving his patients unnecessary dental treatment. Teeth had been pulled out for no good reason, and expensive fillings had been inserted where none were required. It had been a tawdry business, and had led to an arrest only after Ulf, posing as a patient, had submitted to the attentions of this unscrupulous dentist. He had lain back in the dental chair and had allowed the suspect to prepare his drill before he had sat up, ripped off the protective bib, and shown the surprised dentist his identity card. The dentist had stood stock-still, his drill in his hand, and Ulf had wondered whether he might even try to use it as a weapon. He had imagined the struggle, picturing himself gripping the other man's hand in an attempt to ward off the whining needle. But there had been no resistance, and the dentist had submitted meekly, with no more than a muttered, 'Your gums need attention.' Anna had laughed when he told her about what had happened. 'White mask crime,' she said.

The following day, while Blomquist went off with Fridolf to make the formal identification of the stolen house, Ulf, as requested in an electronic memo, reported to the Commissioner's office. He knew what the summons was about: the Commissioner wanted to know the outcome of the personnel rearrangements in the department, and Ulf was now in a position to announce his proposed move. He was not sure if the Commissioner would approve, but he was prepared to make a strong case for his own transfer. He was aware, too, of the fact that the saving represented by his moving would be greater than that which would be generated by a more junior member of staff being nominated. Ulf would take a small pay cut by going to Litter and Waste, as it was a less highly ranked department; that would help the overall police budget, which was always a headache for the Commissioner. For that reason alone, Ulf thought his proposal would be accepted, even if the Commissioner were to express some misgivings.

Ulf had to wait for almost twenty minutes while the Commissioner finished a telephone call with the Minister of Justice. Ulf heard some of the exchange, as the Commissioner raised his voice at several points in the conversation, but he was unable to work out what the topic was. All he could ascertain was that the Commissioner thought the minister was being unreasonable, not that he would ever accuse him of acting that way. 'It's just that your attitude might strike *others* as being a bit unbudging, Minister – not that I take that view, of course – far from it. I think, though, that there could be those who do, and there may be a fair number of them, come to think of it – you know what people are like.'

As she came over to admit Ulf to the office, the Commissioner's secretary leaned forward and whispered, 'I worry about his blood pressure, you know. The Commissioner always turns red when he speaks to the minister. I always know when that man is on the phone.'

'Ah,' said Ulf. 'Blood pressure is something you have to watch.'

'Exactly,' said the secretary. 'And he won't take a holiday, you know. I keep telling him there's no point in working hard all the time and then waking up dead – so to speak.'

'None at all,' agreed Ulf. 'You can't run a police force if you're dead.'

It was a pointless, rather absurd thing to say, and Ulf wondered immediately why he had said it. There were some comments that were simply *noise*, and this was one of them. He was worried that the Commissioner's secretary would think that he was trying to be funny – he was not – and that she might conclude that the comment was in notably poor taste. But she did not, apparently, as she looked at him seriously before saying, with some gravity, as one might do when delivering a carefully considered opinion, 'That's absolutely right, Ulf. Never a truer word spoken.'

Ulf entered the Commissioner's office and was invited to sit in front of the large, uncluttered desk behind which his superior officer sat.

'It's always good to see you, Ulf,' said the Commissioner. He paused. 'I take it I may call you Ulf – as before?'

'Of course.'

'And I'm Felix, as you know.'

'Felix.'

The Commissioner rubbed his eyes. 'I've just been on the phone to that dreadful man, the Minister of Justice. Have you met him?'

Ulf shook his head. 'I don't believe I have.'

'He's a typical politician,' sighed the Commissioner. 'The only thing that motivates him is votes and how voters will react. It's the only question, really, as far as he's concerned.' He paused.

'Where's national interest? Surely that should come into it. Or principle? That could have a bearing. But all we get is an eye on how anything will look "on the street", as he puts it. On the street, indeed! Since when was policy determined by what was being thought on the street?'

Ulf felt tempted to say, 'For a very long time,' but did not.

'Anyway,' the Commissioner continued, 'I gave him a few home truths. He didn't like it – they never do – and he even reminded me of his constitutional position. Things have come to a pretty pass when you get politicians like that reminding you of their constitutional position.' He stopped. 'You have a brother in politics, don't you, Ulf?'

Ulf swallowed. It seemed that everyone knew about Björn, and that there was nowhere Ulf would be able to escape the association. Some years earlier, Ulf had been presented at a police ceremony to the King himself, and the King had looked at him through narrowed eyes and said, 'You're the brother of that Moderate Extremist fellow, aren't you?' The King had rapidly indicated that his comment was not accusatory – kings needed to be scrupulously above politics – but it was clear to Ulf that Björn and his party were not in royal favour.

'He is my brother, Your Majesty,' Ulf had replied. 'But I don't really see much of him.'

The King had picked up the correct implication, and had smiled indulgently. 'We can't exactly choose our relatives, can we?'

It was a profound thing for a king to say, because not being able to choose your relatives when you were in a position like his had major implications. Ulf had smiled. 'I believe you're right, sir.'

'Mind you,' said the King, 'everybody has their role, don't they? If there's nonsense to be talked, then somebody has to talk it, I always say.'

Ulf had pondered this remark for some time afterwards, but had been unable to decide on its significance. It either came from the depths of resignation at having to listen to nonsense being talked – something that every king, Ulf imagined, might complain about – or it was a coded refutation of everything that Björn and his Moderate Extremist party stood for and said. That was possible, of course, but it was never easy to work out exactly where Björn stood on a number of issues, and a succinct countering of their positions was difficult.

Now the Commissioner was waiting for Ulf to respond.

'Yes, I have a brother in politics. My brother, Björn Varg. He's a—'

'Moderate Extremist, isn't he?' said the Commissioner. 'I have a nephew who's keen on them. He keeps giving me leaflets. I throw them straight into the bin, and let him see me doing that.'

Ulf smiled. 'I do the same, I'm afraid.'

'Ridiculous people,' said the Commissioner. 'Not that my nephew sees that. He's a very annoying young man. He's got it into his head that we should all stop speaking Swedish and speak English instead. He says that English is the language of the future and that Swedish simply complicates matters.'

Ulf shook his head. 'There are some very strange ideas going round.' But then he remembered Esperanto, and the faith that some people, at least, had in it. If we had a universal language, they argued, then international understanding would flourish and misunderstandings would die on the vine. Ulf thought of a teacher he'd had as a child – the starry-eyed Mr Lundin, teacher of geography and a firm believer in world government and world language. Ulf had not thought of him for a long time, but now he remembered Mr Lundin, standing at the head of the class intoning *bonan matenon*, which was 'good morning' in Esperanto. Ulf had liked the teacher, and had made an effort to learn a little Esperanto just to please him. Now he remembered nothing, apart from *bonan matenon*, a phrase with which he occasionally greeted Martin – in spite of his deafness – and *mi havas problemon*, which, almost laughably, was 'I have a problem'. But why should one learn Esperanto now, when English had so clearly elbowed its way to being the international lingua franca? One might as well learn Klingon, thought Ulf, and recalled that the only person he knew who could speak even a few words of that strange, constructed language was Blomquist ... It was typical of Blomquist to take an interest in such frankly useless matters, tucking the information away in his mind, alongside all those facts abouts vitamins and garlic and various arcane nostrums. And yet Blomquist should not be discounted, Ulf thought: those who wrote Blomquist off as a bore, given to trivial chatter, were making a big mistake – and were being unkind, too, which Ulf never liked. *Be kind* was his motto. It was a simple and unambiguous rule by which to go through life: *be kind to other people.*

The Commissioner had more to say about his nephew. 'I point out to him that there's no need to get rid of Swedish – we're not like the Chinese. There's a very strong case for them to abandon Chinese and use something simpler.'

Ulf waited for the theme to be expanded upon. The Commissioner was known for his theories, which could be brought into the conversation at unexpected moments.

'It takes an awful lot for Chinese people to learn how to write,' said the Commissioner. 'All those brush-strokes. I don't know how they do it.'

'It provides mental training, perhaps,' Ulf ventured.

The Commissioner sighed. 'When they run everything,' he said, 'we'll have to learn then.'

Ulf said nothing. The Commissioner looked at him through narrowed eyes. 'You think I'm joking, Ulf?'

'No, I don't.'

'Because they're planning it in open sight,' the Commissioner went on.

'I suppose they're ambitious,' said Ulf. 'Most people are, when it comes down to it.'

The Commissioner looked away. 'I don't think we should be discussing China,' he said. 'I didn't ask you here to talk about that.'

Ulf waited.

'It's about the departmental restructuring,' said the Commissioner. 'There's been a bit of a change of plan.'

Ulf looked up sharply. It had not occurred to him that the proposed cut would be rescinded; that was not normally what happened with budgetary cuts: if anything, they were deepened.

'I don't want to give you false hope,' the Commissioner said quickly. 'You still have to lose point seven-five of a person. That's not going to change.'

'Oh . . .'

'However,' went on the Commissioner, 'there is to be a change in where that point seven-five goes. You will recall that we were intending it to be Litter and Waste.'

Ulf nodded. 'So I gathered.'

'Well, that's no longer the case,' said the Commissioner. 'One of the people who was going to retire from Litter and Waste seems to have developed a second wind and wants to stay. I'm a bit annoyed about this, but I've decided it would be difficult for everybody if we forced a retirement. She's the union repre-sentative, you see, and I thought it might be easier just to back off.' He gave Ulf an imploring look, as if seeking validation of his decision.

'Probably wiser,' said Ulf. 'There are enough fights to be fought without creating new ones.'

'Thank you,' said the Commissioner, with some relief. 'In normal circumstances this would be awkward, but, as it turns out, circumstances are not normal. By an extraordinary coincidence, just as that officer in Litter and Waste was digging her heels in, a man in another department altogether announced that he wanted to leave in order to . . .' The Commissioner looked a bit sheepish. 'In order to pursue a career as a disc jockey.'

Ulf shrugged. 'It's an honest job,' he said. 'Bad for the hearing, I imagine. But young people like that sort of thing, I suppose.'

The Commissioner pursed his lips. 'He's forty-eight. Forty-nine next month.'

Ulf smiled. 'Male menopause?'

'Something like that,' said the Commissioner. 'I should have anticipated it. I saw him a few months ago wearing what I thought was teenage clothing – you know, a cap on backwards, a T-shirt with a picture of a superhero on it – that sort of thing.'

'It can be an embarrassing stage,' said Ulf. 'Of course, he may have been in disguise. That's a possibility.'

'There are better disguises for a man in his late forties,' said the Commissioner. 'But be that as it may, what do you know of crayfish? I mean, noble crayfish?'

'I'm in favour of them,' said Ulf. And he thought of crab linguine, and what that had represented in his life recently, and how it now stood for failure and disappointment. People did not eat crayfish with linguine, but they could.

'And eels?' continued the Commissioner.

Ulf shrugged. 'I don't really know much about them. I'm not sure I've ever eaten eel.'

'We all know about crayfish parties,' said the Commissioner. 'August wouldn't be August without them, would it?'

Ulf realised that he had not been to a crayfish party for several years. That is how out of touch I am with ordinary family life, he thought.

The Commissioner was looking at him. 'You live by yourself, don't you, Ulf? You and that dog of yours.'

Ulf nodded. 'I'm seeing somebody at present, but . . .'

The Commissioner waited.

'But, well, I'm not sure if it's going anywhere.'

The Commissioner looked sympathetic. 'Our work can put our personal lives under some strain,' he said. 'I'm very much aware of that, sitting where I sit. It's not always easy to conduct a normal home life when you do what we do.' He paused. 'You must join my wife and me for a crayfish party next month. We go to my brother-in-law's place. They'll be happy to have you.'

'You're very kind,' said Ulf. 'But don't worry about me, Felix. I'm all right.'

The Commissioner looked at his watch. 'I'd better get to the point. Crayfish. Eels. You'll have noticed the connection.'

Ulf frowned. 'Well, there is an obvious one, but beyond that . . .'

'Fishing regulation,' said the Commissioner. 'Word has come from above – and I mean *right* above, that we are to take environmental crime more seriously. In particular, we're to crack down on illegal activities in connection with marine and aquatic life generally. So, there are foreign crayfish being brought into the country illegally. They bring disease and threaten our indigenous Swedish species. Then eels are being trapped indiscriminately, with the result that our eel population is endangered. There are other threats too.'

'It's a familiar story,' said Ulf. 'There are just too many mouths to feed. Nature can't cope.'

'You're quite right,' said the Commissioner. 'But we have to do our best, and Stockholm wants us to try and stop the rot. So I'm going to have to replace this fellow who wants to go off and be a disc jockey. He's in environmental crime. There are 3.75 posts there, and so I need to find somebody to be the .75 – and entirely concerned with fish. At the moment, fish are just a sideshow.' He paused. 'I take it you can give me a name – the person who was going to go to Litter and Waste.'

It took Ulf a few moments to order his thoughts. His mind was racing ahead to the possibility of a neat solution. Of course. Of course.

'Actually,' he said, 'it was me. I was going to go to Litter and Waste.'

The Commissioner looked confused. 'But you can't,' he said. 'You're too senior. You'd be wasted there.'

Ulf explained how he had been reluctant to ask any member of his staff to do what he himself would not do. It was important, he said, for the morale of the department that he should be seen to be shouldering the unwelcome burden himself.

'However,' Ulf went on, 'I think that I see a marvellous solution emerging right before our eyes – a solution that will result in a very contented employee while at the same time meeting your overall needs.'

The Commissioner listened as Ulf explained about Erik. 'He's a very good officer,' he said, 'but he's completely obsessed with fishing. This job will be his idea of heaven on earth.'

The Commissioner shrugged. 'It beats me that anybody can find fishing interesting, but I suppose there's no accounting for taste.'

Ulf agreed. 'And I take it that he will be able to spend the remaining twenty-five per cent of his time in Sensitive Crimes?'

The Commissioner thought for a moment. 'I see no reason why not,' he said eventually. 'We're all encouraged to be flexible – portfolio careers and all that.'

'Then, with your permission, may I tell him?'

'It sounds as if it will suit him,' said the Commissioner.

'It will do more than that,' said Ulf. 'It will propel him to cloud nine. To nirvana. It will make him blissfully happy.'

The Commissioner laughed. 'I really want people to be happy,' he said. 'Sometimes people don't realise that this is how I feel. They think that police commissioners don't want to be loved. They think that we don't care about other people's happiness.'

Ulf recalled that he had assured the Commissioner he was loved on the last occasion they had met. It seemed that reminders were necessary.

'Erik will be immensely grateful to you,' he said. 'I think your decision is exactly right, if I may say so.'

The Commissioner beamed with pleasure. 'We must talk one day about your promotion, Ulf. Before too long, I think.'

Ulf had not expected this, and felt embarrassed. He would never wish to be promoted simply because he had flattered the Commissioner. He did not believe in flattery, and the intention behind his words really had been to make the Commissioner feel better about himself. So he pretended that he hadn't heard what the Commissioner had said, and rose now to take his leave.

The Commissioner, though, had one more thing to say.

'I had a letter from members of your department,' he said. 'They proposed that Blomquist should be sent to Litter and Waste. They suggested that this was the considered view of the department.'

It took Ulf some time to appreciate just what the Commissioner had said. At last, his wits gathered, he asked whether the letter had come from all members of the department. 'No,' said the Commissioner. 'Just two. I assumed they were speaking for everybody.'

'They weren't,' said Ulf.

'Perhaps they need talking to,' said the Commissioner.

'At the very least,' said Ulf.

'I should have asked you,' said Blomquist. 'Do you have a key?'

He was standing with Fridolf outside the front door of the rediscovered house.

'Of course.'

Fridolf responded immediately, but his answer was followed by a rather odd silence – of the sort that sometimes follows the making of a remark that is regretted as soon as it has fallen from the lips. Then, after that moment of silence, 'At least I think I do. Let me check.'

But he *knew*, thought Blomquist. Fridolf knew that he had the key in his pocket, and that must be because he was using it regularly. You did not keep old keys in your pocket – you put them back in the drawer or on the nail on which they hung; you did not carry them around with you.

The key was there. 'Ah,' said Fridolf, unconvincingly affecting surprise, 'here it is. Yes, this is it. I haven't used this for some time.'

The last sentence, Blomquist thought, was the belt and the braces that he needed for certainty. Fridolf had been using the house all along.

The front door having been unlocked, they made their way into the entrance hall.

'It's so good to . . . to see it again,' muttered Fridolf as he looked around him.

Blomquist watched him. 'Yes,' he said. 'Is it more or less as you left it?'

Fridolf nodded. 'Nothing seems to have been moved.'

'That's odd,' said Blomquist. 'You'd think that the thieves – whoever they are – would have put in some of their things.'

Fridolf hesitated. 'Yes, you'd think that, wouldn't you? Yes, I suspect you're right.' He paused. 'Ah . . . That umbrella over there in the corner. See it? That's not right. That wasn't there.'

Blomquist looked to where Fridolf was pointing. A furled black umbrella with a curved cane handle was propped against a wall.

'You don't recognise that?' Blomquist asked.

Fridolf shook his head. 'No. That must have been left by . . . by these people – whoever they are.' He turned to Blomquist. 'Do you have any idea who they might be?'

Blomquist sucked in his cheeks. 'It's best to keep an open mind in these matters,' he said. 'Sometimes the perpetrator turns out to be the *most* unlikely person.' He dwelt on the word *most*, and as he did so, he shot a glance towards Fridolf, who quickly looked away.

Now Blomquist walked over to pick up the umbrella. The

canopy had been tightly wound and then secured by a strap of elastic. This he released.

'I know it's unlucky to open an umbrella indoors,' Blomquist said. 'Were you told that as a child?'

Fridolf was watching him. He did not reply.

'Not that I believe in these superstitions,' Blomquist continued, reaching for the safety catch that would release the canopy. 'I never hesitate to leave my keys on a table, although an awful lot of people in this country will avoid that like the plague.'

'I know,' said Fridolf, his eyes still fixed on the umbrella.

'Do you know the origin of that particular superstition?' asked Blomquist. 'It's to do with the selling of sex. Apparently, people would leave their keys on the table to indicate their availability. That put respectable people off from doing the same thing – in case they were thought to be ...'

'Harlots,' said Fridolf.

Blomquist gave him a reproachful glance. 'That's perhaps a rather old-fashioned word, don't you think?'

Fridolf smirked. 'Words change, Blomquist, but people don't.'

Blomquist did not engage. He had decided that he did not like Fridolf, but he was determined not to show it. A detective lost any advantage he had if he allowed personal animosity to get in the way of his judgement. So now he simply nodded non-committally.

He slipped the catch beneath the umbrella handle and the spring-loaded mechanism pushed up the canopy. He looked up. There was an advertising slogan emblazoned on the canopy material – the sort of display one saw on promotional golf umbrellas.

Bengtsson Bacon.

Blomquist stared at the slogan with unconcealed surprise. Then he transferred his gaze to Fridolf. 'What a coincidence,' he said.

For a few moments Fridolf simply gaped at the sight of the umbrella. Then, in a very thin voice, he said, 'My mistake. I must have left it there.'

Blomquist collapsed the umbrella. 'Easily done,' he said. 'I often forget where I've left things.' He was trying to decide whether this was a genuine mistake, or whether in order to strengthen the story of the theft he had chosen the umbrella simply to get himself out of a corner.

Fridolf was relieved to be given a way out. 'Perhaps we should take a look to see if there's anything else,' he said. 'You never know.'

'No,' said Blomquist. 'You don't.'

He pointed to a door. 'What's behind that?' he asked.

'The kitchen,' said Fridolf. 'Or it used to be.'

Blomquist laughed. 'I don't think the thieves will have done anything quite so fundamental as to rearrange the kitchen, do you?'

Fridolf went first.

'It looks exactly as it was before the theft,' he said. He shook his head. 'These wretched people ... Can you credit it? Stealing somebody's house – I mean, their actual house!'

Blomquist remained cool. 'Do you see anything unusual?'

Fridolf looked around. He opened a cupboard and took out a container of cutlery. 'My wife's silver cutlery's still here. She inherited it from her mother. She'll be very relieved to know they haven't taken that.'

Blomquist saw his opening. 'Do you and your wife see eye to eye over most things?'

Fridolf looked surprised. 'Of course. Why do you ask?'

'Because I like to get the overall picture. And I'm sorry if my question seems a bit intrusive, but when you're investigating a sensitive crime like this, it helps to be as fully informed as possible.'

Fridolf appeared placated. 'My wife and I share views on most important matters. Of course, we have one or two differences at the edges, but which married couples don't?'

'And your previous wife?' asked Blomquist. 'Did you have any major differences of opinion?'

'We went our separate ways,' snapped Fridolf. 'It was all very amicable. And adult, too.'

'It's always better like that,' mused Blomquist. 'It's awkward when there are unresolved issues.'

'Agreed,' said Fridolf. '*D'accord*, in fact.'

Blomquist glanced at him: introducing a foreign phrase was a way of distracting attention from another issue. He knew all about that. '*Alors*,' he said. 'You and your wife . . . is everything all right?'

Fridolf's eyes narrowed. 'Of course it is.' He paused, before continuing, 'What exactly are you suggesting?'

'Nothing,' said Blomquist quickly. 'I was simply checking that all was well.'

'My wife is a wonderful woman,' said Fridolf. 'We are the greatest of friends.' There was a further pause. 'I would certainly never leave her, if that's what you're hinting at.'

'I'm glad to hear that,' said Blomquist. 'There is so much chopping and changing these days. People don't seem to be prepared to commit for the long haul.' He moved towards the other side of the room. 'The fridge is on, I see.'

'The sheer cheek of it,' muttered Fridolf.

'They could come back at any moment, I suppose,' said Blomquist. 'That would give them a nice surprise: finding us in the house would be rather like the story of Goldilocks and the three bears. They came back while she was still in the house, asleep in one of the beds.' He rested his hand on the fridge door. He saw that Fridolf was watching him intently. 'Mind you,' Blomquist continued, 'this whole story has made us think about another story altogether – the story of the three little pigs. Do you remember that one?'

Fridolf nodded. He swallowed.

'*I'll huff and I'll puff and I'll blow your house down.* That was the big bad wolf. Remember?'

Again, Fridolf nodded wordlessly.

'We found what looked like a wolf's footprint outside the house,' Blomquist continued. 'I wonder if there are wolves around here?'

Fridolf had something to say about that. 'Definitely not. That would be a dog's print. I've seen a large dog hanging round ...' He stopped himself.

Blomquist's eyes widened. 'Hanging round here?'

Fridolf shook his head vigorously. 'No, of course not here. In the other place. The original site.'

'Ah,' said Blomquist. 'For a moment I thought you were talking about this place.'

'Well, I wasn't,' said Fridolf, almost surlily.

Blomquist opened the door of the fridge. An interior light came on obligingly, illuminating several well-stocked shelves. Blomquist reached forward and took out a packet of processed cheese. 'This is very much in date,' he said, scrutinising the wrapping. 'Best before the end of next month. Plenty of time.'

He reached for another item. 'And what have we here? A salami of some sort. *Proshute* it says on the label. That sounds a bit like Italian, doesn't it? *Prosciutto*? But this is not an Italian word. Perhaps it comes from a neighbouring country – somewhere nearby.' He turned to look at Fridolf. 'What do you think, Fridolf? *Proshute*? Macedonian?'

Fridolf shrugged. 'Who knows?'

'And what have we here?' said Blomquist, reaching forward to pick up a bottle on the bottom shelf of the fridge. '*Raki*. Well, well. I don't like these drinks, but some people do. Very popular in Albania, I believe. He replaced the bottle and took out a small packet of sausages. 'These look like skinless sausages, if I'm not mistaken. And the label? *Quebapa*. That's an odd word. Have you ever heard of *quebapa*?'

'No,' said Fridolf.

'I can tell you one thing,' said Blomquist. 'That's not a word I know.'

He returned the package of sausages. As he did so, he noticed the opened can of dog food at the back of the fridge. He stared at it. The label, surely, was a joke – a marketing ploy. *Tinned Moose,* it said, *for the wolf in your life.*

He stared at this. This was becoming complicated. Fridolf stood for the wolf; his house being the house belonging to the little pigs. He'd blown that house down – or, at least, moved it. But there must be a dog, too, perhaps one owned by his girlfriend. And where did the pigs come into it? Fridolf was a pig farmer, ultimately, but symbolically he was a wolf. That was strange.

He closed the fridge door. 'I think we can get back to town now,' he said.

Fridolf looked relieved. 'Yes,' he said. 'Good idea.' He hesitated, and then added, 'Wouldn't it make sense for you to leave somebody here? That way, you could arrest the thieves when they came back?'

Blomquist tapped the side of his nose. 'All in good time,' he said. 'Timing is a very important part of police work, you know. If you move too early – before your case is well and truly prepared – you run the risk of compromising everything. Taking your time always gets the best results.'

'I see,' said Fridolf. 'It's rather like curing bacon. Don't remove it from the cure too early.'

'A very good analogy,' said Blomquist. 'Or cooking a goose, I suppose. Don't take your goose out of the oven before it's properly cooked.'

He gave Fridolf a sideways look, which became a smile. Fridolf returned his smile in an unforced way. You are much more relaxed now, my friend, thought Blomquist. You shouldn't be, but you are.

CHAPTER TWELVE

A Memory of Crab Linguine

Ulf was unable to get away from the office the following day until shortly after four in the afternoon. He had received a call from Juni at lunchtime, telling him that she was back at the flat with Martin, and that she was sure Martin would be eager to see him. She said nothing about the operation, other than to assure him that the dog had come round from the anaesthetic without any apparent ill effects and had already enjoyed a substantial meal. When Ulf asked whether the procedure had been a success, she had simply said, 'We can talk about that when you get back,' which meant, in Ulf's view, that it had been a failure.

'I feared there was no point,' said Ulf into the telephone, noticing that Anna was watching him from her desk. 'But, all right: we'll talk later.'

'Martin?' asked Anna, her voice registering her concern.

Ulf nodded.

'Is he . . .' Anna did not complete her question.

'He's still alive,' said Ulf. 'He's home now. It's just that the operation doesn't sound as if it was successful.'

Anna made a sympathetic gesture. 'Oh, Ulf, I'm so sorry. But it
did seem – how shall I put it? – a bit of a long shot.'

'I know,' said Ulf. 'I didn't want it. I was pushed into it,
I'm afraid.'

'By Juni?'

Ulf nodded. He had told Anna about Juni. It had hurt him to
do so, as he was, in effect, telling one person whom he knew he
loved about another with whom he hoped he would fall in love.
That was never going to be easy.

'I'm sure she was only trying to help,' said Anna. 'But there
are limits to what you can do for an animal. And I don't think
we should be doing transplant surgery on domestic pets – not
when there are people who are desperate for some fairly basic
treatments.'

Carl was listening. 'My father did a programme on that,' he said.
'You might have heard it on the radio. He chaired a discussion.
Philosophers and so on. They all agreed: our fellow humans have
first claim on society's limited resources.'

Ulf had said that he was surprised there was that consensus.
There were plenty of philosophers who found it hard to privilege
homo sapiens in that way.

Carl explained. 'My father has a simple policy,' he said. 'When
he draws up lists of people to invite on his programmes, he only
chooses those who agree with him. It's very straightforward, but
he says it makes for good radio and television. People don't want
to see too much conflict. It makes them feel good to see people
agreeing with one another.'

'Is that why he's so popular?' asked Anna. Carl's father, who was
a regular broadcaster on moral questions, enjoyed a wide audience
throughout Sweden. His nickname in the popular press was the
'Popular Professor', a soubriquet that provoked seething jealousy

amongst those of his academic colleagues for whom speaking in a way that was intelligible to the person in the street was incontrovertible evidence of academic superficiality.

'I think it is,' answered Carl. 'People write in to him and tell him what they want in life is calm advice from people who know better than they do. They don't want to think things out for themselves. They want somebody to hold their hand.'

'Don't we all?' said Anna. 'At least, sometimes. Do you know about the English poet, T. S. Eliot? You know what he said: "Humankind cannot bear very much reality." Or something like that. He was dead right. We want to be shown the way.'

'He was American,' said Carl. 'He came from Missouri. We studied him at school. I wrote an essay on him. Then he became English. He worked in a bank in London. He was American, and then he became English.'

'His poems are set in England, not America,' said Anna. 'Where's *The Waste Land*? London?'

'Does it matter?' asked Erik. 'Fish belong to the waters they swim in.'

They turned to stare at him.

'If a German writer came to live in Sweden,' asked Carl. 'Would he become a Swedish writer – even if he never spoke a word of Swedish?'

'Interesting,' muttered Anna. 'It might depend on whether he continued to write in German . . .'

'Which he would have to do,' said Carl. 'You can't write in a language you don't know.'

Anna raised a finger. 'Are you sure about that? I saw a very interesting programme on television about xenoglossy. Do you know what that is? It's when people go into a trance and speak a foreign language they've never learned. There was a woman in America who spoke perfect German when she was hypnotised into a past life. She'd never learned a word of German – not one.

But she spoke all about her life in a Bavarian village – complete with all the details – the baker's name, and so on.'

'Rubbish,' said Carl. 'Impossible. I just laugh at these people who say they've had a past life. They've always been Egyptian princesses or something; they've never been anything ordinary – a Russian serf, for instance, or—'

'Or a salmon,' offered Erik.

Carl burst into laughter. 'So you were a fish in a previous life, Erik? Until you took that worm . . . Big mistake.'

Ulf had listened with some interest to this exchange. It made him proud of the Department of Sensitive Crimes that such a discussion could take place within it. You would never find that, he told himself, in the Commercial Crime or Traffic departments, nor – and perhaps particularly – in Litter and Waste. But this was not what they were paid to do, and so he said, 'Well, we'd better get back to work.' There was a pile of correspondence on his desk, a stack of files on Anna's, and a twenty-page draft report on Carl's.

Anna cast a final look at Ulf. 'I hope Martin's all right,' she whispered. 'I know how important he is to you.'

She had said something similar once before, and Ulf had found himself resenting it. He knew that her remark was well intentioned, but he could not help but interpret it as meaning: *I'm unavailable, but at least you have your dog for company.* He wondered now what her reaction would be to hearing, as he was sure she would, that he and Juni had split up. Because that was going to happen now – he was sure of it – and he would have to tell Anna in due course. Ulf did not want pity – who did? I want love, he thought. I want to drown myself in somebody else – in *her* – but that will never be possible. The one person I want more than any other in this world – the one – is married, is out of bounds. It's so unfair . . . no, he thought, it isn't; it's not unfair because the world is inherently unfair. Fairness is something we create in order to make life bearable. But we know, in our heart of hearts, that belief in fairness is an act of faith. It's Kierkegaardian. It's a Kierkegaardian leap of faith, but that did not mean that it was there. It was one of the many safety nets that we, the trapeze artists, hoped were beneath us, but probably were not. We were alone in our aerial displays – tiny performers, travelling through space on our revolving planet, trying to keep ourselves going with ideas of purpose and justice and so on, when all about us was a void so complete and unfathomable that we could not even contemplate it. Only love mattered in that emptiness – love, and the moments of warmth and purpose that it gave us in our brief and tiny lives. That was what Ulf thought, as he sat at his desk, trying to concentrate on the papers before him. They were deep thoughts – troubling and unanswerable ones, and not ones that the average Swedish detective entertained as he discharged the duties that the state imposed on him. Or perhaps they were. For who knows, Ulf asked himself, what Swedish detectives think, other than Swedish detectives, of course, of which he was one. And yet he was far from sure.

He worked quietly for fifteen minutes or so, but then he closed the file in front of him. He had been thinking of the Commissioner's revelation that Carl and Erik had sent a letter recommending Blomquist for transfer. He had been uncertain as to what to do about this discovery, but now he thought he knew.

He rose from his desk and crossed the room to speak to Carl. 'I'd like to have a word with you and Erik,' he said. 'Outside – in the corridor.'

Carl frowned. 'Now?'

'Yes,' said Ulf. 'Right now.'

The three of them met outside. Ulf noticed that Carl looked anxious – as well he might, he thought.

'I'll come straight to the point,' Ulf said. 'I saw the Commissioner yesterday. He told me he had received a letter from the two of you.'

They both blushed, and any sliver of doubt as to their guilt was immediately dispelled.

'I hope that you both feel thoroughly ashamed of yourselves,' Ulf said.

Carl exchanged a helpless glance with Erik.

'I don't propose to do anything about it,' Ulf went on. 'Your consciences, I hope, will punish you for your unkindness. But I should perhaps add to that by saying that I hope in future you will treat Blomquist with courtesy. In fact, I expect a special effort on both your parts. Do I make myself clear?'

Neither Carl nor Erik spoke. Shame had descended on them like a blanket.

'Yes?' pressed Ulf.

'You make yourself clear,' said Carl.

Ulf nodded. 'Good. And I suggest you remember that there are those who do not have much in this life, who don't have what you have. People like Blomquist. Think about them from time to time, will you? Try to make their lives a bit better. It's not hard, you know.'

Their shame deepened, and seeing that written in the cast of their features, Ulf brought the conversation to an end.

Juni met him at the door. She put a finger to her lips in a gesture of silence.

'He's just dropped off to sleep,' she whispered. 'I was hoping that would happen, but he was quite alert, and it's taken a bit of time. I suppose it's the effect of the anaesthetic – it can disrupt an animal's sleep patterns.'

She pointed through the hall, and Ulf followed her into the living room. There, lying on a blanket that had been spread out on Ulf's IKEA couch, was Martin, a large white bandage tied around his head. He was wearing one of those curious lampshade devices that vets put on dogs to prevent them licking wounds and dislodging stitches.

Ulf crossed the room and stood looking down on Martin. 'Poor Martin,' he muttered. 'Poor Martin.'

Juni was beside him. She touched Ulf's forearm gently. 'He's not in pain. He's had a good dose of painkillers, and Niklas has given me a whole box of them. You've got far more than enough.'

Niklas, thought Ulf.

'What happened?'

Juni kept her voice down as she told Ulf about the operation. 'At first Niklas thought it was going to go well enough,' she said. 'He made the initial incisions without any difficulty.'

Ulf looked at her. 'You were there?'

She nodded. 'I helped him. I am, after all, a qualified veterinary nurse, remember.'

Ulf ignored the reproach. She had not told him that she was going to be assisting in the operation. She should have told him that; she should have.

'And then?'

'And then,' Juni continued, 'once we'd got into the ear canal, things became a bit more complicated.'

We, thought Ulf; we. But his reaction, he decided, was a petty one. Juni was trying to be helpful. He should not resent that. And it had always been clear to him that she felt considerable affection for Martin; one could not fault her on that. And yet, the whole thing had been her idea. She and that rather self-satisfied vet had cooked it up themselves. She had manoeuvred him into selling his Saab to pay for it – and now he had no Saab and a dog who was still deaf.

'So the whole thing was a failure?' asked Ulf.

Juni did not reply immediately. Then she said, 'It depends what you mean by failure.'

Ulf drew in his breath. 'By failure, I mean: it didn't work. An operation that doesn't work is, in my view, a failure. One might call it something else, for all I know, but as far as I am concerned it must be a failure. And if the patient is dead, then you might even call it a profound failure. I don't know. These are just the thoughts of a layman.'

He could sense her eyes upon him.

'You're feeling upset. That's perfectly understandable.'

He drew in his breath again. She was right: he was upset, and now he felt the emotion welling up within him. *Poor Martin. Niklas. My Saab that I loved so much. Love gone wrong. Loneliness.*

Now he said, 'Yes, I'm upset. And I'll tell you why. I'm upset because you've gone off with somebody else. I had been hoping that you and I . . . well, I had been hoping. But now you've gone off with Niklas and it's all over. All over. And there's poor Martin and he's had to put up with all this nonsense for what? For nothing, really.'

The accusation hung in the air – the entire paragraph of it. This was not a few short, sharp words; this was a denunciation.

He felt her beside him. It was a strange sensation – an electrical field, he felt. You could feel things like that – hatred, anger, fear – any of those extreme emotions seemed to be capable of generating an electrical field that could be felt, somehow, even if it was undetectable by any scientific instrument.

He was not sure how she would respond, but now she simply said, 'Yes. And I'm sorry. I didn't think it would happen, but it has.'

'You didn't think you'd fall for somebody else?'

She nodded miserably. 'I really didn't. I wanted it to work between us, Ulf – you have to believe that. And I was happy, you know. I loved it when we used to have crab linguine together.'

'Crab linguine,' muttered Ulf. Is that what they would take from this relationship? A memory of crab linguine?

'Yes, well we did, didn't we? We had those dinners together and we went for walks with Martin, and I thought that . . . well, I thought that we would stay together.' She paused. 'But it didn't work that way – and all because of me.'

He waited for her to continue. He found, now, that he wanted to know more about how it had happened. It was a sort of voyeurism, he admitted to himself, but he wanted to know the details.

He forced himself to ask. 'When did you first become lovers?'

She hesitated. Then she said, 'Straight away.'

Ulf said nothing.

'I know it sounds awful,' said Juni. 'I know it sounds awful that it happened while I was still with you, but I just couldn't help myself.'

He thought about this. At least she was being honest. And what she said about that sounded quite credible anyway. People did that sort of thing. They became lovers because of some urge that they simply could not resist. You may as well fight against gravity, or magnetism, or any of those elemental forces. People did what they were compelled to do in their love lives because that was the way we were constructed. It was biology.

He found himself saying something that he would have rather not said. 'I take it that you preferred him to me as a lover?'

She looked away. 'I didn't say that.'

'But it's true, is it?'

She resisted. 'I don't think I need to answer that.'

On his sofa, Martin stirred.

'He's waking up,' said Juni.

Ulf knew at that moment that there would be no further discussion of what had happened with Niklas – or of their relationship. This was the end. It was happening just as it had happened to him before, *mutatis mutandis*, of course.

'Let's leave it,' he said. 'Let's call it quits. I'm sorry if I've done anything to disappoint or hurt you. And I don't want you to be unhappy. I'm pleased if you've found somebody you like in Niklas.'

She was staring at him in disbelief. 'Do you really mean that?' she asked. 'You aren't angry with me?'

He shook his head, and he meant it. Anger seemed to have passed him by – and Ulf was a good man, a kind man, who meant

168

what he said when he expressed the wish that somebody should be happy: he meant it.

Martin opened an eye and looked up at Ulf. He whimpered, and his tail wagged slightly.

'He loves you so much,' said Juni. 'And I'm not surprised. Dogs can tell when people are good.'

Ulf glanced at her, and saw that the compliment was heartfelt. She reached out and put an arm around him. 'I'm so sorry,' she said.

He nodded. 'I told you: we should just call it a day. We're adults.'

'I know, but . . .'

'There's no point in doing anything else,' said Ulf.

He bent down to touch Martin's flank. The dog whimpered again.

'Niklas has refunded the money,' Juni said. 'He was able to return the device to those Dutch people. The only expense has been the pills, which I've paid for.' She reached into her pocket and took out a cheque. 'This is it,' she said.

Ulf took the cheque and examined it. It was for the precise sum he had handed over. It represented his Saab.

'I'm really sorry you sold your car,' said Juni. 'And now you can't get it back, I suppose.'

Ulf shook his head. 'I'm all right with the Volkswagen,' he said.

'A Volkswagen is never going to be a Saab,' said Juni.

'That's true, I suppose,' agreed Ulf. 'But let's not worry about it. I'll be all right.' He paused. 'You can get on your way now, if you like. I'll look after Martin. Mrs Hogförs will take him tomorrow, I imagine.'

'I saw her,' said Juni. 'She said that she would stand by for tomorrow. She was very concerned.'

'She loves him,' said Ulf.

CHAPTER THIRTEEN

The Allocation of Drawers

The atmosphere in the office of the Department of Sensitive Crimes the following morning was markedly cheerful. In spite of his disappointment over Erik's behaviour in the Blomquist letter affair, Ulf had informed Erik of the Commissioner's decision that he could, if he wished, take up the fisheries protection post, and Erik had, as Ulf expected, accepted the position without hesitation.

'I told the Commissioner that I thought you'd welcome the move,' Ulf said.

Erik threw his hands in the air. 'Welcome the move? Ulf, I'm . . . I'm blown away by this. Really blown away. If I ever had to design my ideal job, this would be it.' He paused. 'And I want you to know that we – that's Carl and I – feel very sorry about how we behaved.'

Ulf nodded. 'Thank you for telling me that,' he said. 'None of us is perfect, although some of us are more or less perfect than others, so to speak.'

Erik inclined his head. 'Absolutely,' he said.

'Anyway,' Ulf continued. 'The past is the past. I've spoken to Personnel, by the way, and they say you can transfer immediately, if you like. They say that all you need to do is go and see them about the special allowances.'

Erik looked interested. 'Special allowances in the new job?'

'Yes,' said Ulf. 'They said that you're entitled to a specialist duties allowance for the purchase of fishing equipment and clothing.'

Erik's mouth opened wordlessly. Ulf watched him: he had never witnessed a lottery winner being informed of a major win, but this, he imagined, was more or less how that would look.

'Apparently, you can buy yourself a fly rod and all . . . all the line and reels . . .'

'And nets,' interjected Carl.

'Yes, nets too,' Ulf continued. 'All the things you need. It's so you can blend into the angling community. You'll need to do that, I imagine, to get information about what's going on.'

Erik beamed with pleasure. 'This is very cool.'

'They also said something about magazine subscriptions,' Ulf continued. 'They said that you're entitled to get up to five fishing periodicals so that you can monitor what's being written in them.'

'That will be very useful,' said Erik. 'This is a seriously good job.'

'And I'm sure you'll do it extremely well,' Ulf said, looking about him and seeing that Carl and Anna were both nodding their assent.

'Well done, Erik,' said Anna. 'You've really fallen on your feet.'

'Yes,' said Carl. 'This is it, Erik. This is the big one.'

Erik shook his head in a gesture of disbelief. 'I don't know what I've done to deserve this,' he said.

'Kept your nose clean,' said Carl. 'Served your time. Rocked no boats. There are any number of reasons why people eventually get what they want in this life.'

Erik gave Ulf a grateful look. 'It's thanks to you, I suspect.'

Ulf denied this. 'The Commissioner required no convincing. I didn't have to go out on a limb, or anything of the sort.'

'But you still made it possible,' insisted Erik.

Anna glanced at Ulf, and saw that he was feeling embarrassed. 'We're going to miss you, Erik,' she said. 'For those four days of the week you're going to be away.'

'And I'll miss you people too,' said Erik.

Carl smiled. 'The department won't be the same without you at your desk there. It'll seem . . . a bit empty, I suppose.'

'Not as empty as you fear,' interjected Ulf. 'It's policy not to leave desks unoccupied. So there's going to be somebody sitting there while Erik is off fishing, or whatever the new job entails.'

They all looked at him. Then Carl asked, 'A person?'

'Of course,' said Ulf. 'What did you expect? A dog?' For a moment he pictured Martin sitting at the desk, sniffing at papers.

Carl looked at Ulf reproachfully. 'I was just wondering who it would be,' he said.

'Somebody from Commercial Crime downstairs. You know how they're always going on about not having enough desk space.'

'If you let them in,' said Anna, 'you won't get them out. They'll gradually encroach on all our space. We'll be out in the car park before we know where we are.'

'Blomquist,' said Ulf.

This was greeted with silence.

'As you know,' Ulf went on, 'poor Blomquist doesn't have a proper desk. He has, at most, a table, and even then he doesn't have a complete table. It's point three-five of a table, I think, or something like that. It has no drawers. None. None.'

They listened politely. When Ulf finished, with the word *none* echoing like the tolling of a funeral bell, the silence was a heavy one. Carl was the first to speak: 'That's very sad, I agree. It's bad luck only having point three-five of a table. I'm glad that we'll be able to help Blomquist to get more desk space.'

'Absolutely,' said Erik.

Ulf told them what he had planned. 'Blomquist can sit at Erik's desk on the days that Erik is off on his fishing duties.' He turned to Erik. 'Erik, I'd like you to clear three drawers for him. You have four drawers, I think, and you're going down to point two-five here in Sensitive Crimes. That means you're entitled to one drawer, and Blomquist can have the rest.'

He gave Carl and Erik a glance, as if to ascertain whether anybody was contemplating arguing. Nobody was. They are good people at heart, he thought, but every one of us is capable of unkindness to others, especially to people like Blomquist, especially when it comes to the seemingly petty things of this life: desks, drawers and the like. And yet those things are of immense importance, because they stand for something much bigger.

Ulf suddenly found himself on the brink of an emotional wave, carrying him in a direction of which he was quite unsure. Was he upset over Juni? Of course he was, and yet he knew that there had been no acceptable route out of that relationship other than the one he had chosen. He had not wanted recrimination and accusations, and he had ensured that there were neither. Was he worried about Martin? Of course he was, because although he had no reason to believe that the dog would not recover, he did not like the thought of his being in discomfort, even if his pain was dulled by the drugs that Juni had left for him. And then he realised that what he was really missing was his Saab. It was only a collection of metal and wires and leather seats. At one level it was only a somewhat inefficient method of getting from place to place. But at another, it was much more than that. It was his companion. It was his little bit of Swedish engineering history. It was a tiny part of his country's soul – and he had signed it away for a pile of krona for which he had no particular affection or use. That was what was making Ulf sad.

*

Ulf had made an appointment for coffee with Irena Falk, his friend from Commercial Crime, that morning at eleven. They would meet, he suggested, in the coffee bar across the road and he would invite Blomquist to join them, if Irena did not mind. She did not.

'I like Blomquist,' she said to Ulf. 'I know there are others who . . .' She left the sentence unfinished.

'I know what you mean,' said Ulf. 'People are unkind to him just because he has a tendency to go on a bit.'

She did not mind that at all, she said. 'A lot of what he says is really informative, you know. The problem is that there's just a little bit too much of it. If he could only divide by four, or something like that, then that twenty-five per cent would be very interesting – even useful.'

'Oh, I know,' sighed Ulf.

'But one thing I'd say is this,' Irena continued. 'If I had the option of having Blomquist in Commercial Crime, I'd take him like a shot.'

Ulf was surprised. 'Would you really?'

'Yes, because he's a first-class detective. He has a better nose for what lies behind things than virtually anybody else in the force – present company excepted, of course.'

Ulf laughed. 'I'm very happy to yield to Blomquist. And I'd agree with you, you know. He comes up with unexpected solutions. He's done it time and time again – but he very rarely gets the credit.'

'Because life rewards the wrong people,' Irena said. 'That's one of the first lessons I learned. I was eight, maybe nine, at the time and we had a boy in our class at school called Tommy Sunderberg. He wasn't very bright, but he was terrific at copying other people's work. He got top marks in everything as a result. And he was in all the sports teams because he would hang about near the goal and intercept somebody else's shot so that it looked as though he'd scored it.'

'I know the type,' said Ulf. 'What became of him?'

'He went to Uppsala and came out covered in academic honours – all thanks to plagiarism, I imagine. His career thereafter was a great success. He had promotion after promotion – all unmerited, from what I heard. An ascendant star is an ascendant star, you see, even if there's nothing behind it.'

Ulf shook his head. 'What can one say?' he asked.

'Nothing,' said Irena. 'Except, possibly, "Oh, well."'

'And then there are people like poor Blomquist,' said Ulf, 'who do all the work and get none of the credit.'

They had reached the café by now, and through the window Ulf saw Blomquist sitting inside, waiting for them. 'We can continue our discussion some other time,' said Ulf. 'There's Blomquist over there.'

Blomquist rose to greet them. Irena took his hand and then leaned forward to plant a kiss on his cheek. 'You're looking so well, Blomquist,' she said.

It was the wrong thing to say – Ulf knew that, and he realised that Irena probably understood that too, as it triggered an immediate response from Blomquist.

'That's very good to hear,' he said. 'We're on a new regime, my wife and I. We're eating a lot of kale. You've probably read about how kale can lower cholesterol. Have you?'

Irena sat down. 'That's news to me. Actually, I rather like kale.'

'So do I,' enthused Blomquist. 'We used to have it now and then, but now ... well, we have it every day – sometimes twice. Kale goes quite well with poached eggs, you know – just as spinach does. So we have kale at breakfast time – and we also have kale tea. Did you know that you can buy that now? You don't have to make it yourself.'

'That must be more convenient,' said Irena. 'I must say that I tend to have coffee at breakfast time.'

'Which is no bad choice,' said Blomquist. 'People used to be defensive about drinking coffee, but there are plenty of benefits. Same thing with chocolate – as long as you stick to the ninety per cent brands. The others have far too much sugar in them – far too much.'

Ulf cleared his throat. 'Irena probably has information for us,' he said.

'Not about chocolate or kale or anything,' said Irena, with a laugh. 'Not as interesting – but interesting nonetheless.'

Ulf signalled to the woman behind the bar while he asked, 'Coffee everyone?'

The order was taken, and he turned to Irena.

'Anything about our friend Fridolf?'

She reached into an attaché case she had brought with her and extracted a piece of paper. 'Fridolf Bengtsson,' she announced, 'is Mr Bacon – or one of the several Mr Bacons we have in this country. His outfit started in a smallish way, but he now employs eighty-five people. That makes him medium-sized, I suppose.'

She glanced at the paper. 'As far as I can see, the company is not in trouble – at the moment, at least. However . . .'

Ulf looked interested. 'However, it had a rocky patch about three years ago. They were badly advised as to tax liability – very badly, apparently. It was in the financial press, and there were red faces in one of the big accounting firms. They might have been able to sue the accountants, but these things are bitterly contested and can take years to resolve. So Fridolf decided not to, and instead he got his father-in-law to bail the company out with a long-term commercial bond – more or less interest-free but with a flexible repayment term. I managed to get the details – effectively the father-in-law could pull the plug, demand repayment, and liquidate the company if he so desires. He hasn't, of course – he seems happy to let things go on as they are.'

'So they're out of the woods?' asked Ulf.

'As long as father-in-law is happy,' said Irena.

Blomquist was stroking his chin. Ulf thought he might be about to ask a question, but he did not.

'Where does the father-in-law get the funds?' asked Ulf.

'Pulp,' said Irena. 'Nothing exotic – just pulp for paper mills. He supplies several big mills in Austria and southern Germany.'

'I see.'

'So, let's get this straight,' Ulf said. 'According to what you've discovered, there's no evidence of financial difficulties in the Bengtsson household.'

Irena shook her head. 'None. And just to be on the safe side, I asked a financial journalist friend whether he knew of anything, and the answer was pretty much the same. He's more than solvent. He gave some money to the Nationalmuseum last year and this year he part-funded a scholarship at the University of Agricultural Sciences – for potential bacon people, I suppose. So he's not hard up – not specially wealthy, but comfortable, one might say. If you're looking for a financial motive for whatever it is you're investigating, then I doubt if there is one.' She shrugged. 'Which leaves the other obvious area of inquiry.'

Ulf frowned, but Blomquist looked up with a broad smile. 'Exactly,' he said. 'Sex. If it's not money, then it's sex. Always, always. Or, *almost* always.' Their eyes turned to him, and his smile broadened.

'What you've just said, Irena,' he began, 'very much ties in with what I've discovered.'

Ulf was surprised. He had not been aware that Blomquist had been doing any private investigations into the case – there was no reason why he should not, but it was customary to tell one's colleagues, and he had not done so.

'So, Blomquist – tell all.'

Their coffee had arrived, and Blomquist took a sip of his. The milk left a small white moustache on his upper lip, and Ulf signalled this to him.

'Sorry, Blomquist,' said Ulf. 'But it's best to tell people about these things.'

Blomquist wiped at his lip with his handkerchief. 'I should avoid full fat milk,' he said. 'They'll do coffee with soya milk, you know, but I've been avoiding that for the last few months. They're cutting down trees in South America to plant soya. It's going to end in disaster.'

'What about almond milk?' asked Irena. 'I rather like that.'

'Almonds require a lot of water,' said Blomquist. 'And they grow them in the wrong places – where the water table is depleted anyway.'

'You were going to tell us something,' Ulf interrupted.

Blomquist took another sip of coffee. 'You told me that you heard at your school reunion that—'

'That Fridolf had a girlfriend? Yes.'

'And that your friend . . .'

'Harald. Yes, he told me that she worked in a coffee bar called the Bar Tirana.'

Blomquist nodded. 'I happened to find myself driving past it, so I went in. I hope you don't mind.'

'Any information helps,' said Ulf.

'Well, I went in and it was full of Albanians – all talking in Albanian. One or two of them looked at me a bit suspiciously. They don't like strangers, I suppose.'

'You have to be careful in unfamiliar bars,' Irena said.

Blomquist nodded. 'I was. There was a woman behind the bar – a young woman. Blonde. Lots of make-up. A . . .' He looked apologetic. 'A brassy type, I suppose one might say.'

Irena laughed. 'I'd use the same words myself, Blomquist. You don't have to worry.'

'It's just that there are so many people ready to jump down your throat if you say the wrong thing. It's difficult to describe anybody – or anything – if you're not allowed to be judgemental.'

Irena snorted. 'Ignore all that,' she said. 'If somebody looks like a thug, don't be afraid to say it. Don't assume that they *are*, of course – treat them fairly, but for heaven's sake, if we're to suppress all personal observations, how can we possibly do our job?' She thought of something. 'We had a fraudster in the other day; we brought him in for questioning. You should have seen him. He looked like a weasel – nasty little eyes.'

Ulf was cautious. 'You still have to be careful. Lots of murderers look very mild. They don't look as if they'd hurt a fly.'

'That's true,' said Irena. 'But I still think Blomquist should be allowed to say that this coffee-bar woman looked brassy. We all know what that means. She might be a part-time student at theological college, but she could still look brassy.'

'She was no theologian,' said Blomquist. 'I talked to her. I told her I was a friend of Fridolf. I took a risk, but it paid off.'

They waited.

'I said that Fridolf had invited me to go round for a meal in a week or two at his country place.'

Ulf's eyes widened. There were police rules about lying, but they were vague at the edges. This was probably all right.

'I mentioned where it was. I said I knew somebody who lived nearby.'

Ulf frowned. 'Do you mean where the house is now, or where it used to be?'

Blomquist had the air of one about to make a dramatic disclosure. And it was. 'Now,' he said.

Ulf wanted to be absolutely sure. '*After* the theft?'

Blomquist nodded. 'She said that she was looking forward to seeing me up there. She said that she was very fond of the house. She said that Fridolf was the best of hosts and loved firing up the barbecue.'

'She sounds like quite the talker,' said Ulf.

'Yes. She's that, all right. And all of this, of course, ties in with

179

what I found when I went there with him yesterday. I was writing up my report when you asked me for coffee, and so I thought I would just give it to you when we met.'

Ulf invited him to give them the details, and Blomquist reported on his visit to the house with Fridolf. 'I came away certain of three things,' he said. 'The first was that he knew exactly where the house was. And the second was that he's been using it. And the third thing is that he's been going there with somebody who likes Albanian food. The fridge was full of it, including a special sort of Albanian skinless sausage.'

Ulf thought about this. There was only one conclusion, and he now advanced it as a theory. 'He's having an affair,' he said. 'It's perfectly obvious. He's been taking his girlfriend there.'

'Yes,' said Blomquist. 'She told me how much she loved the place.'

'Ah,' said Irena. 'So he moved the house to enable him to carry on using it with her – a portable love nest, so to speak.'

'Because he has to keep on the right side of his wife,' said Blomquist. 'Because the father-in-law controls the bacon business and he couldn't have him calling in his loan.'

Irena laughed. 'Men,' she said. 'The things they get up to. Are you going to arrest him?'

Ulf was silent. He was thinking.

'Yes,' said Blomquist. 'I think he should. Right now.'

Ulf shook his head. He turned to Irena. 'You said that he employs quite a few people?' And then to Blomquist he said, 'And he has a child with this new wife, doesn't he?'

'I think so,' said Blomquist.

'I'm not sure how many lives we should let this man ruin,' said Ulf. 'Sometimes, a bit of damage limitation is the best policy.'

'So what are you going to do?' asked Blomquist.

Ulf admitted that he had no idea.

Irena looked at Ulf admiringly. This, she decided, was what she liked about him: there were far too many people who were so disconcertingly *certain*, who knew what they wanted to do, who were never plagued by doubts. Ulf was not one of them. She admired that, his ability to look at things in the round, and, most of all, his reluctance to cause further hurt. If only there were more men like him, she thought, and if only he and she had not for years been in an amiable workplace relationship. It was impossible, she thought, to change the nature of those relationships without losing the one quality that made them so special: simple friendship. Besides, she had heard rumours that Ulf had been in love with somebody else for a long time and that he pined for someone who was unavailable. In her experience, people like that never recovered, and while one might feel sympathy for them, it was best not to get involved.

Ulf thanked her for the information she had shared with them, and offered to buy her a box of chocolate eclairs from the shop two doors down. But Irena shook her head. 'Fattening,' she said. 'Too many carbs.'

Blomquist greeted this with approval. 'You're quite right,' he said. 'Chocolate eclairs are lethal. Don't even look at them. Ever.'

It was a relief to Ulf when he rang his neighbour's doorbell that evening and he heard Martin's welcoming bark. Mrs Hogförs had spent the day fussing over the recuperating dog, having put his bed in the living room along with his favourite objects – his tattered security blanket, his half-chewed tennis ball and the ancient rubber bone that Ulf had given him for his last birthday. These were strewn about the floor when Ulf entered the room and bent down to scratch Martin's back.

'He's had a good day,' Mrs Hogförs said. 'I wasn't going to take him out for a walk – but I decided that it would do him good to go to the park. He loved it and he even made a half-hearted attempt to chase a squirrel. I think he'll be back to normal in a couple of days.'

'He's in no discomfort?' asked Ulf.

'He has his pills,' said Mrs Hogförs. 'And the wound seems to be healing nicely. I changed the dressing this afternoon.'

'He's a very fortunate dog to have you as his neighbour, Agnes,' said Ulf.

'I love all dogs,' said Mrs Hogförs. 'When Hogförs was alive, you know, we always had a dog. He had been brought up with them. He was remarkable at communicating with them. He said that dogs tell you a lot through their facial expressions – and their eyes.'

Ulf reached down to slip the lead onto Martin's collar. As he did so, Mrs Hogförs said, 'Are you all right, Ulf?'

He straightened up. He looked at her. She searched his face. Men tell you a lot through their facial expressions too, she thought – and their eyes. Now she said, 'You aren't, are you?'

Ulf saw no reason to dissemble. There were people for whom he would always put on a brave face, but not Mrs Hogförs, who was too like his mother, his aunts – all his senior female relatives, in fact – for him to pretend to her. He shook his head.

She reached out and guided him to a chair. 'Sit down here, Ulf.'

'I have to be on my way,' he said. 'I have to tidy the flat – I have to get things organised.'

'Nonsense. What for?'

'Because . . .' He could think of no reason.

She said, 'It's Juni, I take it. Is that over?'

He lowered his head; and that was an answer.

'She's gone off with somebody else?'

'Yes.' He wondered how she knew. Had it been obvious to her that he would somehow be unable to keep the interest and commitment of a glamorous, vivacious young woman? Was that something that could be sensed by a woman even if he himself was unaware of it? He found himself smarting, and for a moment he flirted with the idea of victimhood. He was the wronged party here, and if there was one dominant strand in the zeitgeist it was the proposition that victimhood should be made the most of. Of course there were victims in this life – as a detective, Ulf had come across any number of people who had been wronged by the callous and selfish and, sometimes, by the downright wicked. But not all of these allowed their victimhood to dominate their lives; not all of these sought to extract the last drops of sympathy that might be offered by the world. No, thought Ulf: I am not going to be a victim, because victimhood can be a downward spiral, a dead end from which escape becomes difficult.

Mrs Hogförs asked, 'Did you part as friends? I hope you were able to do that?'

'Yes,' said Ulf. 'It was nobody's fault.'

She looked doubtful, but said nothing. Now she looked at her watch. 'Could you give me an hour, Ulf? I have a few things I need to do. Then I thought I might come and cook dinner for you – if you don't mind my doing that. I have a very nice halibut steak – easily big enough for the two of us.'

Ulf looked at her with affection. Halibut was just what he wanted. 'That's very kind of you. I'd love that.'

'And I have a bottle of wine that somebody gave me. A Swiss white wine, from one of those hills above Lake Zurich. It's very light.'

'It'll go with the halibut.'

'That's what I thought,' said Mrs Hogförs.

He led Martin out of the room and made his way to his own apartment. I am a fortunate man, he reminded himself: I have an interesting job; I am largely my own boss; I have a loyal dog; and I have a neighbour who offers to cook halibut steak for me. I am *not* a victim. If there is anything that I lack, then I can do something about it. If I need somebody else in my life – and I must admit to myself that I do – then I can find somebody. There are plenty of nice women in Sweden, and although I am nothing special, women seem to find me acceptable. I shall find somebody, but this time I shall not go for a good-looking glamorous woman. I shall go for a quieter type – somebody who has not had all that many offers and perhaps feels that she is now on the shelf.

He stopped himself: that was such a cruel expression – *on the shelf* – but perhaps it might be re-evaluated. Perhaps it could even be turned round, and those who were on the shelf could make the most of it, might be relieved that at last some man was taking an interest. He thought of this as he unlocked his door. He wondered if some sympathetic person might establish a bar for women who were on the point of giving up hope of finding a partner. They could be bold – they could show some spirit. The bar could be called On the Shelf and the seats could be bench seats, designed to look like shelves. And the men would come in and meet women who would treat them well, who would not run off with other men, and who would appreciate even the most unprepossessing of males. And there could be an equivalent bar for men, called The Last Chance Saloon, perhaps, in which women might find men who had almost given up; men whom nobody would normally notice, who would never turn any heads; men of the sort one might find frequenting those rather sad men's sheds one read about; men who would make extremely dull but very loyal husbands, and who would be grateful that at last they had found somebody who would appreciate them, in spite of everything.

The thought cheered him up, and when Mrs Hogförs arrived with the halibut, a bag of accompanying vegetables and a thin bottle of Swiss white wine, he told her about his brief fantasy. She listened and smiled, but said nothing. She had a good sense of humour – he knew that – but it was not the same as his. Absurdity, he thought, might perhaps be something that she did not take to. Was that true, and if it was, was it because for so many women, over the aeons of our development, life had been just too difficult to leave time to contemplate the absurd? He was not sure, and he could not be bothered to think any more about it. A more pressing need was for the glass of Swiss white wine that Mrs Hogförs was now offering him in one of his best smoky-green wine glasses.

'Oh, my goodness,' said Ulf, as he took a sip of the wine. 'This is really good.' He glanced at the wine bottle's label, with its watercolour picture of Lake Zurich. He looked more closely, and saw that the building depicted on the shore was the Bollingen Tower, where Jung had lived. Dr Svensson had been there, and displayed a picture of that very house in his consulting room.

'Jung's house,' he said to Mrs Hogförs, pointing to the picture.

She looked at the label. 'Was he the one with the dogs?'

Ulf thought for a moment. Did Jung have a dog? And then he realised what she was referring to. 'That was Freud,' he said. 'Freud had those chows – those big, furry dogs.'

'Very light,' said Mrs Hogförs, taking a sip of wine. 'I like it, but Hogförs preferred something with more body.' She paused. 'He was a great man,' she mused.

Who was a great man, Ulf wondered. Freud? Jung?

It was Hogförs. 'He liked dogs, you know, and we had one for years. Then it died. You know how they die.'

They did. Ulf glanced at Martin. He did not want him to die. And Martin looked back up at him, and Ulf realised that Martin must feel the same about him.

'Your husband must have been a very great man,' said Ulf, not really knowing why he said it.

'He was,' said Mrs Hogförs. 'But just about everybody was great in those days.'

The halibut and its accompanying vegetables cooked in minutes. After the main course, Ulf served water biscuits with a truffle cheese he had come across in the local delicatessen. As he sat there, he felt a sudden urge to share with Mrs Hogförs the details of the Bengtsson case. Ulf, of course, was well aware of the requirements of confidentiality, but on occasion he made what he called a 'consultative exception' and would sound Mrs Hogförs out for her advice. He knew that she would never pass on to anybody else the information he divulged, but, more than that, he valued her insights and advice. Standing too close to a case, one might easily miss something that an external, uninvolved eye might spot. Every detective knew that, and, because of this knowledge, just about every detective would occasionally share the facts of a puzzling case with a partner or spouse. Doing that was an inevitable concomitant of human nature – of the need to share our burdens – and it some-times brought results. *Pillow talk*, thought Ulf, that most intimate of conversations – and that, he suddenly realised, was what he wanted so desperately. He wanted somebody to share not just this flat, this routine, this *domesticity*, but the things that lay in his heart. Everybody wanted that in this brief . . . brief . . . what was it? And it came to him: this brief *accident* that was life. It was an impossible, unlikely development – the emergence of consciousness from all that primal chaos, that churning soup of atoms that had coalesced into a tiny, hospitable planet, and then, as an afterthought, into a seething, living mass that included *us*. It was a fleeting and tran-sitory moment, and yet we took it all so seriously and thought it would last forever. It would not. It came, flickered briefly, and then would disappear into cold inertia, into nothingness.

'You look thoughtful.'

Mrs Hogförs was staring at him.

'I was thinking some rather large thoughts,' said Ulf. 'And I wanted to speak to you about some of them.'

'That's what neighbours are for, Ulf. You know you can speak to me.'

'I do. It's about a case – one that we were working on today. We solved it, actually, so it's not a case of my wanting you to give your views on that. We know who did it.'

'That must be very satisfactory.'

He nodded. 'Yes, it is. I know who committed the . . . theft, in this case. But that doesn't mean I know what to do about it.'

Mrs Hogförs looked puzzled. 'Surely if you know who's responsible for stealing ... what was it that they stole?'

Ulf grinned. 'You won't believe this,' he said. 'A house.'

Mrs Hogförs chuckled. 'Come on, Ulf, you mean the *contents* of a house, surely.'

'No,' said Ulf. 'I mean what I said. A house was stolen. It was picked up, put on a trailer and then taken somewhere else. It was dropped down in a clearing in the forest. That's where we found it – thanks to some rather smart detective work by my colleague, Blomquist.'

'Very odd,' said Mrs Hogförs. 'But why would somebody want to steal somebody else's house?'

'Not somebody else's house,' Ulf corrected her. 'His own house.' And then he said, 'I'll start at the beginning, perhaps.'

She sat back on the sofa, allowing Martin to come up beside her. He laid his head, lampshade and all, on her lap. If dogs could purr, in the way of a contented cat, that is what he would have done.

Ulf told her of his first encounter with Fridolf Bengtsson and of the visit that he and Blomquist had paid to the site of the robbery. He described their disbelief on seeing the empty plot of land, and the surgical precision with which the house appeared to have been removed from its foundations.

But Mrs Hogförs seemed only to be half listening to the main thrust of the story. 'Bengtsson,' she interrupted. 'Bengtsson, Bengtsson ...' And then, 'Bacon people, of course. Maja Bengtsson. Same family. Of course. Bacon. Of course.'

Ulf stopped. He should not have given the name; he should have anonymised the story. But it was too late. As in any country, parts of Sweden were a village.

'You know the family?'

She nodded. 'I know his mother.'

Ulf waited for the details.

'She plays in a bridge club I go to,' Mrs Hogförs said. 'You know the club. I've mentioned it to you on occasion, I think.'

Mrs Hogförs had explained that there were some afternoons when she took Martin with her to a bridge club of which she was a member. Ulf had stressed to her that she should not hesitate to leave him behind, as he did not want her offer to babysit him during the day to become a burden to her, but she had insisted. 'He likes bridge,' she said. 'He sits beside me – on the floor, of course – and watches the cards. He seems to find it interesting. And he picks up the excitement when somebody bids – and makes – a grand slam.'

'Anyway, carry on,' she encouraged Ulf. 'What happened? How did you find the house?'

Ulf told her the rest of the story.

'Your friend, Blomquist, is very on the ball.'

'He is,' said Ulf. 'He never gets the credit, of course. Life isn't like that, is it?'

It was not, she agreed. 'Hogförs made a great deal of money for a company he worked for,' she said. 'Did they ever thank him? They did not. Did they even acknowledge what he had done?' She shook her head. The world was full of ingratitude, she said. It was everywhere. There was no justice. People got away with things. Look at the Russians; just look at them, she said.

Ulf knew that she had long-held suspicions about the Russians, and he smiled. 'At least they were not involved in this business.'

'Perhaps not,' she said, before adding, 'On the face of things.'

'You have to be careful about blaming whole groups of people for the actions of a minority,' he said. 'Don't be too hard on the Russians, Agnes.'

But she shook her head. 'History, Ulf,' she said. 'Never forget your history.'

Ulf steered the conversation back to the house. He explained how they had concluded that Fridolf had stolen the house himself

188

in order to create a love nest for himself and his lover. That seemed quite credible to Mrs Hogförs.

'That's what men do,' she said. 'They do that sort of thing.'

'He wants to have his cake and eat it,' said Ulf.

'That's what men do,' repeated Mrs Hogförs.

'That's as may be. But what am I to do? If I set a prosecution in motion against Fridolf, the whole thing comes out. His wife discovers the affair, as does her father. The company goes to the wall – sold, I imagine – but what about the people working for it? And the child that Fridolf has with his wife?'

She thought for a few moments before responding. Then, 'That's what happens when men have mistresses. It just does. Everything's wrecked.'

'Or women,' said Ulf. 'It's not always men who wreck things.'

'Maybe not,' she conceded. 'Sometimes it's women, but in my view that's much rarer. Women like to keep the home going. Men have . . . well, they have a different sort of eye. It's just the way it is.'

'Well, the point is: what do I do? Bring everything down about Fridolf's ears?'

'He's asked for it, hasn't he?'

Ulf agreed that he had, and yet, he said, 'If only he'd see sense and drop this Albanian woman.'

'You could go and tell him that,' said Mrs Hogförs. 'You could tell him that unless he goes back to his wife, he'll be prosecuted for—'

'For making a false report to the police. Yes, that's an offence. And it can be a serious one. The courts don't like it.' He hesitated. 'I'm afraid I can't have that conversation with him. It's called blackmail. I'd be committing an offence myself.'

She looked incredulous. 'You can't threaten him with the consequences of his own actions? What sort of justice is that, Ulf?'

'Formal justice,' he replied. 'I can't get people to do things by threatening to prosecute them if they don't. I can threaten them with prosecution if they break the law in some way, but that's different. Here I'd be using the prosecution process to achieve an incidental objective.'

She wrinkled her nose. 'You sound like a legal textbook, Ulf. You really do.'

'That's the way it is, Agnes. I'm a police officer. I *have* to sound like a legal textbook.'

She stroked Martin's neck as she thought about this.

'It's difficult,' she said. 'And I wish I could come up with a suggestion. But I can't. I can't think of anything you can do, other than do things according to the book. If that leads to a lot of unhappiness, then that's just the way it is.'

He muttered her phrase: *it's just the way it is*. It would make a good motto for a coat of arms or a departmental mission statement. *It's just the way it is.* So many of those mottoes were high-sounding and aspirational. This was different, and a much truer reflection, therefore, of how things were.

He rose from his chair. 'I'm going to make us coffee,' he said. 'I shouldn't burden you with all this.'

She declined the coffee. 'It will keep me awake,' she said. 'I'm reading a book at the moment that is very good at sending me off to sleep. It's an autobiography, but the person who wrote it has yet to do anything interesting. In fact, so far, he's done nothing interesting at all and he's already twenty-eight.'

'There must be many lives like that,' said Ulf.

'Not yours,' said Mrs Hogfors. 'Nor Martin's, for that matter.'

Martin looked at her. He had been lip-reading, and had caught the word *Martin*, but that was all. Biscuits? he thought. His head was sore. Something had happened to him – something he did not understand. But that did not matter. God was here, in the room with him. God was getting up. Walks? No, apparently not.

CHAPTER FOURTEEN

The Joyful Barking of Dogs

U lf had two days' leave that he was obliged to take before the
end of the month, or face losing them. It was an irritating
feature of the leave arrangements that short-period entitlements
could not be carried over to the following quarter, and as a result
members of the Department of Sensitive Crimes sometimes found
themselves having to take the odd day of leave at a time when
they did not particularly want to be at home. On the evening of
his dinner with Mrs Hogförs, Ulf suddenly discovered a note in
his diary reminding him that he had two days due to him, and
that if he did not take them by the end of that week they would
be lost. So it was that the following morning he telephoned Anna
before she went into work and explained to her that he would be
on leave that day and the next.

Anna asked whether there were any matters that she could take
over on his behalf. Ulf thought for a moment: it was tempting to
pass on the Bengtsson case – he was still uncertain what to do
about that, and if he handed it over to his colleague he would be

spared the doubts and indecision that was bedevilling the whole affair. But he knew immediately that he could not do that – Ulf was not one to avoid an uncomfortable decision. There were occasions, and this was one, when he allowed himself a bit of procrastination – 'contemplation space', as he called it – but at the end of the day he always shouldered whatever responsibility was to be borne.

'There's nothing that can't wait,' he said to Anna. 'Blomquist and I are involved in that house theft case, but we're pretty much at the end of that.'

'Poor Blomquist,' said Anna.

Ulf bit his tongue. Why did people keep saying, 'Poor Blomquist'? It was condescending and would certainly upset Blomquist if he heard about it. There were policies in place about bullying, and condescension, Ulf thought, could well fit into some category there. Was it an act of micro-aggression? That was a very broad concept – rather too broad, Ulf thought – as it meant that acts that were, on the face of it, entirely innocent, could suddenly take on a sinister complexion. He had even heard of a complaint being brought against somebody on the grounds that his name amounted to a micro-aggression. The name in question was Thor, a name that was hardly unheard of, but was thought, by the complainant, to be threatening. After all, Thor was the god of thunder, and how would you, it was asked, like to receive a memo from somebody called by that name? Was there not an implicit threat in such a signature?

Ulf had laughed when he heard this story, but his amusement had turned to alarm when he heard the outcome. Although a direct sanction was not imposed, the Thor involved had been 'invited' to 'consider' adopting a name that did not make others feel uncomfortable. Not only that, but he was directed – not invited – to enlist for a three-day course of sensitivity training. Even if he declined to change his name, at least he would then be aware of the discomfort that his presence could cause others in what was referred to as their 'personal space'. Thor, of course, had his own personal space, but that was another matter altogether. The fact that he was a volunteer at a Lutheran soup kitchen and a scout leader was not the point: this was not an issue of what he was; this was an issue of how he appeared to be.

Now he said to Anna, 'Blomquist's all right, Anna. No need for the *poor*. He's okay.'

There was a brief silence – a reproach? Ulf wondered. But then she said, 'Of course. You're right. Blomquist is pretty good at his job when all is said and done.'

'I'm glad you see that,' said Ulf. 'People sometimes misjudge him.'

He asked her to see how things went in the office in the absence of Erik, who had just started his new assignment. Blomquist might be moving his things into Erik's desk, and he hoped that would go smoothly. 'They'll get used to him,' he said.

'Just as one gets used to the weather,' said Anna.

'You could say that. But listen, Anna, don't let anybody get at Blomquist. Make sure they're nice to him, please.'

There was the slightest hesitation at the end of the line. Then she said, 'Of course I will. I promise you.'

He could tell that she meant it, and he brought the conversation to an end after a brief enquiry about her girls' latest swimming achievements. They had been selected for a regional team, she said, and she was very proud of them. 'It's a lot of hard work,' she said. 'But it's worth it, Ulf. It makes it all worthwhile – everything else one has to put up with.'

He wondered what she meant by that, and he pondered it well after the end of the telephone call. Did *everything else one has to put up with* include her marriage? It sounded as if it might, and if it did, then was it possible that once the girls left school and went off to university or whatever lay ahead of them, there would then be a chance that he and Anna might get together? He imagined the scene: a sort of Hollywood-inspired landscape – a field of wildflowers, perhaps, across which the two of them would walk, hand tentatively in hand, and she would turn to him and say, 'At last, Ulf. It's been so long, but all those years of separation are over now.' And he would reply, 'Yes, it's been a long time, but the waiting is over.' He mulled over those words; they were somewhat bland, as words spoken at moments of intense significance can sometimes be. What was it that one of those lunar astronauts said when he first radioed back his impressions. 'The moon is essentially grey,' he had said. Could he not have managed anything better than that? Of course, the moon *was* essentially grey, and there are some truths that are best unembroidered. And what had President Nixon said on being taken to the Great Wall of China? 'This surely is a great wall.' That was oddly eloquent, in its way.

He stopped himself from thinking about Anna. He should not allow it. Like a medieval monk struggling with temptation, he consigned the Devil to his quarters. I shall not be tempted. I shall not think about her.

He took Martin for a walk and stopped at a nearby café for a cup of coffee. One or two other dog owners were there – members of a fraternity that recognised one another and exchanged news of canine interest. Martin's lampshade and bandage were an obvious talking point, and Ulf spent some time discussing the surgery with various concerned dog owners. The reaction was sympathetic – how sad, they said, that the whole thing had been in vain, but Martin was happy enough, was he not, in spite of his disability? And they knew about his lip-reading, too. It was a source of pride in dog-owning circles in Malmö that one of their number should have achieved the distinction of owning the only lip-reading dog in Sweden, if not all Scandinavia.

He had an early lunch, and watched a small amount of daytime television – a delicious sin, in spite of the tedium of the programming. Two teams of hairdressers were competing with one another to see who could bring about the most complete transformation of volunteers with unprepossessing hairstyles. *Hopeless Hair* was a programme that Ulf had not seen before, and could imagine becoming addicted to. Those who benefited from the hairdressers' attention were certainly pleased with the results. 'I can look in the mirror again,' said one. 'For the first time in years, I can look in the mirror.' And Ulf thought: if this nonsense achieves that, it is worth all the bother – all the electricity used to broadcast it to the nation; all the studio time and complimentary cups of coffee; all the assistants with clipboards and a sense of importance; all the taxis and kisses.

At five that evening his doorbell rang. Martin growled, the lampshade acting as a megaphone, amplifying the sound. Ulf went to open it to a man somewhere in his late sixties, wearing a dark, double-breasted blazer. It took Ulf a few moments to realise that he knew who this was. This was Jurien, the purchaser of his Saab.

'I'm sorry if I looked blank,' Ulf apologised. 'When I opened the door, I wasn't expecting you. It took me a few moments to remember.'

Jurien smiled. 'I would have called first,' he said. 'But I didn't have your number. Edvard said he'd lost it, but he gave me your address.' He paused. 'I hope you don't mind.'

'Of course not,' said Ulf. 'I hope the Saab isn't giving you any trouble.' It must be, he thought; that was the only reason why Jurien should come to see him.

Jurien was looking at Martin. 'This is your dog?'

'Yes,' said Ulf.

'The one who had the operation?'

Ulf sighed. 'Yes, poor fellow. He's not quite right yet – but he's getting there.'

'Those lampshade things look so ridiculous,' said Jurien. 'I hate to think how embarrassed dogs must feel.'

'Martin's quite a good patient,' said Ulf. 'He's a stoic at heart,

195

I think. He had a very uncomfortable operation on his nose not all that long ago. A squirrel almost detached it.'

'Ouch!' said Jurien, feeling the top of his own nose, as if to reassure himself it was still there.

'Unfortunately, this last operation didn't achieve what they hoped. But still – Martin's on the mend, which is the important thing.'

Suddenly Ulf realised that Jurien had revealed he knew about Martin's operation. How had he come by that knowledge? Had Edvard told him? But then Ulf thought that he had not told Edvard why he had needed to raise the money.

'Did somebody mention Martin's operation?' Ulf asked. 'Did Edvard say something?'

Jurien hesitated. 'No, not him. Actually, I do know all about it. Your girlfriend, you see, came to have a word with me.'

Ulf frowned. 'Juni?'

Jurien nodded. 'Yes. She got in touch. She told me all about why you sold the Saab in the first place. Then she told me about Martin's hearing problems and the operation he had to undergo.' He paused. 'I'm so sorry it didn't work out.'

'These things happen,' said Ulf. 'It was very much an experimental procedure. I'm not sure that it's entirely suitable for dogs.'

Jurien gave a sympathetic nod. 'At least you tried.'

'I suppose so.'

There was a brief silence. Then Jurien said, 'I'd like to return your Saab. If you want it back, that is.'

Ulf stared at him in astonishment. It had not occurred to him that he would ever get the chance to recover the Saab. He had accepted that he had lost it. And yet, did he want it back? Of course he did.

'I couldn't ask that of you,' he said. 'Not that I don't appreciate it – I do.'

'All I would ask is for the purchase price to be returned,' Jurien went on. 'Of course you might have used up some of that already, but Juni told me that the fee for the operation was waived.'

'I still have the money,' said Ulf. 'They refunded me.'

'In that case, I'd return the car to you with a discount – to cover the enjoyment I've already had from it. I'll return it in exchange for the price I paid minus, let's say, twenty per cent.'

It was an astonishingly generous offer, and it triggered Ulf's public service antennae. As a public servant you had to be very careful about accepting the largesse of others. He shook his head. 'I can't accept that,' he said. 'Not in my position. But if I return the whole sum, then . . .'

'That's up to you,' said Jurien. 'I wouldn't want you to do anything inappropriate.'

Ulf scratched his head. 'Do you mind my asking why you're doing this?'

Jurien did not hesitate. 'You may recall,' he said, 'my mentioning that you were very kind and supportive to my cousin when she was being stalked by her hairdresser. She's never forgotten that. I'm very close to her and it would give me particular pleasure to do this thing for you.

'And there's something else,' Jurien continued. 'I'm getting on a bit and my eyesight is not what it once was, you see. I'm going to be doing less driving.'

Ulf crossed the room to his window and looked outside. There was the Saab in all its ineffable Saabness. His heart gave a lurch. He wanted his car back; of course he wanted his car back.

'You'll see that I'm parked down below,' said Jurien. 'Illegally.'

They both laughed.

'So, it would be best if you took back ownership of the car as soon as possible so that any parking fines can be laid at your door, not mine.'

They laughed again. Martin, looking up through his lamp-shade, barked; a sound that, magnified by the shade, reverberated around the room. *How loud is the joyful barking of the dogs* . . . Ulf muttered the line of poetry, which came from somewhere he had forgotten, and which he would probably never remember. Had he learned it at school, along with all the other facts and scraps of facts that constituted an education? There were so many poems that were lost to us now, ephemera that we had once learned and that lodged somewhere deep in our minds. *How loud is the joyful barking of the dogs* . . .

He turned round to give Jurien his answer. 'I'm very grateful,' he said. 'I'd like to accept.'

Jurien reached in his pocket for the keys to the Saab and gave them to Ulf. 'I'm glad you said yes,' he said. 'I would have been unhappy keeping it.'

'I was missing it,' Ulf confessed.

He offered Jurien coffee, but his visitor had an engagement that evening. 'It would be helpful if you could run me home, though.'

Ulf drove Jurien back across town to the comfortable detached house he occupied in a wealthy suburb. Martin sat in the rear seat. He was clearly pleased to be back in the embrace of the smells of the Saab. Volkswagens smelled different; even the human nose could detect that. They did not necessarily smell worse – just different.

Jurien gave Ulf a brief tour of his other Saabs, all housed in a large wooden garage at the edge of the property. 'A temple to engineering,' muttered Ulf, as he surveyed the cars.

'Exactly,' said Jurien, making a strange, S-shaped gesture, as if conferring a benediction on the stored machinery. Ulf had never seen that sign before, and wondered whether he had imagined it. Perhaps, he thought, this is a mystery to which I am not yet fully admitted.

Back in the house, where Ulf made arrangements for the repayment of the purchase price, he was introduced to Jurien's daughter, Karin. She was a teacher, Jurien said, and she was living with him and his wife, as she had just taken a new job nearby. Ulf looked at her. She must be about Juni's age, he thought; perhaps a year or so older. She had light-brown hair and a slightly retroussé nose. She smiled at Ulf warmly.

'Karin has been busy organising a crayfish supper for us,' said Jurien. 'Next month. Not a very big affair, but there's always rather a lot to do.'

'Do you like crayfish?' asked Karin.

'I do,' said Ulf.

'Perhaps you might care to join us.'

The invitation came from Karin, but Ulf could tell that Jurien endorsed it. Ulf hesitated. He wanted to meet new people; he wanted a new beginning – one that might lead to a new relation-ship. And now here was an invitation that on the surface was one to a crayfish supper, that most innocent of Swedish traditions, but seemed to have the potential to become something actually rather more.

'I would love to,' he said.

On the way back, Ulf reflected on what had happened. He was touched that Juni should have done this – that she should have bothered to contact Edvard and told him about the failure of Martin's operation. And Juni had, Ulf assumed, asked Edvard to contact Jurien to see whether he might consider returning the car. And both Edvard and Jurien had gone along with the scheme because they were good men of fundamentally kind disposition. That was the most heart-warming thing of all: that there were plenty of people like that in the world, no matter how cynical we become about human nature.

'A very good outcome, Martin,' said Ulf over his shoulder as he drove back towards the flat.

Martin did not respond, as he had not heard what Ulf had to say. For his part, he was breathing in deeply, savouring the smell of the old leather seats, thinking of nothing in particular, but aware, at some level at least, that he was happy, which is the most that any of us, dog or man, can realistically hope of the world.

The following day Ulf took Martin for his check-up at Dr Håkansson's clinic. He had mixed feelings about going – he felt that seeing Juni so soon after their break-up could be as awkward for her as it would be for him, and yet he wanted to thank her personally for what she had done. Even if she had rather cajoled him into agreeing to Martin's operation, and even if she had preferred Niklas to him, her subsequent behaviour had shown consideration and kindness. People parted – they just did, and there was no point in recrimination. You either loved somebody or you did not – blame did not really come into it, as long as there was no deception.

She greeted him warmly. 'I'm glad you came,' she said. 'I've been worried.'

'I wanted to thank you,' he said.

She lowered her gaze. 'Jurien came to see you?'

'He did.'

She looked up. 'I'm glad he did that,' she said. And then she added, 'It was all my fault – the whole thing. The operation was a silly idea. Then letting you sell your car – I can hardly believe I did that.'

'I did it of my own volition,' said Ulf. 'I'm not blaming you for anything.'

'You'd be within your rights if you did,' she muttered.

'This is not a question of rights,' said Ulf. 'We've gone our separate ways. People do that. These things don't always work out.'

'No, they don't, but—'

He took control. 'I think we need to draw a line.'

He reached across her desk and took her hand. 'We can at least shake hands. Friends. All right?'

Her gratitude was unmistakeable. 'Friends,' she said. And then, to Martin, 'And you, darling Martin, how are you doing?'

'He's feeling a lot better,' said Ulf. 'I can tell. He just ... well, he just *looks* better.'

'I think I can tell that too,' said Juni.

Dr Håkansson was of the same opinion. He gave Ulf a further supply of painkillers, but suggested a much smaller dose. 'Increase the dose if he looks uncomfortable,' he said. 'Otherwise reduce it further after another couple of days.'

'And the lampshade?' asked Ulf.

Dr Håkansson looked thoughtful. 'Two more days,' he said. 'Then you can try him without it. If you see him scratching at his wound, then put it back on.'

Dr Håkansson cast an anxious glance at Juni. 'And you two ...' he began.

'We're being very adult about it,' said Ulf.

Dr Håkansson laughed. 'That's a great relief,' he said. 'And I'm sure Martin will appreciate that. Dogs pick up tension between people, you know. They can tell.'

That was a Wednesday. On Thursday, Ulf returned to work after his two days of incidental leave. He drove the Saab into its customary parking place and stood for several minutes admiring it once outside. It was a beautiful car. That's all there was to it, and it would have been a beautiful car even if it were not a Swedish icon. It expressed confidence, purpose, harmony and, most importantly, courtesy. This was not an aggressive car, as some cars were. Nor was it brutal – as a modern SUV might be. This was a gentle, *sympathetic* car. And it occurred to Ulf, as he stood there admiring the vehicle, that a car manufacturer looking for the name of a new model might do worse than to call it a Simpatico or, perhaps Simpatica: drivers might choose according to their gender. Yes, that sounded just right. *What do you drive?* I drive a Ford Simpatica. Or even a Fiat Simpatico. That sounded entirely plausible – a Fiat Simpatico. If I weren't a detective, Ulf thought, I could be one of those people who names products for market. I could do it, he thought. I could change my career. I could do it right now. For a moment he was tempted. He did not have to spend the rest of his life in the Department of Sensitive Crimes – there was a world out there that had nothing to do with human failings, a world ungoverned by departmental memos and quotas and closely watched leave entitlements; a world in which disagreements about desks, of all things, would be completely unknown. Perhaps he should join that world, and have much more RAM. That odd memory made him smile: people actually were envious of others who had more RAM than they did. It was risible. It was absurd. But then life itself was risible, and even absurd, and there was no point in standing apart from it in a superior way and saying that none of it really mattered. It *did* matter – at least in the context of our tiny lives and our limited outlook. In so far as there was any meaning in life, it emerged in relation to these small things, these things that made up our daily lives, our *local* existence.

He tucked the keys of the Saab in his pocket and turned away. He had arrived early – intentionally – and he was looking forward to a half-hour or so in the coffee bar, catching up on the news that he had missed over the last two days. He knew the gist of what the paper would say, of course, but there was always a slightly different angle on the familiar diet of disagreement and political machinations. And, of course, there was Björn's column, too, which he thought he would only glance at because he knew that it would spoil his day if he read everything that his wayward brother had dreamed up.

The coffee bar was quiet, and he was able to sit at his favourite table in the window. And he was there, immersed in his newspaper, when he looked up to see Blomquist enter the café, glance around, spot him and come immediately over to his table.

'I hoped I'd find you,' said Blomquist.

Ulf laid aside the newspaper as Blomquist sat down.

'I see your brother has something to say about climate change,' Blomquist said, nodding towards the paper.

Ulf groaned. He was unsure what his brother's views on that issue would be, but they would certainly be controversial. 'I haven't read him yet,' he said. 'And, frankly, I'm not sure that I shall. What does my brother know about climate science? Well, I can tell you: nothing.'

Blomquist smiled. 'He says that there should be a special climate tax on beef.'

Ulf sighed. 'Well, he has a point about methane, and I suppose one has to start somewhere.'

'He also said that air travel should be stopped completely.'

Ulf digested this. 'He goes to Majorca three times a year. And he's always flying off to conferences. He was in Rotterdam last week at a meeting of the Dutch Semi-Revolutionary Party.'

Blomquist laughed. 'I've read about them.'

'They have a lot in common with the Moderate Extremists,' said Ulf. 'Bjorn's always going on about them.' He sighed. 'I wish that my brother wouldn't ... well, just *wouldn't*.'

'You don't choose your relatives,' said Blomquist. 'That's what they always say, I believe. Mind you, if I had to choose a brother, I think I'd choose you.'

It took Ulf a moment or two to appreciate the profundity of Blomquist's compliment. People were slow to express their admiration for others, and it came as a surprise on those rare occasions when it happened. He looked at Blomquist now, and felt a surge of affection for him. 'That's a very kind thing to say, Blomquist.'

'I mean it,' came the reply.

'And I would willingly exchange my brother for you,' Ulf went on. Ulf thought: we are like two ten-year-old boys pledging blood-brotherhood, but what did it matter? So many men were lonely – there were dozens of articles in the press that made that point. Men had fewer friends than women; men suffered from changing work patterns that gave them fewer colleagues; men were not very good at keeping in touch with one another – the problem was a vast one, and seemingly getting worse. And so, occasions like this, when one man was able to speak frankly and say to another how much he appreciated his friendship, should be savoured and cherished.

But Blomquist had another agenda, and he now leaned forward and confided in Ulf. 'I had a telephone call yesterday from our friend.'

'Which friend?'

'Fridolf. He called me at four yesterday afternoon. He wants to speak to you this morning.'

Ulf raised an eyebrow. 'Did he say what for?'

Blomquist shook his head. 'I assume it's about getting his house back.' He looked at Ulf enquiringly. 'Have you decided what to do?'

Ulf shook his head. 'Not yet.'

'Should I put him off, then?' asked Blomquist. 'I tentatively arranged for him to come in at ten. I've booked an interview room.'

Ulf hesitated. He would have to make a decision, and putting off an interview with Fridolf was simply delaying the inevitable. 'No,' he said. 'Let's bring him in. Let's hear what he has to say.'

'Probably more lies,' said Blomquist.

'Well, we're used to hearing those, aren't we?' said Ulf.

They drank their coffee. Blomquist had a story to tell Ulf about how his neighbour had caught a high heel in the grating of a drain and was suing the local council. Ulf listened with half an ear – he was mentally rehearsing what he knew he would have to say to Fridolf, and weighing, too, the evidence that he had against him. The solution to the disappearance of the house, as suggested by Blomquist, seemed feasible enough, but what actual proof did they have? The idea that Fridolf had gone to all that trouble simply to cater to a girlfriend's desire to have continued use of a favourite love nest – or wolf's den, perhaps – seemed ridiculous, and yet middle-aged men with younger girlfriends *did* behave in ways that were utterly ridiculous. That's what they did; it never occurred to them that their conduct would strike others as pitiful – Ulf had seen so many cases of it. Passion distorted judgement, made children of mature men, ruined the lives of the innocent. There were no limits to the power of sex to upend the rational and the considered, and Fridolf's behaviour in this case was just another illustration of that. Nobody should be surprised by it. And yet proof was still needed. It was all very well to say it was quite possible that Fridolf had acted in this way, but that was only the beginning of the proving of the case.

At the conclusion of the story about the heel stuck in the drain, Ulf shook his head in sympathy. 'Poor woman,' he said. 'It can't have been easy.' He looked at his watch. He needed time to gather his thoughts and prepare for the interview with Fridolf. He would invite Blomquist to sit in, as he was entitled to do as one of the investigating officers. 'We'll think of something to say,' he told Blomquist. 'We might even just let him dig a hole for himself. An awful lot of people do just that, you know.'

'We had someone near where I live,' Blomquist began, 'who was digging a hole in his garden. He was planning to plant a mature tree, you see, and so he started digging this hole—'

Ulf rose to his feet. 'Perhaps later, Blomquist. I don't want to be rude, but we need to get back over the road.'

Blomquist took a last quick sip of his coffee. 'All I was going to say was that he dug down deep and then discovered he couldn't get out. He'd dug himself into a hole.'

Ulf stopped. 'How very unfortunate,' he said.

'Yes,' said Blomquist.

'But they got him out?'

Blomquist shrugged. 'I don't know. I didn't hear about it directly, you see.'

Ulf made towards the door. How odd it must be to be Blomquist, he thought; how odd to inhabit that particular universe. But then all of us were odd in our own way, and getting through life was mostly just a question of managing our oddness. That was the secret, Ulf thought – if there really was a secret, which he sometimes doubted.

Blomquist showed Fridolf into the interview room. Ulf was already seated behind a small rectangular table; there was a seat for Blomquist beside him and one for the interviewee on the other side.

Ulf noticed that Fridolf was formally dressed, in a pearly-grey suit, dark tie and scrupulously polished shoes. He wondered whether that was his normal working dress, or would he change into the apron and jaunty white hat of the sort that butchers wore. For that, in effect, was what Fridolf was: he was a butcher, even if a very successful one. Not that Ulf looked down on any honest occupation: his distaste was reserved for those who did nothing, or who leeched on the hard work of others. He had no reason to suspect Fridolf of anything like that. And yet, as Fridolf came into the room, Ulf found himself thinking, I don't like you, after all. He was careful about such conclusions, as they could cloud and interfere with detective work, but occasionally his intuitive ability to judge the moral stripe of others asserted itself. And it was rarely wrong, Ulf reflected.

Fridolf sat down, at first crossing his legs uneasily, and then uncrossing them.

'There are a few questions I need to ask you,' Ulf began. 'I was going to get in touch with you, but then—'

'But then I contacted you,' interjected Fridolf. 'Yes, there are things I need to say.'

Ulf paused. 'Would you like to go ahead, then?'

Fridolf cleared his throat. Ulf noticed that he was looking up at the ceiling, avoiding direct eye contact with both him and Blomquist.

'I've come to apologise,' Fridolf said. 'Unreservedly.'

Ulf had not expected this. He glanced at Blomquist, who shrugged. He had obviously also been unaware of Fridolf's intentions.

'Yes,' Fridolf continued. 'I have wasted your time. I have misled you.'

'Perhaps you can tell us how you've done all this,' suggested Ulf.

'My house was never stolen,' said Fridolf. 'I moved it myself.'

Ulf did not want to give the impression that they had already worked this out. He remained impassive.

'I did this because I've been having an affair,' Fridolf went on. 'My . . . my friend very much liked the house, and yet my . . . my wife liked it too. You cannot have two ladies sharing the same—'

'Same man,' uttered Blomquist.

Fridolf gave him a sideways look. 'The same house. So I decided to move it and then tell my wife—'

'Lie to your wife,' muttered Blomquist, adding 'and to us.'

Fridolf faltered. 'This isn't easy for me.'

Ulf gave Blomquist a nudge. 'Let him be,' he said.

'So I moved the house and pretended that it had been stolen. That way, everybody was happy – in a manner of speaking. My wife thought the house had been stolen, and my friend was able to enjoy it in its new setting.'

'And insurance?' asked Ulf.

Fridolf shook his head energetically. 'I have never made a false insurance claim,' he said. 'And I made no claim in this case.'

Ulf sat back in his chair. 'What do you expect us to do?' he asked. 'Do you imagine that we'll condone this waste of our time – this making of a false complaint? Do you really think that?'

Fridolf hesitated. He was now looking directly at Ulf, and Ulf saw that there was an imploring look in his eyes.

'I have ended my affair with Adriana,' he said. 'I have gone back to my wife. I shall not let her down again.'

Ulf remained impassive. 'From what I understand, you are no stranger to affairs.'

Fridolf looked down towards the floor. Then, raising his eyes to meet Ulf's gaze, he said, 'Yes, that's true. But I want you to know something, I had ended the affair before I was . . .' He hesitated, and Ulf could see that it was hard for him to say what followed.

'Before?' Ulf enquired.

'Before I was found out.'

'Before your mother discussed it with you?'

Fridolf looked away. 'How did you know that?'

'We know things,' said Ulf. 'And we aren't at liberty to tell people how we know them. It's best just to assume that we know everything.'

'My mother made me act, but I had already made up my mind to end the affair even before she spoke to me.' He paused. 'The truth of the matter is that Adriana isn't easy. She's very demanding, you see. She threatened me.'

Ulf frowned. 'How did she threaten you?'

'She said that she would get some of her friends to deal with me if I didn't do what she wanted. She made me steal the house, you see. I agreed to do it, but then there were more threats. These came the day after I had moved the house. It all happened so quickly. She said that I would have to leave my wife.'

'And you didn't stand up to her?' asked Blomquist.

'She's very persuasive,' said Fridolf. 'You have to be careful with her.'

'I see,' said Ulf. 'And when you ended the affair – how did she react? Did she put her friends, as she calls them, on to you?'

Fridolf sighed. 'I paid her off,' he said. 'I gave her eight hundred thousand krona. I sold a painting I owned. I did it discreetly. There was a dealer who had asked me several times if I would sell. He took it on the spot.'

'Your wife wouldn't have wondered why you were selling the painting?' asked Ulf.

Fridolf shifted in his seat. 'I'm having a copy made. There's a Polish art student in Gothenburg who can copy anything. Most people would be unable to tell the difference between the original and the copy – he's extremely talented. I told my wife I was having the painting cleaned.'

'You lied to her?' said Blomquist.

'Yes. A final lie, though.'

'Carry on,' said Ulf.

'I've commissioned this student. He's making it now. I should get it in a couple of weeks.'

Fridolf gave Ulf a challenging look. 'I've done nothing illegal,' he said. 'I haven't defrauded anyone. The painting was mine to dispose of if I wished.'

Ulf considered this. 'No, deceiving one's wife is not a crime in Sweden.' He let this sink in. Then he continued, 'Your father-in-law knows nothing of this?'

Fridolf shook his head vigorously. 'He does not. And I beg you not to tell him. I beg you.'

'Is that because of what he might do? Because he might insist on the repayment of his loans?'

The effect of this question was immediate – and striking. Fridolf's jaw dropped; he had not expected Ulf to know anything about this. Any vestiges of pride or confidence that had been present when he'd entered the room now disappeared. 'It would be the end of my business,' he said. 'My father-in-law is a stern man.'

'And your wife?'

'She never knew about the affair, although I think she may

have suspected something. Anyway, I'm making it up to her. I am going out of my way to be pleasant.'

'Flowers and so on?' said Blomquist.

Fridolf nodded. 'Yes. And a trip to the Amalfi coast.'

'So, what are you asking of us?' said Ulf.

For a short while there was silence. Then Fridolf said, 'Mercy, I suppose.'

Ulf looked at Blomquist, who gave nothing away. Then Ulf said, 'May I ask you one thing? How do you imagine your mother heard of what you were doing?'

'Somebody told her,' Fridolf answered.

'And do you know who that was?' Ulf asked.

Fridolf shrugged. 'Heaven knows.'

Ulf looked at Blomquist, and noticed his look of mild amusement.

'A man has to obey his mother, doesn't he?' said Ulf.

Fridolf blushed. 'I don't want to cause her unnecessary distress.'

There was a final matter to be resolved. 'How did you get the house to its current position?' he asked.

Fridolf explained that they had used a trailer and a crane.

'I know that bit,' said Ulf. 'But the house is quite wide. How did it fit down that track?'

Fridolf stared at him. 'We took the porch off, of course.'

'Of course,' said Ulf.

Blomquist was shaking his head. 'You are a very foolish man, Bengtsson,' he said.

Ulf gave Blomquist a disapproving look. It never helped to insult suspects, even after they had admitted their guilt.

'I know,' said Fridolf. 'I know that. But ...' He spread out his hands in a gesture of resignation. 'I've learned a lesson. Can't we be allowed to learn lessons as we go through life?'

'Yes, we can,' said Ulf. 'And I think you have done just that.' He paused. 'When will you return the house?' he asked.

'It's being lifted today,' said Fridolf. 'As we speak.'

'And how will you explain it to your wife?' asked Ulf.

Fridolf stared at his feet. 'Just one more little untruth will be necessary. I shall tell her it was removed by a contractor by mistake. A faulty sat-nav reading, I think.'

Ulf stared at him. He felt almost sorry for this man now, but at least he was trying to do better, and he deserved some credit for that.

'I suggest, then, that we draw a line under this most unfortunate business,' said Ulf, rising to his feet.

Fridolf looked up with relief. 'You're very kind,' he said. 'I don't know how to thank you.'

'Do what you've said you'll do,' said Ulf. 'Don't add to the unhappiness out there. Do you think you can manage that? Is that simple enough?'

Fridolf blushed again. He had been told off, as a child might be scolded, but he realised that he deserved it. He nodded, but said nothing. Then the three of them left the room. As he left, Ulf found himself thinking that he did not dislike Fridolf as much as he had at the beginning of the interview, which was further proof, if proof were needed, of the dangers inherent in making up one's mind too quickly, and sometimes, indeed, in making it up at all.

When Ulf collected Martin from Mrs Hogförs late that afternoon, he was pleased to see that the protective lampshade had been removed, as had the bandage around his head. The wound, made visible by the shaving of Martin's surrounding hair, appeared to have healed, the skin around it being dry and unswollen. Martin greeted him as he always did – with enthusiastic barks, jumping up to lick his hands and nuzzle into his master's trouser leg.

'This is not a sick dog,' said Mrs Hogförs. 'Look at him, Ulf – the old Martin has come back, just as we hoped he would.'

Ulf bent down to pat Martin's back, and the dog wriggled with pleasure under his touch. 'Thank you, Agnes,' said Ulf. 'I'm sure you've contributed to his recovery.'

'I haven't done much,' said Mrs Hogförs. 'But at least Martin knows that I've been here for him.'

Ulf looked out of the window. 'I think I might take him for a walk,' he said. 'It's such a fine evening.'

Martin had been watching Ulf's lips, and he saw the word *walk*. He gave another excited look, and rushed into the hall to retrieve his lead.

'Such a clever dog,' said Mrs Hogförs.

Ulf fixed the lead to Martin's collar. 'By the way, Agnes,' he said. 'Have you by any chance seen your friend, Mrs Bengtsson, recently?'

Mrs Hogförs pretended not to hear, and so Ulf repeated the question. Now there was no escape, and Mrs Hogförs, trying to sound as casual as possible, said, 'Recently? No,' and then, in a smaller voice, 'Not since yesterday.'

'But you played bridge with her yesterday?'

Mrs Hogförs continued to affect insouciance. 'Yes, I believe I did.'

'Well,' said Ulf. 'That's interesting.'

She looked at him out of the corner of her eye.

'I assume she threatened Fridolf,' Ulf went on. 'Mothers don't mince their words, do they?'

Mrs Hogförs could hardly escape. 'Possibly,' she said. 'I believe she might have given him an idea of the alternatives open to him. Behaving himself or losing the company and being prosecuted. I would have thought it would not have been a difficult decision to make.'

Ulf thought about that. 'No,' he mused. 'Possibly not.' Then, after a short pause, he continued, 'You should be very careful about being party to blackmail, Agnes.'

'I would never blackmail anybody,' she protested. 'The very thought!'

'Hmm,' said Ulf.

Mrs Hogförs returned to her flat, and Ulf began his walk. Halfway to the park, his mobile phone rang. It was Karin, Jurien's daughter.

'I'm planning our crayfish supper,' she said. 'And that made me think of fish restaurants. I have a couple of friends who are getting up a party to go to a fish restaurant and then on to a concert of Finnish folk songs. Would you be interested in joining us? It's next Wednesday.'

He took no time to reply. 'I would love that.' The fish restaurant and the Finnish folk music was neither here nor there from Ulf's point of view – but the same did not apply to Karin. So he repeated, 'I would really like that – and thanks so much for thinking of me.'

They made arrangements, and then rang off. Ulf felt exhilarated. The evening sun was touching the tops of the trees; the sky was empty, blue and infinite. Martin was sniffing at the air and suddenly raised his head and uttered a bark of sheer joy. If I were a dog, thought Ulf, I think I might well do the same myself.

Alexander McCall Smith is the author of over one hundred books on a wide array of subjects, including the award-winning The No.1 Ladies' Detective Agency series. He is also the author of the Isabel Dalhousie novels and the world's longest-running serial novel, 44 Scotland Street. His books have been translated into forty-six languages. Alexander McCall Smith is Professor Emeritus of Medical Law at the University of Edinburgh and holds honorary doctorates from thirteen universities.